EVERLASTING

THE UNRESTRAINED SERIES: BOOK SIX

S. E. LUND

ACADIAN PUBLISHING LIMITED

S. E. Lund Newsletter

Sign up for S. E. Lund's newsletter and gain access to updates on upcoming releases, sales and freebies! She hates spam and so will never share your email!

S. E. LUND NEWSLETTER SIGN UP

❀ Created with Vellum

CHAPTER 1

KATE

Drake Morgan was the sexiest, most intelligent and most romantic man I'd ever met.

And he was mine – every beautiful inch of him.

He leaned against the hotel bar, his arms spread out on the counter behind him, one knee bent, his slick black boot on the foot rest. He wore a crisp white linen shirt, open a few buttons, over black leather jeans. I could see the thick metal belt buckle beneath his shirt, which was untucked. His leather jeans were slung low over a very ample package.

He watched me intently from under thick black lashes, his bangs falling in his eyes in this incredibly sexy way while he waited for the bartender to fix our drinks. The corner of his mouth quirked up in that characteristic way, a gleam in his blue blue eyes.

Before he went to the bar to order for us, he leaned down to me, his mouth by my ear. "I have so many plans for you tonight, Mrs. Morgan," he whispered. "I hope you're ready."

Of course, he had to know that his words would make me more than ready and in fact, just moments after he said those words, I was already wet and aching deep inside. I'd be so ready that I doubted it would take me any time to orgasm when he began touching me later that night. It had been over ten days since we made love – ten days during which time I'd been sick with a stomach bug and Sophie had been sleepless due to teething. Drake had been working five days straight, twelve hour shifts in the ER at UCSF, the evening shift from three in the afternoon to three in the morning.

We were both exhausted and feeling incredibly deprived of each other.

He returned to the table with our drinks and we held them up and clinked glasses.

"To us. To trying to make up for ten days of deprivation."

"To us," I replied and took a sip of my vodka cooler. Drake had a vodka martini with a twist of lime. We agreed to have one drink before dinner, then we'd go to the dining room and eat a meal and spend some time walking outside as the sun set. We were staying at the Ritz-Carleton in Half Moon Bay, which was a glorious hotel over-looking the ocean a few miles south of our place farther up the coast closer to San Francisco. We'd driven by it on our travels and had planned to come and stay for weeks.

Now here we were.

Drake promised me a night of pleasure. I knew he'd deliver.

Sophie was with my dad and Elaine at our new house along the coast. When we first moved to California, we'd originally located in Monterey to be close to my father but when Drake's supervisor asked him to work at UCSF instead of the hospital in Monterey because of a staffing issue in the ER, Drake had been willing. It meant he'd either commute the two hours each way five days a week or we'd have to move closer to San Francisco.

I hated the thought of Drake on the highway every day, so we found another house along the coast closer to SF. It meant we were farther away from my father and Elaine, but it was safer that way and less strain on Drake. His schedule was already grueling.

As a result, our trips to visit my father were less frequent but we made a point of driving down to spend time with them on Drake's days off. They drove up and stayed at our place every couple of weeks so that Drake and I could spend some alone time with each other.

My cell dinged to indicate an incoming text. I checked and saw it was from Elaine.

ELAINE: Sophie just went down. I gave her some Tylenol and she was happy to go to sleep. Just thought I'd let you know so you can relax.

I texted her right back after showing Drake my cell.

KATE: That's good to know. I hope you two are comfortable and have a good night. She usually sleeps through the night but sometimes, she wakes up especially now that she's teething.

ELAINE: We'll be fine. You two enjoy yourself. Drake works so hard and long and you've been sick so you need grownup time.

KATE: We do. Thanks so much. Give my dad our love.

ELAINE: I will.

I smiled and put my cell away.

"Thank God, they're so willing to sit for us or we'd probably never get a night alone."

"They love it," Drake said and popped a pretzel into his mouth from the bowl on our table. "Don't kid yourself. Elaine loves indulging herself by looking after Sophie. And Ethan wants to get as much Sophie time in as he can."

Drake didn't say *because he's worried about how long he has left to live* but I knew what Drake was thinking. My father had fallen and had a stroke that left him partially paralyzed. He wanted to spend whatever time he had left in a warm climate so he could spend more time outside. We'd moved to California to be closer to him and to Liam, who was living in San Francisco with Maureen and Chris.

We'd been in our new place just south of San Francisco for two months, getting settled after a brief stay in Monterey. Everything was still all new and felt like we were on an extended vacation – except for the long hours Drake worked in the ER. Other than that, when he had his five days off, we were adjusting but we'd barely had any time alone since we arrived. It was the fate of most new parents and we were no different.

We had a nice meal, and then walked hand in hand along the cliff that bordered the ocean in Half Moon Bay. Down below, the waves crashed against the beach. We watched the moon setting and the stars peeking out from thin noctilucent clouds.

Drake took my hand and kissed my knuckles, looking deep into my eyes.

"Time to go back, Katherine."

That was the signal that I was to fall into submissive mode with him and I was surprised, because we hadn't done a scene for so long, I could barely remember how to do it.

I didn't say anything, but I smiled, a thrill going through my body at the thought Drake was going to take thorough control over me, which I knew meant a night of pleasure.

He pulled me against him so that I could feel his body. "I hope you'll remember your manners," he said, his eyes narrowed. "Or I might have to punish you."

I widened my eyes, trying to act confused.

"Punish me, Sir?" I said, innocently. "I leave that up to you."

"Yes," he said and ran a hand down my back to my buttocks, which he gripped firmly through the thin fabric of my sundress. "I might have to deny you an orgasm. Only two instead of three."

"That would be so cruel, Sir. I assure you that I will obey you in all things from here on in."

I leaned against him, looking up into his eyes, which were heated.

"I hope so," he replied. "Because I was planning on making you come at least three times and I don't like to have to change my plans."

"I'm yours," I said, resting my head against his shoulder. "To do with as you please, Sir."

"You are, Ms. Bennet. You are."

I *was*.

I was so totally his that my knees were weak at the prospect of us doing a scene. As we made our way back to the hotel, I wondered what he'd do because I hadn't seen him pack any implements and saw no ties in his suitcase.

What could he do that would involve kink?

As much as I wanted to ask him what he had planned, I didn't. That wouldn't be keeping in character and showing proper submission to his desires. Whatever he planned, I knew I'd enjoy it so I finally just let myself go, turned off my mind, and let him lead me back to the hotel, our hands clasped. He took me to the bank of elevators and we waited for the next one to come when we saw another couple enter the one that opened.

"We'll wait," Drake said and pulled me over to the wall across from the bank of elevators. He stood facing me, his eyes glued to mine, one hand on the wall beside my head.

When the next elevator arrived and we were alone, we got inside and as soon as the doors closed and Drake had entered our floor number, he turned to me and pressed me back against the wall.

He kissed me, one hand sliding up along my thigh to my hip and then my breast.

I couldn't help but see the security camera in the corner of the elevator.

"Drake," I whispered, tilting my head to the side, trying to alert him about its presence.

"Shhh," he commanded.

"But—."

He held a finger up to my mouth, his eyes intense. "*Katherine...*"

Then he began kissing me again and I shut my eyes, trying to obey.

"It'll give them a thrill," he murmured against my neck, his tongue wet against the skin at the base of my throat. He pressed his hips against me so I could feel his erection and that sent a huge wave of lust through me, making me dizzy.

When the elevator chimed, indicating we'd reach our floor, Drake moved away, leaving me breathless from desire.

He grabbed my hand and pulled me outside and I couldn't help but smile at the thought that some security guard sitting in a small dark room in the parking garage might see us and imagine what was going to happen next.

I doubted they'd be able to guess because even I had no idea.

Drake unlocked the door to our hotel room, which was the deluxe suite with a panoramic view of the ocean and a private balcony. It was far larger than we needed but it was private and it had an amazing view

Drake pulled me inside, closing the door behind him after putting the DO NOT DISTURB marker on the handle.

He didn't waste any time, pushing me through the entry and living room to the huge bedroom with windows overlooking the ocean. We were on the top floor and had a magnificent view of the ocean and sunset. It was marvelous.

I didn't get any time to appreciate the view nor did I want the time. Instead, I was focused on Drake, on his hands on my body, his lips on my jaw, my chin, my throat. I was at the side of the bed before I could even take off my sandals. When I reached down to remove them, he stopped me.

"No, don't," he said and stepped back a few feet, his arms crossed, his expression like a wolf about to devour his prey. "Keep them on."

I stopped and stood up straight, waiting.

"Pull down one strap."

I did and he stepped closer, his fingers trailing down from my jaw to my neck and then tracing lightly over the swell of my breast. I smiled as he began kissing my neck and jaw, closing my eyes and letting him do whatever he wanted to me. He slipped the other strap down and pulled it lower, kissing the other breast while one hand cupped it.

"Did I ever tell you that your breasts are perfect?"

He glanced up in my eyes while he exposed my entire breast, my nipple hardening in the cool air. While he kept his eyes locked with mine, he took my nipple between his finger and thumb and tweaked it, eliciting a gasp of breath from me. He repeated this with my other strap of my sundress, so that both my breasts were fully exposed.

"Perfect," he said and stood there, his knee between my thighs, his eyes on my breasts, his hands cupping them. When he bent down and took one nipple into his mouth and sucked hard, my back arched in pleasure and I moaned softly in response.

"This is going to be fast," he said, his voice throaty. "I need you, now. Turn around so I can take your dress off."

I turned and waited while he unzipped my sundress and let it fall to the ground. I stood in my heels and thong, my breasts free with him standing close behind me.

"Take your thong off as well."

I did as he commanded, making sure to bend down extra deep and slowly remove my thong, pulling it off me and stepping out of it.

"Beautiful," he murmured. "You have a perfect ass and it's all mine."

I stood up straight, but he put one hand on my back and kept me bent over so I complied, waiting for him to do whatever he would do.

I heard the zhrrr of his zipper coming down and the jangle of his belt being unbuckled. He was going to fuck me, right then and there. No preliminaries.

I didn't need them at that point, my body already swollen and wet.

I felt him step closer behind me and then his hard cock slide against my pussy, the head stroking my clit. I couldn't help but push back, wanting more stimulation.

"Stop," he said. "Let me do everything."

I stopped and closed my eyes, trying hard to stand still. I felt his arm go around my waist and his fingers find my folds, spreading me wide and stroking his cock over my slit.

"Nice and wet," he said, his mouth beside my ear. "Almost ready."

He stroked his cock against me slowly, back and forth, until I was breathing rapidly, aching to feel him enter me and start to thrust. I wanted so badly to press back against him, to find the head of his cock and feel it press inside of me, but fought to obey his order to remain still.

"Do you want it?" Drake asked in a husky voice.

"Yes."

"Tell me what you want, *Katherine*."

"I want you to fuck me, Sir," I said, my voice shaky, remembering my manners.

"What else do you want?"

"I want to have an orgasm, Sir."

"You will have one, Katherine. You'll come on my cock while I fuck you. Do you want that?"

I gritted my teeth as he stopped his motions while he waited for my answer.

"Yes, please, Sir. Please let me come on your cock while you fuck me."

"You have my permission, but tell me when you're close. I want to time my own orgasm to come when you do."

"Yes, Sir," I said, biting my bottom lip, waiting for him to finally slide inside of me and give me the relief I needed.

He continued stroking his cock over me, rubbing the head against my clit while I remained bent over, my hands pressed against the wall in front of me. I smiled to myself, for as much as he suggested we'd do something kinky, he couldn't wait.

"I'm going to fuck you now, Katherine," he said and I felt the tip press against my pussy, searching for the entrance to my body. When he slipped inside a few inches, I groaned and couldn't help but press back, wanting to feel him fill me up entirely.

"Stop," he said, his voice shaky. "Don't move."

I remained still and waited while he slid fully inside and remained like that, not moving. I knew he was relishing the sensation of filling me entirely. My body contracted around his length, hungry for sensation.

"You are impatient, Katherine," he said, a touch of amusement in his otherwise-aroused voice.

"I'm sorry, Sir," I said. "I need you, badly."

"I know what you need, Katherine.

"You do, Sir," I replied, my eyes closed, trying to keep a smile off my face. Luckily, he couldn't see my face, but I was certain he could hear the hint of humor in my voice, no matter how hard I tried to sound contrite.

He leaned over me, one hand sliding around my body, his fingers on my clit. He began to stroke me while we stood still, our bodies joined, his cock inside me as deep as it could get.

"Nice and hard," he said when he stroked my clit, eliciting a delicious ache in my core. I would be quick, once he started thrusting.

When he removed his fingers, I groaned at the loss of sensation, but I was so ready that I didn't need additional stimulation. It felt so good with him inside of me, filling me, that I knew it wouldn't take too long to come.

He gripped my hips and began thrusting, slowly at first – agonizingly slowly, withdrawing completely only to enter again, angling his cock so that the head struck a sensitive spot inside of me over and over.

Soon, I felt that familiar buildup of sweetness inside my core, and I knew I would come with only a few more thrusts.

"I'm ready," I managed to say, forgetting to add the "Sir" part of the equation, but Drake seemed not to notice – or care – for he began to thrust in earnest now, pumping, entering me and filling me up. When my orgasm began, my whole body tensed as white hot pleasure coursed through me, spreading from my core down my legs and up into my chest.

"Oh, God," I gasped, my breath caught in my throat, my body spasming around his cock. He thrust harder, faster, with my hips still in his grip, then he slowed his motions and thrust slowly through his own orgasm, his body shuddering over top of me.

When he was finished, he slipped his arm around my waist and raised me up, supporting us both with a hand against the wall.

"Fuck, that was good," he said, his voice next to my ear.

"It was."

"I planned to tie you up and fuck you slowly, but I needed to fuck you fast and hard."

I smiled to myself. I had thought he'd do a full scene, since we would be alone for the entire evening and had the time and ability to focus, but fast and hard had been just as good.

I knew that it would be the first of many.

A WEEK after our glorious night at the Ritz-Carleton, life was back to normal.

I awakened just as the sun was rising and the first rays of sunlight beamed through the crack between the curtains. Dawn was my favorite time of the morning. The house was quiet and Drake and

Sophie were sleeping. This morning, she lay between us on her back, her little arms spread wide, her pacifier in her mouth. Although she fell asleep in her crib hours earlier, she started babbling and the sound from the monitor woke me, so I went into her room and brought her into our bed where she quickly settled down. Now, I lay beside her and just watched her sleep. Her hair was starting to grow in and was soft light brown wisps, curling over her ears and down the back of her neck. She was such a beautiful happy baby that I felt I couldn't deny her the comfort of sleeping with us. We'd moved our bed into the corner so that she couldn't fall out if she woke up and crawled around. A safety bedrail had been attached to the foot of the bed so she couldn't crawl out without waking Drake up.

Beside us, Drake slept on his stomach, naked except for his boxer briefs, a pillow over his head. He worked late last night, kept busy by the surfers and motorcyclists, skateboarders and highway speeders whose antics ended up in trips to the ER and a call to Drake to consult when a brain injury was suspected.

When we arrived, we thought Drake's workload would be lighter than in Manhattan since he wouldn't be taking on any patients outside of those who came in through the ER, but that hadn't turned out to be the case. The brain injuries were constant, and Drake had been busy.

That was good – he needed to be busy to take his mind off what has been going on back in Manhattan.

The trial made news almost daily with salacious bits of gossip about Lisa Monroe's sex life, Derek Richardson's sex life and Drake's sex life before I met him. Drake had been portrayed as Manhattan's Mr. Grey, even though nothing could be further from the truth. He hadn't faced the daily onslaught he did while he was still in Manhattan, so that had been a relief.

I slipped out of bed, crawling around my two sleeping beauties, and went to the bathroom for a quick shower. When I was dried off and dressed in my sundress, I tiptoed to the great room to make my cup of coffee and start the day. While Drake and Sophie slept, I squeezed some oranges for fresh orange juice. After making toast and peanut butter, I sat on the patio and watched the ocean. Even from our house, I could hear the surf roar in the distance. A few seagulls flew up and down the coastline, looking for their next meal.

I loved it here.

I pulled out my bullet journal and wrote for a few moments, listing all the things I was grateful for in my life – first, Drake. The love of my life. My soulmate and the man who made me realize how loved I was. Second was Sophia and her sunny disposition. Every day I thanked the universe for sending me a baby who was so easy, despite her difficult beginning. Finally, I was thankful that I had been raised by parents who loved me and now I truly appreciated that I was part of an affluent family where I never lacked for anything. I realized that everything was still open for me. I could go back to college and finish my MA when I felt ready. I could paint. I could become a freelance journalist and write about whatever I wanted. I could devote myself to charity, given Drake's money inherited from his father and from the business.

I closed my bullet journal after writing down some goals for the day: enjoy Sophia, show my love to Drake, and check out the studio space in downtown San Francisco.

Life was good.

I heard Sophie making noise on the monitor and went back to the bedroom to retrieve her so Drake could continue to sleep. When she saw me she smiled, her pacifier falling out of her mouth.

"There you are," I whispered as I picked her up where she sat up in bed, playing with her pacifier. "Time to get up."

S. E. LUND

I carried her to her bedroom and quickly changed her diaper before taking her to the kitchen island for her breakfast. She sat happily in her high chair and played with the toys I placed before her while I fixed her cereal. I dropped a few Cheerios on the high chair tabletop and Sophie was happy to pick each one up and pop it in her mouth.

I heard sounds from the back of the house and realized that Drake was up. I checked my watch – it was still far too early for him to get up, but he was a light sleeper and liked to spend the mornings with us when he could. Later, I'd take Sophie out for a walk and he'd go back to sleep, but for now, we'd have our breakfasts together.

Drake emerged down the hallway, wearing a pair of khaki shorts and nothing else, his hair still mussed from sleep. Seeing him half naked still did it for me. He was such a gorgeous man, tan and fit, his dark hair and blue eyes still making my knees weak.

"Good morning, Mrs. Morgan," he said when he came to my side at the stove. He kissed me and I could taste toothpaste on his tongue. He stroked my hair, smiling down at me. His eyes were still a bit bleary, but he looked somewhat refreshed after his sleep.

"Good morning, Dr. Morgan," I replied and kissed him again, a quick peck on the mouth because my bacon needed flipping. "Would you like bacon and eggs?"

"Sounds fabulous," he said and went over to Sophie, leaning down to kiss her and stroke her head. "My two girls."

Then he sat beside Sophie at the island and fed her a spoonful of cereal. He turned to me after he finished the second spoonful.

"What's on your agenda for today? Are you going to check out that studio space?"

I nodded, eager to look at the space in an old warehouse near the waterfront in San Francisco.

14

"Elaine's coming over this afternoon to watch Sophie for me so I can go and see it. I saw pictures online, but it's always nice to see the space in person."

"It's exciting," Drake said with a smile. "You'll get to meet a few other artists and make friends."

"I'll be happy just to have a space for myself," I said, feeling a little guilty still that I'd be leaving the house, but Elaine insisted that it would be good for me to create my own life outside of family. "Time to focus on my collection."

"You need it," Drake said and I was so glad he was so understanding. "Being a new mother is a lot of work. You need to be Kate, the artist or writer as well as Kate the mother and wife."

I removed the bacon from the pan and then went over to where he sat reading the morning paper.

"I'm happy to be a wife and mother, but I feel like moving here has opened up so many possibilities for me and for us."

"It has, strangely enough. I never thought I'd want to move away from Manhattan, but after the whole business with Lisa, I honestly couldn't wait to get away."

I leaned into his arms for a moment and stroked my fingers through his hair. "I'm sorry all this happened to you. You've sacrificed so much because of her."

"I sacrificed nothing," he said and kissed me. "I have everything I could ever need or want right here."

We kissed again and smiled at each other.

"Do you want your eggs scrambled or fried?" I asked when I left his embrace and went back to the stove.

"Scrambled," Drake replied and returned to reading his paper. Beside him, Sophie fingered her Cheerios and munched away happily. I nodded and quickly scrambled his eggs, before fixing him a plate. I placed it in front of him and sat beside him with my own and together, the three of us ate our breakfasts and watched the view through the picture window as the sun played on the ocean.

My cell rang and I grabbed it from the counter and checked the caller ID. It was my dad.

"Hey, Dad," I said, smiling at the thought of him.

"Hey, sweetheart, how are you today? How's the little family?"

I glanced at Drake and Sophie side by side. "We're great. What's up?"

"Elaine said we'd come by and sit with Sophie whenever you're ready and you can go into the city and do your business. We'll be happy to have her at our place for a few hours if you and Drake can come over for dinner tonight."

"Drake's working evenings so he won't be able to, but Sophie and I would love to have you stay at our place for dinner."

My father called out to Elaine. "Katie wants to know if we can stay for dinner. Drake's working so he can't come down. We could stay if you don't mind driving back later."

I heard Elaine respond and then my dad spoke.

"She says yes. Just tell us what time to come by and we'll be there whenever you're ready."

"Okay, thanks Dad. I appreciate you and Elaine sitting for me while I go out and check on the studio. I was planning on going sometime after three when Drake goes for his shift."

"No problem. I'll let Elaine know. We love to do it and you know it."

I said goodbye and ended the call.

16

"Too bad you can't join us," I said with a sigh. "You've worked so since we came to California."

"Gotta pull my weight," Drake said and held up his cup of coffee. "If I do, I might get a better shift next time. I hate sleeping during the mornings."

I nodded in sympathy. "You're far too successful to be putting in time, but I understand it was the only position open that fit."

We tidied up once we were finished eating. Drake kissed us both and went back to bed for a couple more hours of sleep before heading to the hospital to check on his patients.

On my part, I got us ready, packing up everything I'd need for a walk along the beach. When I was ready, I took the stroller out of the garage then packed Sophie in, her tiny pink sunhat fastened around her chubby cheeks. We stopped on the beach a mile down from our house and Sophie played in the sand. I sat beside her and got in some sun, enjoying the morning. There were only a few people walking the beach that morning, collecting shells and walking their dogs. I saw the same older couple out for their morning walk and we smiled at each other. People were generally friendly and often stopped to say hello to Sophia.

When I'd had enough sun and Sophie had crawled around, getting sand in her hands and her playsuit wet, we made our way back along the beach to the house. All in all, we were out for about an hour and a half. I wanted the house to be quiet so Drake could sleep longer. Because she was wet, I changed Sophie quietly and then we took a drive to the store to pick up a few items we needed. The local Whole Foods had great organic vegetables that I used to make Sophie baby food and so I did some shopping while Sophie sat in the cart and sucked on her pacifier. I picked up a cup of coffee from the local Starbucks, and then sat in the window seat with Sophie beside me in a high chair, and we watched people on the street while I planned my afternoon.

I looked at the calendar on my cell and thought about what I'd do if I liked the studio space. I'd get the keys and pay the deposit and the year's rent, then I'd start to move in my supplies. I was so excited that I had butterflies in my stomach. I was planning to finish the rest of the series of paintings from Africa and hoped to get the collection shown at a local gallery. I didn't care about selling my work, but I would be happy to feel like a real artist.

When I was done with my coffee, we drove back to the house and I hauled in the groceries and Sophie. She sat happily in her chair while I put the groceries away.

For the next couple of hours, I amused myself with Sophie, watching television and eating a light lunch. Finally, around two o'clock, I heard water running in the back of the house. Drake was up and was having a shower before he went to work. He emerged from the bathroom, wearing only boxer briefs, his hair still damp, and came right over to where I stood by the island reading my emails.

"I hate to leave you," he said, his arms slipping around me. "I wish we could go and lie down for a while."

"Me, too," I said and turned around in his arms, sliding my arms around his neck.

We kissed and it was a tender kiss that could have become passionate if we let it, but Drake would be leaving in a few moments and so we didn't go there.

The kiss ended and we stood together for a while, our foreheads pressed together, our arms around each other.

Drake sighed heavily. "Two more days," he said softly. "Two more shifts and then I'm all yours."

"I can't wait."

We kissed again and then he pulled away reluctantly and went to the bedroom to finish changing for his shift. When he emerged from the bedroom, he was wearing a pair of blue scrubs that made him look devastatingly handsome, highlighting his deep blue eyes.

"Gotta go," he said and kissed Sophie on the top of her head, running his hands over her hair before kissing me once more. I followed him to the door and watched him go to the SUV and get inside. He slipped on a pair of sunglasses and then backed out of the driveway, waving at me as he did.

Then he was gone.

Until Elaine dropped by to pick up Sophie, I busied myself getting her diaper bag ready and my art supplies in order in the office. Sophie played in her chair, grabbing at the toys I placed strategically around her.

The doorbell rang and I picked up Sophie and went to the door. Elaine and my father came in, he in his wheelchair. Luckily, the house was easily accessible for him. Once inside, we all hugged and kissed hello.

"Come in," I said and led them to the living room. I kissed Sophie and pulled went to the door, watching as Elaine took Sophie and placed her into my dad's arms.

"Sophie was just having some playtime. She could have a bottle in about thirty minutes and then you can put her down for a nap if you want. I probably won't be too long."

"Don't rush on our account," Elaine said. "Your father's looking forward to playing with her," she said and I watched as he kissed Sophie's cheek. "We haven't seen our little angel for almost a week."

"I'm on my cell if you need me," I said and went to the door. "I'll see you when I get back."

"You have fun. Don't rush because of us. Take your time and meet the other artists who work there if you can."

"I will," I said. "I hope the space is as nice as it looked on the website. I can't wait to get started back painting."

She smiled and I waved at her as I drove off, making my way up the coast to San Francisco, through the winding streets to the city and the Dogpatch area to Minnesota Street, renowned for its warehouses used as galleries and artist studios.

THE WAREHOUSE WAS DIRECTLY across the street from a converted building that functioned as a gallery for local artists. I was excited as I met with the building manager and went inside to check out the space that was open. I was lucky that the person who originally wanted the space pulled out at the last minute and so it was available and I was next in line, otherwise I might not have been offered a space. It was so in demand.

We walked through the halls to a studio facing the bay and the manager opened the door to admit me. I walked inside and glanced around. It was basic – a long narrow room with windows at one end and a small area with a sink, cupboard and countertop. We would share washroom facilities with the rest of the building tenants.

"I love it," I said, turning around in a circle and taking it in. The walls were a bit battered and there were marks on the wall where paintings had been hung but I didn't care.

"We can paint it white before you move in," he said. "That way you can start with a clean slate."

"No, that's fine. I like the way it looks. Makes it feel like a real studio."

"Okay, but if you change your mind, the offer stands. Just give me a day to arrange a painter to come in and it's done. We don't usually get people willing to pay for a full year up front, in addition to the security deposit, so we're happy to do it if you want."

"I'll be happy to be here looking out at that view of the bay, especially with the natural light."

We talked about the building facilities and then he handed me the magnetic card that I could use to get into the building and a key to my space. I left, and on my way out, decided to go to the gallery across the street and see what they had on display. I entered and walked around, looking at the paintings and collages and sculptures as well as installations. It inspired me and I felt giddy as I walked through the building, imagining that one day, I could have my work displayed there as well.

I had to finish my Africa collection and that was first on my agenda when I finally took possession of the studio.

As I was on my way out of the gallery, I passed a wall of notices of upcoming exhibitions, as well as requests for studio space. I saw one flyer, glossy, with a photo of something that looked familiar. At first, I couldn't remember where I'd seen the painting before but then I realized it was Sefton deVilliers.

Sefton was holding a traveling exhibition in the next month, that went across the country from Manhattan to LA and then up to San Francisco and Seattle before going to Canada. The poster featured him standing beside a large easel. On the canvas, a scene from the savannah. I could almost imagine it was from our time on the art safari. I checked the dates – in two weeks, he'd be in San Francisco after a week in New Orleans and then a week in Los Angeles. He'd already spent a week in Charlotte, North Carolina and another in DC. Before that, he'd been in Manhattan.

I got in the SUV and drove back to the house to pick up a few things for Sophie in case she needed a change of clothes, then I went to my father's place for supper. On the way, I thought to myself that I certainly didn't want to run into Sefton.

It wasn't that I felt anything for him. I never did, but he brought back painful memories of Drake's and my time in Africa and the whole business with Sefton and Sam.

I was glad that was behind me and would make sure that I didn't go to the exhibition he was holding while he was in town.

He was the last person I wanted to see.

CHAPTER 2

DRAKE

I ARRIVED at the hospital just before my shift and spent a few moments in the staff lounge, getting a last cup of coffee before I went to the ward to check on patients I'd seen the previous night. After that, I'd go to the ER to see how my new patients were doing. I was lucky that I got to follow patients from the ER to the wards and knew their outcomes. Many ER docs saw a patient in the ER and then didn't hear about them again.

I loved my job.

I never thought I'd want to work in the ER, preferring the calm and steady world of the neuro OR, but I did. I found it exhilarating to enter a room and try to figure out what was going on with a new patient. When I was pulled into a neuro consult, it could be for any number of reasons – a stroke, an aneurism, a traumatic brain injury, epilepsy, you name it. It kept me on my toes in a way that a very predictable and regular office practice and surgery practice didn't. I had to be ready to see anything and intervene on the fly when a patient decompensated.

Maybe there was a bit more of my trauma surgeon father in me than I realized. Maybe I was becoming less and less of a control freak.

If so, I credited it all to Kate and how she gave me what I really needed – love and a family.

I chatted with a few of the ER residents, enjoying their enthusiasm for their latest rotation and we talked about the cases we'd dealt with the previous night. I seemed to take on a natural teaching role with the residents and was happy to give my opinions on cases and make suggestions as well as offer encouragement.

Earlier in the evening, I'd texted Kate to see how she and Sophie were doing. Ethan and Elaine were at our place for supper.

KATE: Things went well today. I loved the studio space and can't wait to get set up in it. How is work?

DRAKE: Exciting, as usual. Who would have thought? I figured it would be too much excitement for an old neurosurgeon like me, but I love it. It's a real challenge.

KATE: Good. I'm glad you're enjoying it. I hope it doesn't burn you out. You're keeping quite a pace...

DRAKE: I'm off for a couple of days so I can rest up and spend time with my girls.

During a break, I went to the cafeteria and bought my supper, which consisted of a chef's salad and some yogurt, and sat by myself, reading over the paper while I ate. I was absorbed in a story when one of the staff physicians came over with his tray in hand and stopped my table.

"Drake Morgan, right?" he said and held up his tray. "If I'm not interrupting, do you mind if I join you?"

I pointed to the chair. "Be my guest. I was just finishing up and reading the headlines."

He sat and I saw his name tag, which read Dr. Roger Phillips. He was wearing a lab coat with the hospital logo on the lapel and I vaguely remembered from my orientation that he was an administrator in addition to being a staff physician.

He put his tray down and extended his hand. We shook and introduced ourselves and he began unpacking his sandwich.

"I thought I'd drop by and see how things are going. I haven't had the chance to sit down with you and have a chat. Markham's taking a leave to do some training in LA so I'm taking over for him and I'll be supervising the Neurosurgery Department. I was also on the review committee for appointments and remembered seeing your application. Markham was eager to hire you, and from your CV, I could see that you were top rate. You seem to be working out well, according to the staff I've spoken to so far."

"I appreciate the interest. If you had anything to do with hiring me, let me say thank you."

He gave me a strange smile. "Well, actually, I didn't," he said and bit into the sandwich. "I was away at a conference the week the decision was made, but I did see your application. I've also been reading about the trial in Manhattan."

I wiped my mouth after swallowing a mouthful of yogurt. "Oh, really?" I shrugged. "Something I'd much rather not have been involved in, believe me."

"So, it's true that the woman who attacked your wife was also involved in the murder of your friend. Richardson, right? A wealthy businessman? We normally have very little drama so this is quite the topic among the staff."

I leaned back and glanced at him, trying to read him but it was hard. He seemed friendly enough, but he brought up the case.

"I had no idea. No one has said anything to me about it, if it's the subject of gossip."

"I asked staff not to talk about it in front of you. Out of respect for your privacy so if you haven't heard anything, that's good. I wanted to check to make sure you were doing well and adjusting to things here."

"Yes, I am. I'm really enjoying my work here."

"Good. Like I say, early reports suggest that both the staff and patients like you, so we're glad to have you fill in. So long as there's no intrigue at his hospital, things will work out okay."

"In other words, keep my nose clean and down to the grindstone and I'll be okay?"

"Something like that." He smiled – a self-satisfied smile.

He'd just given me a warning that he and the hospital wouldn't tolerate any drama on my part. They really must think I was some kind of rogue.

I finished my food and checked my watch. "Well, my break is up so I better get back. Thanks for joining me and for the head's up. I appreciate it."

"No problem. Any time you have any questions or concerns, you come and speak to me."

I took my tray and placed it on the conveyor belt that went into the kitchen dishwasher, and threw the garbage into the trash can and left the cafeteria. As I left, I felt aware for the first time of a few heads that had turned my way. I never thought about it before, assuming I was just a new doctor and people were curious who I was, but now I realized they knew who I was and what was going on back in Manhattan with Lisa and the trial.

Of course, the trial was the topic of national news so they may have recognized me, but when I started working at the hospital over a month earlier, I didn't think it was that recognition which explained all the turned heads. I thought it was the fact I was a new face.

If I hoped to escape the whole business by traveling across the country and getting a new job, I was wrong. Lisa's attack on Kate and her involvement in Derek's murder had followed me to UCSF Hospital. No doubt the staff had read all about my participation in BDSM and my sexual relationship with the woman who tried to kill my pregnant wife.

What a scandal. I could imagine the staff talking behind my back while I was out of the staff room, and quickly shutting up and smiling at me, acting as if nothing was going on. Phillips warned them not to ask me about it, and that was probably the only reason no one had approached me with questions just yet.

I thought it was because I was free of my past, but I was wrong.

I WENT BACK to my desk in the office space I shared with several other ER doctors and read over some patient files, checking on test results and trying to focus on work instead of my personal drama, but it was hard and unsettled me for the rest of my shift. In the back of my mind from that time onward, I felt people's eyes on me and wondered if they knew and what they were thinking.

Kinky Doctor Morgan. Master D. Doctor Dangerous.

I wondered if anyone would say something to me about my past, and hoped they didn't.

My little talk with Roger Phillips had ruined my peace of mind.

I spent the rest of my shift seeing patients in the ER and popping in to check on patients on the wards and before I knew it, the evening was over and it was time for me to leave and go home to a sleeping Kate and Sophie.

At least I knew I wouldn't face any drama at home.

I ARRIVED JUST BEFORE four in the morning and parked the car, letting myself into the house as quietly as I could manage. I went to the bedroom to find Kate was asleep with Sophie beside her, sucking intently on her pacifier. The two of them looked so peaceful, I had to smile while I undressed. Before I got into bed, I had a quick shower, scrubbing the day off me, not wanting to bring any germs into my family bed.

After I dried off, I slipped into bed wearing only clean boxer briefs and snuggled next to Kate, trying not to wake up her or Sophie. She stayed asleep, luckily, and so I lay in bed for a while and tried to decompress after the shift. It took me a while, for my mind was caught in thoughts of Roger's conversation with me earlier in the night and how I now felt unsettled.

Would I never be able to work somewhere without my past coming back to haunt me?

Sleep was a long time in coming...

I WOKE in the morning when Sophie started grousing, clambering around on the bed. When I glanced out from under my pillow, I saw Sophie playing with Kate, sucking on her pacifier and pulling on Kate's locket. As usual, Kate picked up Sophie and took her out of the bed, not wanting to wake me up. It was too late, for I was awake and wanted to say good morning to Kate before I went back to sleep.

"Come back here," I called out. "Give me a kiss you two."

She came around the other side of the bed and sat on the edge, holding Sophie down so she could give me a kiss.

"Kisses," Kate said and I got several wet sloppies from Sophie before a kiss from Kate.

"How are my girls?" I asked, stroking Kate's arm and then Sophie's curls.

"We're fine. Had a nice time with Grandad and Grandma and then slept almost all night. How was your night?"

I tucked my pillow under my head and stroked Kate's hair. "It was good. Busy. The time passed really quickly."

"Anything interesting?"

I nodded. "It's all interesting in the ER. Had a first seizure come in. Typical head injuries from car accidents. An accident at a school playground. A stroke that needed immediate intervention."

"Do you want to get up and have breakfast with us?"

"Sure," I said and sat up in bed. "Might as well."

Kate took Sophie to change her and then after a trip to the bathroom, I went to join Kate in the kitchen. Sophie was sitting in her high chair at the island in the kitchen while Kate squeezed juice and made some French Toast using a loaf of French bread, topping it off with real maple syrup.

While we ate, I talked to her about the studio.

"You'll never guess what I found out," Kate said, raising her eyebrows. "Which artist that we both know is on a national tour, with an exhibit coming up in San Francisco?"

I frowned and chewed on my French Toast. It had to be only one person.

"Sefton."

She nodded, her lips pressed thin. "Yep. He'll be here in two weeks for a week and will be exhibiting in the gallery across the street from my studio."

"Remind me not to visit the gallery that week," I said with a snort.

"I know," she said and stared off in the distance. "I'll have to lay low that week just in case I see him on the street. I do want to go to an opening, but maybe the week before or after he's gone."

I shook my head. "Don't let him keep you from living your life. He has nothing on us and holds no power over you so ignore him. Go to the studio. You have to do what you love and you can't let other people derail you."

She leaned over and kissed me. "I love you, Dr. Morgan. You're always so reasonable and calm about things. I thought you'd be angry."

I frowned. "Why? You have no control over what he does."

She shrugged. "Of course, but just thinking about him brings back all these bad memories of what happened in Africa."

"Nothing happened in Africa," I said and leaned closer to her, stroking her cheek. "He wanted you and you didn't want him. He lost. I won." I kissed her lips. "You're mine."

"I am," she said with a smile. "Thankfully. I was afraid that you might have believed what Claire said and turned to Sam for solace."

"Ha!" I said with a laugh. "Not likely. I never felt anything for Sam other than she provided a convenient place to put my dick."

"Drake!" Kate grinned at me, punching me playfully in the shoulder. I mock-grimaced although it didn't hurt. "The poor girl was infatuated with you."

"I have no control over who finds me irresistible." I leaned over to Sophie and kissed her plump cheek. "Isn't that right, Sophie? You can't resist me either."

Sophie grinned at me, her mouth filled with Cheerios, her cheeks wet with milk.

"Speaking of who finds me irresistible, apparently, people at work are all filled in on the latest gossip about me, or so the new head of the Neurosurgery Department informed me. Roger Phillips took over as head from Vince Markham and told me last night during my supper break."

"What?" Kate frowned, her expression horrified. "People know about the case?"

"Apparently," I said and sopped up the syrup with a hunk of French Toast. "Roger told them to keep it down and not mention it to me. But everyone knows."

"I'm so sorry," she said and leaned in and kissed me tenderly. "They'll realize that you're nothing like the papers portrayed you."

"Really?" I said, only half-jokingly. "The papers portrayed me as, and I quote, a Dashing Devilish Dom, if I recall correctly..."

"You are a Dashingly Devilish Dom, but you are definitely not a Secret Sadist Surgeon," Kate replied, quoting one very notorious gossip columnist.

We laughed together, and it made me feel better to see Kate brush it off, but I still felt uneasy about the staff knowing my personal business. There was nothing I could do about it now, so I decided to just keep my head down and do my job.

We finished our breakfast while Sophie played with her food, managing to eat only half of it. The rest ended up on the floor or on top of her head. I helped clean up after breakfast, then I kissed Kate and Sophie and went back to bed, needing a couple of hours sleep if I hoped to make it through another night at work.

Despite being tired, I tossed and turned, my mind still caught up in the meeting with Roger and the way staff looked at me – or the way I realized staff had been looking at me since I started my new job. It ruined what had been a great shift.

There was nothing I could do about it so I tried to shut off my mind and fall back asleep but once again, it was a long time coming.

CHAPTER 3

KATE

DRAKE WENT BACK to work just before three that afternoon, and on my part, I packed up the car with boxes of my supplies and canvases. Before I left, I put Sophie in her car seat and drove to my father's place down the highway. I wanted to go back to the studio but didn't want my father to have to make the trip. It was an hour there but I didn't mind.

After I dropped Sophie with Elaine and my dad, I drove up the coast to the studio and parked on the street outside. For the next few minutes, I unloaded boxes, carrying them into the building one at a time. Before I was finished, a guy about my age saw me struggling with some canvases and offered to help.

"You're the new tenant?" he asked, taking a couple of canvases up the stairs.

"Yes," I said and we stopped on the landing. "I'm Kate."

He extended his hand. "Marco," he said. "I'm in the studio across the hall."

We shook hands and it was slightly awkward. "I see you do naturalist art," he said and held out one of my unfinished canvases featuring an elephant drinking out of a waterhole.

"Yes, I went on an art safari in Kenya and started the series last year."

"Cool," he said. "I do acrylics. Urbanscapes."

When I frowned in confusion, he added. "The urban landscape."

"I'd love to see your work," I said, eager to meet other artists in the building and become part of a community."

"Come on over when you can. I'm right across from you. I share my studio space with my girlfriend, Serena. We'll be having some hot tea soon and you're welcome to join us."

"Hot tea?"

"She's British. They drink hot tea. I got in the habit."

"I love hot tea," I replied. "My mother was from Poland and they drink a lot of it."

I smiled, glad that he was attached so that there'd be no misunderstanding about my intentions or his.

"Sounds great."

We finished carrying up the boxes and canvases and I went into my studio and he into his.

I closed the door and stood in the empty space, glancing around, imagining it once I had everything settled. I turned around in a circle. The room was bright because of the west-facing windows, but it was indirect light and filled the room. Overhead incandescent lights added to the brightness. Several of my blank canvases leaned against one wall. I was eager to finish my current work and move on to my other plans.

There was a workbench against one wall with a shelf. I could stack my paints and brushes and other paraphernalia there. I needed to go to the local art supply store for some fresh paint thinner and a few other supplies before I could get started. I wanted to get a high stool so I could sit at the workbench and use my computer if I wanted. Plus, I wanted a small television so I could watch news if I wanted while I worked.

For the next hour, I unpacked my supplies and tried to arrange them in some logical fashion, and then wrote down a list of what other supplies I'd need. I decided to leave and do some shopping. I could return the next day and maybe get my easel set up and start back on my current work in progress.

I picked up my unfinished painting and studied it in the bright light from the window. The elephant was sketched in and half-painted. Beside it, I'd sketched in a wildebeest, which stood knee-deep in the water, a white bird on its back. In the distance was a copse of baobab trees, their spindly branches reaching up towards the white-blue sky. The white hot African sun beat down on the scene. I could almost feel the heat from memory, smell the dust, hear the wind whipping through the tall grass.

I was pleased with the painting so far and with the studio space, I couldn't wait to get back to work on it. In fact, I couldn't have asked for a more perfect setup. The only thing missing was a sound system so I could listen to music while I worked.

I checked my watch which read close to 4:30 P.M. and so I decided to pop over to check out Marco's space and see what he meant by urban-scapes. I grabbed my bag and locked the door, then went across the hall to his studio, knocking on the door hesitantly. I still felt a bit nervous meeting new people but he seemed nice.

The door opened and a woman in paint spattered blue-jean overalls answered, her dark hair pulled back with a blue head band, long braids falling over her shoulders. She smiled at me.

"You're Kate, right?" she said with a slight British accent.

"Yes, I am. You must be Serena."

She opened the door and ushered me in.

"Marco told me you might pop by. Come in. We have some tea brewing if you want some."

"Thanks."

I entered the space and saw that it was divided in two, with Marco's work on one side and Serena's work on the other. Marco was busy applying gesso to a new canvas, bending over the frame and using broad strokes to cover its surface. He stopped and smiled at me.

"I'm just about done. Take a look around. Serena's brewing some tea."

"Thanks, I will," I replied and peeked at his canvases. Half a dozen lined the walls. They were quite different than I imagined. Bright colors and broad strokes of downtown San Francisco streets. At first, the colors seem positive, vibrant, but then I examined the subject matter and found it was all back alleys, empty parking lots. Garbage bins overflowed, discarded bottles lined gutters, a homeless man sat against the brick wall in an alley, a hat partially shading his craggy and weathered face.

Marco was talented. His choice of subject was critical. It seemed like he was making a comment on the forgotten, the discarded.

"These are really good," I said, honestly impressed.

"Thank you," he said. "I grew up in that neighborhood. It's pretty rough."

"You've really captured it. I feel a sense of desperation in these."

"There's a lot of hardship on those streets."

I glanced over at Serena's half of the space and saw that she did portraits. Her canvases were all people and were impressionistic. The colors were muted, and the people's faces were dirty and their hair messy. I didn't honestly know what to think of her work, but it was clear she had a point of view and was talented.

"Who are your subjects?" I asked.

"They're street people," she said. "Marco and I are activists. We're trying to show the people and places everyone forgets."

I nodded in understanding.

We had a cup of tea together and the two talked about their work and how they met in an art class at UCSF. It was a real love story. They seemed to be really in love by the way they looked at each other when they talked. It was sweet.

It made me feel a pang of regret that Drake had been so busy at the hospital working the evening shift that I hardly spent any time with him alone or with Sophie since we arrived in San Francisco.

I was determined to change that. Drake had a couple of days off coming up and I was going to make them memorable. We hadn't really made love for a while and I missed him. I missed that easy sexuality we shared. I loved Sophie madly but we were both so tired all the time that it was hard to find the perfect time for sex.

And we hadn't done anything kinky for a long time.

After our tea was finished, I said goodbye to Marco and Serena and left the building, driving back down the coast and to my father's house to pick up Sophie.

When I arrived, she was playing on the beach with Elaine while my father sat on the patio and watched.

I bent down and kissed my father on the cheek. "How are you?"

He squeezed my hand on his shoulder. "I'm great. Sophie and Elaine are down on the beach. They're having a great time. How are you? How's the studio?"

"It's wonderful," I said and sat beside him for a moment. "I honestly couldn't have asked for a better space. I can't wait to finish getting set up so I can start to paint again."

"Great to hear," he said and smiled. "You need to make a life for yourself outside of Sophie and Drake. If you do, it will make your time with them both so much more meaningful."

"You think so?" I said, sighing. "I was feeling guilty taking time away from them both, like I was denying them."

"Not at all," my father said and pointed to the beach. "You're allowing Sophie time with her grandparents. That's something great. You're allowing Drake time to spend with Sophie alone so he can establish his own bond with her. A father and daughter have a special relationship. I can't explain it, but it is special."

"I know," I said and squeezed his hand back. "I guess I feel selfish wanting time to myself to paint."

"Don't feel that way. You're more than any one thing. You're more than an artist. You're more than a mother and wife. You're more than a daughter. You're all those things together and more. You are more than the sum of your parts, Kate."

I kissed the top of his head. "How come you always say the right thing to take me out of my funk?"

He frowned. "Are you in a funk?"

"No," I said, correcting myself. "I was just feeling guilty and wanting to spend more time with Drake alone. It seems we're always too tired to be a couple anymore and when we do feel great, we have Sophia.

Don't get me wrong," I said quickly. "I wouldn't change things, except maybe have a bit more time with Drake."

"It gets better," he said and nodded in understanding. "I remember when your mother and I had you and Heath and I was busy trying to make a name for myself as a district attorney and worked late every night. We barely saw each other for a few years. It was hard. But you and Drake should be able to spend more time with each other by choice. He doesn't have to work. Neither do you."

"Drake has the bad shift that no one else wants so he's awake when Sophie is sleeping and is sleeping when she's awake. It's hard enough for him to spend time with her, let alone with me."

"He can get a different shift eventually. Try to enjoy what you can enjoy and don't shoot for perfection. It doesn't exist."

"I know," I said, feeling rather selfish for expecting perfection. "I'll try."

We watched as Elaine gathered up the toys and stuffed them into the tote bag and then picked up Sophie and returned to the house.

I took Sophie from her arms and kissed her. She seemed happy and had some color in her otherwise super fair skin.

"Are you staying for supper?" Elaine asked as she put the toys away. "After all that driving, you need a rest. We're having something delivered. Just some seafood and salad from the local restaurant but you two are welcome to stay."

I smiled. "That sounds good," I said and took Sophie in so I could change her and wash the sand off her legs and clothes.

I SPENT the evening with Elaine and my father, ate a meal with them, and then Sophie and I drove home around eight thirty, after the last rays of sun set across the ocean.

When I got back home, I was able to put Sophie in her crib without a complaint, her toys surrounding her, the mobile on the crib moving around in a circle, a lullaby playing on the tiny speaker. Her eyes were still closed when I left the room and closed the door.

I went to the kitchen and made myself a cup of hot decaf coffee and stood in front of the picture window, watching the ocean as the sky darkened and the stars began to peek out of the blackness.

My cell dinged, indicating a text.

I picked up my cell from the kitchen island counter and was rewarded with a text from Drake.

DRAKE: Hey, sweetheart. How are you and my favorite little girl?

I smiled and texted him back.

KATE: We just got back from my parents. Sophie is asleep and I'm drinking a cup of decaf and being thankful for the wonderful life I have with you.

DRAKE: I miss you. I'm off tomorrow so I hope the three of us can try to have some fun and enjoy a few days of peace and quiet.

KATE: Sounds good. Elaine said we could leave Sophie there overnight so you and I could have a romantic interlude if we wanted.

DRAKE: That sounds fantastic. Maybe not tomorrow night because I'm sure I'll still be wildly out of sync with your sleep schedule and would probably keep you up all night... wait a minute... ;)

KATE: You could keep me up all night if you want. I won't complain...

DRAKE: I just might plan on it.

KATE: I wait for your plans with bated breath and beating heart. See you in the morning.

DRAKE: I love you, Mrs. Morgan.

KATE: I love you, Dr. Morgan.

I read over our texts and then put my cell away. I imagined Drake sitting in a staff room in the hospital, wearing his scrubs, reading my texts and smiled to myself. He was irresistible in those scrubs, a stethoscope around his neck. I imagined that a number of female staff would be drooling over him and felt a twinge of jealousy that they would get to enjoy him while I wouldn't. Of course, I had him during the few hours of the day between him waking and going for his next shift. Hopefully, our few days off together would make up for some of the deprivation I felt due to his busy schedule. We'd drop off Sophie at my parent's place overnight so Drake and I could have a romantic date night together.

I could hardly wait...

CHAPTER 4

DRAKE

My shift in the ER passed quickly due to a larger than normal number of traumatic brain injuries.

A single accident led to two patients, each needing my skills to rule out anything more than a concussion. Some idiot decided to ride on a motorized skateboard without a helmet and was knocked down in a crosswalk by a pedestrian. The pedestrian was fine but the skate-boarder was unconscious and had a real injury to his temporal lobe. Surgery to relieve pressure on the man's brain was necessary, which kept me busy for most of the evening and watching him overnight. The usual assortment of neuro cases rounded out the evening and by the time my shift was over, I barely realized twelve hours had passed.

Before I left, I checked over each of my patients from the previous night and spoke with the nurses on the neurosurgery ward to make sure things were under control.

Then I went to the staff room and had a shower at work instead of waiting until I got home. I wanted to be able to slip right into bed with Kate – and possibly with Sophia if she was in the bed with Kate – without running a shower or making any noise.

I took a clean set of scrubs I kept in my shared office space and went to the shower facilities set aside for staff and had a quick shower. After dropping off my dirty scrubs in the laundry, I popped into the staff room to grab one of the donuts I saw there during a break and ran into Clint Blackstone, a trauma surgeon, who worked the same shift as I did and who was in a *tete a tete* with one of the nursing staff.

"Hey, Drake," he said and waved me over. "Christy was just telling me that she knew your wife back in Manhattan before you two were divorced."

I glanced at the woman, but didn't recognize her. She was on the short side and a bit portly, with dark eyes and her brown hair pulled back in a bun. If she knew Maureen, she'd know all about our divorce and probably my sordid past in Manhattan.

"Hello," I said hesitantly. "I don't believe we've met."

Christy smiled at me – an obviously forced smile. "I worked with Maureen before you two split and I came out here just after your divorce. Maureen put in a good word for me and I've been here ever since."

"Good to meet you. Well, I'm off for two days," I said to Clint, "so I won't see you until next week."

"Have a good one," Clint said. "Remember that we're going to play a round of golf someday soon."

"It's on," I replied and pointed to him. "Next week."

"Sounds good."

I smiled and left the two of them in the staff lounge, wondering what stories Christy would tell. I could only imagine that her opinion of me would be bad.

I left the hospital and walked through the still-crowded ER parking lot of the staff section to my car. Before I could get inside, I heard footsteps and turned to see Christy walking briskly behind me. She was obviously trying to catch up to me.

"Oh, Drake," she said and was slightly out of breath when she reached my car. "I wanted you to know I hold no ill-will towards you over your and Maureen's divorce."

I frowned, and opened my door, surprised that she'd followed me all the way out like that.

"That's nice, Christy, but I don't know why you'd hold any ill-will towards me. It was Maureen who wanted the divorce because she was having an affair."

I raised my eyebrows, not really caring anymore about what she thought.

"That's not what she told me. She told me you were a control freak and that she had to get a restraining order," she responded tartly. "I also know all about your wife's unfortunate run in with your ex-submissive so..."

She let her voice trail off suggestively.

Damn... The last thing I needed was a busybody like Christy telling people all about my past.

"So?" I said. "What's your point? You know about my past."

I couldn't stop myself. She had a lot of nerve following me out into the parking lot to tell me she knew my private business.

"So, the point is that I know about your past and I wanted you to know that we have a policy of no fraternizing with the staff."

"I'm married. Happily."

"That's fine but there can be no missteps with any of the staff. I'm on the hospital's sexual harassment committee and I keep tabs on these things. That's all."

"What?" I could barely believe what she just said. "What the hell do you mean, you keep tabs on these things?"

"Exactly what I said," she said and put her hands on her hips. "We have a committee. I'm on the committee. It's made up of people concerned with the welfare of our female staff members. People are aware of your past and have advised the new nurses and the student nurses to beware. There's gossip that you also had an affair with one of your students in Africa when you taught in Nairobi."

I stood in awed silence for a moment at the self-satisfied expression on her face, and struggled for a response. Then, I realized that there really was no response, so I shrugged, trying hard to keep my calm.

"That was the past. Now, I'm a very happily married man and father of a toddler. You can rest assured that I have no interest in the nursing staff – or anyone else, for that matter."

Then I sat inside, slamming the door before she could respond. I gave her a big smile and I heard her talking to me through the window but her words were muffled by the sound of my car stereo. I turned up as loud as I could and while I drove away, I saw her point her finger at me, her face screwed up in anger.

What a witch...

She'd obviously taken it upon herself to be the protector of the nursing staff from dangerous threats like me. She was one of

Maureen's friends? I could imagine it. Maureen still disapproved of me all these years later, even though I saved Liam's life.

I drove through the darkened streets of the city, a little faster than I should have, and must have been caught up in a speed trap for as I was flying along the road, I heard a siren and saw lights flashing behind me.

Damn...

I pulled over and stopped my car, already reaching for my driver's license and registration so I could easily hand them to the police officer. Then, I put my hands clearly on the wheel and waited for the officer to come over to my open window.

When he got out of his vehicle, I saw him checking out the car, one hand on his weapon. He walked up to my door and bent down, peering into the car and at me, no doubt sizing me up. I had on a clean pair of hospital scrubs and my hair was still a bit damp.

I smiled at him. "Hello, officer."

He checked me out, nodding in response. "Driver's license and registration please."

I pointed to the dashboard. "It's there. I'm reaching for it now."

I grabbed it and handed them to the officer and waited. He checked them over and handed them back to me.

"Dr. Morgan, are you aware you were traveling fifty miles per hour in a thirty mile per hour zone?"

"I'm sorry, officer. I just got off my shift in the ER at SF General and must have lost track of my speed."

He nodded, his expression not changing at all. "It's late. You should try to obey the speed limit even this late at night when the streets are empty. I'll give you a warning this time, but the next time, I'll have to issue you a ticket."

"Thanks," I said. "I'll be more careful from now on."

He nodded and returned to his vehicle. I put on my signal and merged back into the lane and drove the rest of the way home more cautiously, making sure to keep my speed in check.

By the time I got home, it was four in the morning. I pulled up in the driveway just as the first faint sunlight was visible along the eastern horizon. I entered the house as quietly as I could, and stripped off my clothes down to my boxer briefs. I stood beside the bed and just watched for a moment. On the bed lay a sleeping Kate and beside her Sophie, who was facing the wall, her thumb stuck in her mouth, an empty bottle on the bed near her hand.

I slipped into bed beside Kate, trying not to wake her but she was a pretty light sleeper and woke when I snuggled closer. She rolled over into my arms and I kissed her on the forehead, and pulled her closer.

"What time is it?" she asked, her eyes still closed.

"It's just after four thirty. I was late getting out and was pulled over for speeding on the way back."

Her eyes blinked open at that. "Oh, Drake," she whispered, her voice less sleepy. "What happened?"

"I had a run-in with a nursing supervisor on the sexual harassment committee so I must have been pressing a bit too enthusiastically on the gas pedal. The cop was nice and let me off when he realized I was an ER doc just getting off shift."

"What do you mean, you had a run-in with a nursing supervisor on the sexual harassment committee?"

Then I told Kate about meeting Christy, how she had been a friend of Maureen's in Manhattan and what she told me about watching me for the committee.

"Oh, God, Drake! What a total bitch," Kate said, her voice filled with sympathy – and a bit of anger.

"My words exactly," I replied and squeezed her more tightly, so glad that I had her and that she understood. "I told her I was happily married and wasn't interested in the nursing staff."

"You should go to your supervisor and let him know what she said."

I shook my head. "I think it's best to lay low.

"You're too good," she said and kissed my chin. "If it were me, I'd have told her off. What nerve! To follow you in the parking lot and insinuate that she was warning the nursing staff about you? What does she think you are? A stalker?"

"She thinks I'm Christian Grey and that I'm going to tie up and whip the nursing staff in the broom closet."

"She wishes," Kate said with a laugh. "She's probably fantasizing about you tying *her* up."

"I think she hates me," I said, smiling at Kate's defense of me. "She was Maureen's friend so that's pretty much guaranteed."

"Well, she's wrong. Maureen cheated on you. If anyone deserves to feel bad, it's Maureen for cheating on her husband and never telling you that she was pregnant with your child. She had your baby for years and didn't tell you until she needed you to save your child's life. That's what people don't know about Maureen."

"Did I tell you that I love you?" I said, my throat choked up from the passion in Kate's voice.

"You did, but you can do it again as many times as you want."

Then I kissed her and my heart swelled with love for her, my fierce defender. I would have liked to make love to her at that moment, but Sophie snuffled beside us on the bed and Kate turned over, slipping out of my arms so she could put Sophie's pacifier back in her mouth.

"Tomorrow night I'm going to fuck your brains out, Mrs. Morgan, and make you orgasm at least two times," I whispered, slipping my arm around her waist, snuggling against her. "You can count on it."

"Only two?" she replied, a saucy note in her voice.

"Don't get too greedy," I said with a laugh. I squeezed her, and then closed my eyes, smiling, happy to be back where I belonged with my beautiful loving wife and cherub of a baby.

I SLEPT THROUGH THE MORNING, barely opening my eyes when Kate and Sophie got up and left me alone in the warm bed, a pillow over my head to blot out the light. The house was so filled with sunlight from every angle that I needed a pillow to be able to fall back to sleep. I'd sleep through breakfast and have lunch with them, because I'd be able to spend the next couple of glorious days with the two of them non-stop.

When I finally woke up for good, I smelled coffee brewing in the kitchen and heard the television, tuned to CNN and whatever passed for breaking news. It was just audible over the sound of water running in the laundry room. Kate had been busy. I rose from the bed and went to the bathroom to have a quick shower. I needed to feel the hot stream of water to wake me up completely. Five days of consecutive twelve-hour shifts had worn me out. I'd need a day or two of solid sleep to catch up.

I dressed in a pair of shorts and light t-shirt and went to the kitchen to fix myself a cup of coffee. In the distance, I saw Kate and Sophie on the beach below our house. Kate was standing beside Sophie, her hands on her hips, watching the ocean. Sophie played in the sand with her toys, her little floppy brimmed hat on to shade her face from the sun.

It was a peaceful domestic scene and made me feel it was all worth it. The long hours at the ER, the lack of sleep, even the hassles of trying to fit into a new environment and learn new procedures and rules. Not even Christy and her busy-body-in-my-business warning could ruin my mood when I saw what waited for me on the beach.

I took my cup of coffee, slipped on my sunglasses and joined Kate and Sophie on the beach. When I reached her side, I pulled Kate into my arms and kissed her on the mouth.

"How are you today, Mrs. Morgan?"

She smiled and squeezed me. "Wonderful, as usual. How did you sleep?"

"As well as can be expected. How's my little Sophie?"

"She's good. We're so lucky to have such a good baby."

"We are."

I knelt and watched Sophie play. She had a shovel in her hand and was flapping it against the sand. She smiled up at me around her pacifier and that smile made me smile even larger. For the next fifteen minutes, we built a sand castle, or should I say, I built one and Sophie smacked it with her shovel.

"Are you hungry?" Kate asked. "I was going to make us some lunch if you are. What do you feel like?"

I sat back and glanced up at her. "Anything you want."

"I have some leftover chicken curry and rice if you want me to heat it up."

"Like I say, whatever you feel like. I'm used to cafeteria food so I'll eat anything if it's homemade."

Kate left the two of us on the beach and went back to the house to fix lunch. For the next ten minutes or so, I stayed and played with Sophie, taking her down to the water and letting her stand in the surf, our feet wet while I walked her around, her little hands clasped tightly in mine.

I gathered up the toys and then carried Sophie back up to the house, glad to be able to spend lunch with them instead of sleeping. The rest of the day was ours and I wanted to soak up the family life while I could.

When lunch was ready, we sat down at the island and ate our food. Sophie sat in her chair and I spooned some food into her mouth between a spoonful of my own lunch into mine.

"Are you going to your studio this afternoon?" I asked, remembering that Kate had a few things to get for her studio. "You might as well while Sophie has a nap."

"Do you mind?" she replied, biting her lip like she felt guilty. "I'd love to finish getting a few things from the art supply store and I need a stool so I thought I might pop by. Then, we can spend the rest of the day together until we drop Sophie at my dad's for the night."

"That was my thinking."

Just then, my cell dinged, indicating a text message.

BRENDA: *Do you have a minute? Wanted to pass something by you.*

"Who is it?" Kate asked, leaning over my shoulder to check.

"It's Brenda. She sent me an email saying that she's in town staying at Maureen's and probably wants to know if Liam can come for a visit."

I connected the cell number beside Brenda's contact and waited for her to answer. She came on the line after the first ring.

"Oh, Drake, thanks for calling. I'm in town for a couple of weeks and have something delicate to discuss with you, but I can't right at this moment."

Her voice was soft like she was trying to hide her conversation with me.

A surge of adrenaline went through me at the possibility that Liam was sick.

"What's the matter? Is Liam okay?"

"He's fine. I really can't talk now, because he's here for lunch, but if you could come by and meet me for a coffee so we could talk while he's in school, that would be great."

"Sure, when would you like me to come by?"

"If you're free this afternoon, that would be best. Liam gets out of school after three and I usually pick him up at that point."

"What's this about, Brenda? I need to know something."

"It's about Maureen and Chris. Just come by and I'll explain everything."

I sighed. "Okay. I'll be there at two o'clock."

"That should give us enough time before Liam gets out of school," Brenda replied. "Thanks, Drake. I appreciate this. I know it's cloak and dagger but I don't want to say anything in front of Liam."

"You could text me the gist of it."

"Okay, sure. See you later."

I hung up and waited for her text. Within five minutes, my cell dinged and I read her text.

BRENDA: Chris is unhappy back in California and wants to go back to Indonesia. Maureen wants to go with him. She doesn't think Liam can come because of his medical needs. I offered to keep him with me for part of the year, but that means he'll be coming to Manhattan with me. As his father, I think you're the logical one for Liam to live with, even if only part time. Maureen's not happy about that, but I think she's really depressed and isn't thinking straight. We need to talk strategy.

I showed the text to Kate and she gasped, her eyes wide.

"Oh, my God, Drake. How could she leave Liam like that? How could she consider it?"

I shook my head. "She must be depressed. People who are depressed sometimes can't think clearly. "She thinks she can't live without Chris."

"How can Chris force this kind of decision? He doesn't deserve to have Liam as a stepson."

I shrugged and texted my reply.

DRAKE: I understand. She wants to go with Chris but can't take Liam because he's still under close observation and his remission is being monitored. Maybe after we're sure his remission is more permanent, he can go and stay with her for a while. He should be able to fly there and stay for a short time, but if it interferes with his school it might be best to stay with me in California. I'm sure Kate and I would be happy to have Liam stay with us, either permanently or part time. Up to you and Maureen and I to work it out. But I'd hate to see him bounced around between Manhattan and San Francisco.

BRENDA: Thanks for being so sensitive about this. I'm at my wit's end with Maureen. I only want what's best for all of us but my life is in Manhattan. I'd be happy to have him stay with me but if you're here, and Liam is in school and loving it, I think he should be here. One place or the other. Since you're his father, it's best he stay with you.

DRAKE: *See you in thirty minutes.*

I put my cell away and looked at Kate.

"Would you be okay if Liam came and stayed with us?"

Kate leaned closer to me and ran her fingers through my hair. "Drake, he's your son. Of course, he can come and stay with us. Whatever you want."

We kissed and I was so glad that I had such an understanding wife.

"I'm sorry if this means you can't go to your studio."

"No, that's no problem. This is important. I can go to my studio any day."

I kissed her. "You're so wonderful. I better get ready and leave so I can be there in time."

I kissed Sophie and Kate once more.

"Maybe Sophie will grow up with a big brother after all," she said hopefully.

"It would be great for them both but I have a feeling it's going to be a long hard battle with Maureen. She doesn't like the idea of me having anything to do with raising Liam other than parental visits now and then. But if Brenda takes Liam back to Manhattan with her, it'll be even harder for me to see him. I can afford to fly there whenever I want, but still. It's a huge inconvenience considering I'm living here now."

"I know. I'm sorry this is happening."

I kissed her and after changing into something more appropriate, I gathered my wallet and keys before leaving the house, wondering as I drove along the highway to Maureen's place farther south on the coast how things would work out.

Having Liam live with me had been something in the back of my mind since I found out he was my son.

I ARRIVED at Maureen's place in the southern sector of San Francisco and knocked on the door once I arrived. Brenda greeted me and I entered the cool dark interior of her bungalow.

"Come in," she said and gave me a quick hug. "We have about an hour before Liam comes back from school. Can I get you a cup of coffee or a drink of something? Lemonade?"

"Lemonade sounds good. I just had coffee."

She mixed me a tall glass.

"You have to understand I'm really mad at Maureen over this," Brenda said and I could hear the emotion in her voice. "I just don't understand how she could even imagine going with Chris and leaving Liam behind. It's horrible of her."

"She must be very unhappy to consider it. I know she loves Liam."

Brenda shook her head and slipped on a pair of dark sunglasses. Then, the two of us went to the deck and sat on a pair of lawn chairs under an awning. Across from us, the view of the harbor was fantastic.

"She's selfish, plain and simple. Chris is selfish if he insists on leaving. Why can't he be happy here? He must know this is forcing Maureen to choose between him and Liam."

"He's not Liam's biological father. I would think there's a sore spot in him because of that."

"He raised Liam all those years, thinking Liam was his."

I shrugged. "People are different. I never knew Liam was mine, but I'd take him tomorrow and make sure he had the very best family life I could give him."

"I know," Brenda said and reached over to take my hand and squeeze it. "I'm so glad you feel that way. I'd be willing to keep Liam here, but you are his father and he deserves to be with you. Since we're both here, we can both see him while Maureen is away. Maybe she'll come to her senses and move back, realizing that Liam is more important than Chris."

I shook my head. "I can't imagine being forced to choose between Kate and Sophie. I couldn't do it."

"I had to when Maureen's father left us. I made sure to stay in the same neighborhood so that Maureen could grow up with her friends and stay at her school. It was only when she went off to college that I finally was able to come back to California to live, at least part of the year. I feel like Maureen should be able to make the sacrifice and stay here. She could always fly to Kuala Lumpur for a week or two at a time and leave Liam with me, but she's afraid that the distance will break them up."

"They say absence makes the heart grow fonder."

"I told her that but she replied 'out of sight, out of mind'. She thinks it would be inevitable that Chris would find someone else."

"He might. Liam will always be her son. Look, I know how hard it is to lose a mother. I survived, but I wouldn't want to force a child through it."

"She mentioned you and said that you were able to be a success even though your mother left. She said that a lot of children spend long periods of time with their grandparents and besides, she said she'd fly home frequently on holidays to be with Liam."

"It's not enough," I said, frowning, angry at Maureen for doing this to Liam. "Holidays are never enough."

We sat in silence for a while and I sipped my lemonade, wondering how upset Liam would be when he learned she was leaving. I remembered crying for days when my mother left and my father was no help. He kept trying to reassure me that she'd come back for visits, but she never did. She sent me cards for the first year or two but even they stopped when she got a new life and moved on.

It hurt.

Who knew how much losing my mother shaped me into the man I currently was? I was wound up so tight growing up, trying to keep my emotions in check, fearing that if I didn't, people wouldn't like me. My father loved me, but he only showed it by doing physical things with me, like working on a car or bike or taking me on trips where we didn't talk about things that really mattered.

I didn't want Liam to grow up with a father like that. I wanted him to know I loved him because I showed it and told him so.

I did love Liam, even though I barely knew him. I felt an incredible wave of emotion as I sat there with Brenda and thought about Maureen leaving him to go to Indonesia. My eyes brimmed and I had to bite my inner cheek to stop it, the pain washing away some of my emotions.

"I'll do whatever Liam needs," I said, my voice choked up. "If he wants to come and stay with us, I'll be happy to have him and so will Kate. I know Sophie would love to have a big brother. You can see him as much as you want."

"I want you to know that Maureen will fight you having custody."

"What?" I said and turned to face Brenda. "If she's going away, she has to let me have him. He needs a parent. It's great he has you, but he needs a father and a mother. Kate and I will give him that. How could she fight it?"

"The trial," Brenda said and sighed. "She thinks it would be bad for Liam to be living with you while the trial is going on. She doesn't want him to know his father is involved in anything sordid."

"I'm not. Kate was attacked by a psychopath who imagined a relationship between us."

"I know that and you know that, but Maureen has this thing about you, Drake. I just wanted you to know that if you want custody, you'll have to sue for it."

"I will," I said, my anger rising, making my heart pound. "I'll sue for custody and I have some of the best lawyers money can buy."

"I know," she said. "I'm sure you do. The courts can be tricky when it comes to custody, especially if parents have been involved in anything..." she hesitated. "Questionable, sexually. Just be prepared."

"I will."

Then I left, my heart heavy at the thought that Maureen would leave Liam for so long. If I had anything to do with it, he'd come to live with me.

I was his father.

CHAPTER 5

KATE

D RAKE LEFT Sophie and me and took his car down the coast to Maureen's. Instead of spending the afternoon with him before I went to the studio as I had planned, it would just be Sophie and me, alone as usual.

I felt bad for Drake and Brenda, having to work together to try and figure out how to deal with Maureen's depression and desire to leave the country with Chris, but if Drake could get shared custody, maybe this would give him the chance to really be a father to Liam. He saved Liam's life and now, maybe he'd be able to get to know him as a son. My heart squeezed to think of how sad Liam would be to see his mother leave. How could he feel anything but rejected and abandoned? Maureen had to be completely depressed to be willing to leave Liam behind and go with Chris. I couldn't understand it.

But then I remembered – that's exactly what happened to Drake.

Drake's mother left him when he was only ten years old. She'd never recovered from the loss of Drake's older brother, Liam. Was history repeating itself?

I promised myself that I would be a real mother to Liam, if he came to live with us. Drake grew up without a mother. He had a succession of nannies and housekeepers who looked after him well enough but of course, they likely didn't love him the way a mother does.

I wouldn't let Liam grow up without a mother, if it came to that. I felt tears fill my eyes at the thought that Maureen could even consider leaving Liam, and hugged Sophie tightly while she sat in my lap and drank her afternoon bottle before her nap.

What a cruel world it was that little children grew up without mothers...

Sure, maybe some were better off without their mother if she was abusive, but still...

I spent the afternoon hugging Sophie, unable to imagine leaving her. She fell asleep in my arms with her bottle and I let her sleep with me on the sofa instead of moving her to her crib, just because I felt a need to have her with me. When Elaine called, I whispered into my phone, hoping to let Sophie sleep longer.

"Hi, can I text you? Sophie's asleep with me."

"Sure, I'll send you a text."

"Thanks, bye."

I ended the call and read Elaine's text, holding the cell with one hand while the other held Sophie beside me on the sofa.

ELAINE: *Just calling to check on you two coming for supper before leaving Sophie with us.*

KATE: *We're so thankful you agreed. We haven't been alone since our stay at the Ritz-Carleton. Drake's out right now but we'll come by later.*

ELAINE: *Where's Drake? I thought he had the day off. Don't tell me he's back at the hospital...*

KATE: *No, Drake is at Maureen's talking to Brenda about Liam.*

ELAINE: *What's up?*

KATE: *Maureen wants to go to Indonesia with Chris. Wants to leave Liam behind with Brenda but in Manhattan. Drake wants him to come and stay with us.*

ELAINE: *Oh, poor Liam! What's the matter?*

KATE: *Chris is unhappy in the U.S. Maureen doesn't want to stay without him but can't take Liam due to his medical needs.*

ELAINE: *Oh, dear. Chris just moved back. Poor Liam. I hope she lets Drake take him. Are you okay with that?*

KATE: *I can't imagine him not coming to live with us! It makes me cry to imagine Liam losing his mother and then moving back to Manhattan when Drake is here. It will make it just that much harder for Drake and Liam to form a real relationship.*

ELAINE: *I know. Me, too. Poor child. Do you want me to come up and pick up Sophie while you go to your studio? Then you two could come for supper or not – it's up to you.*

KATE: *That would be so nice of you. I'll talk to Drake about it.*

ELAINE: *Okay, I'll come by and pick up Sophie.*

KATE: *Thanks. I'd like to stop by the art supply store and pick a few things up. I wouldn't stay for long. Maybe an hour or so.*

ELAINE: *I'll see you soon.*

KATE: *Thanks, Elaine. I appreciate it.*

I sighed and put my cell away, slipping Sophie's pacifier back in her mouth when she shifted in my arms. She kept her eyes closed and didn't wake up when I stood up with her, so I took her to her bedroom and laid her down in her crib, tucking her blanket up around her. She didn't move a muscle.

Then, I got ready to go to the studio.

AFTER ELAINE ARRIVED and took Sophie, I drove into San Francisco. I parked my car about a block from the art supply store, which was in the same neighborhood as my studio, and went inside to check out the supplies. I should have been excited about the trip, but I felt so bad for Liam and there was a bit of a damper on my day as a result. Still, I needed some new paint thinner and brushes, as well as other supplies, so I spent the next fifteen minutes selecting what I needed, gathering them in a basket before going to the checkout.

"Are you a member?" the cashier asked.

"No," I replied. "Is there a membership?"

She handed me a brochure, which explained that members paid an annual fee but got 10% off all supplies. I signed up on the spot. Not that I needed to worry about price, but I wanted to support the store and my $25 was nothing. Plus, it would make me feel like a real member of the community to have the little card and use it when I visited.

I finished the paperwork, paid my fee and then left. On my way out, I saw the flyer about Sefton's exhibition taped to the front window. Apparently, it was a big enough thing that it was advertised even in the local art supply stores.

I shrugged and carried my new card and supplies out to the car. Then I drove to a small office furniture store a few blocks away so I could pick up a stool. I needed something to use to sit at the workbench and found the perfect chair on rollers that was higher than normal and was adjustable. Satisfied that I had the perfect choice, I paid for it and then went back to the car, driving the few blocks to the studio. I parked and carried my packages inside, eager now to get the studio space better organized, my mind occupied for the moment and off the issues Drake and I faced back home.

The studio would be my personal escape from life. I wouldn't spend much time there, but it would be enough to keep my artistic pursuits alive. One day, when Sophie went to school, I'd have more time to spend painting – if that was what I wanted to do. I even considered finishing my MA, if the time came when I felt the drive to do so.

I was damn lucky and I knew it. Most women didn't have my options.

I WORKED AWAY in the studio, organizing my supplies and unpacking the stool, getting it set up and adjusted to the right height. Then, I couldn't resist setting up my easel and considering my current canvas. I got out my paints and started working on the elephant, getting my paints mixed just right. My mind was completely occupied with the painting and I forgot about the time as I worked away. When my cell dinged, I was brought back to the present and checked my watch. I'd been gone for an hour and a half.

It was Drake.

DRAKE: *Hey, I came home and found Elaine here with Sophie. I assume you're still at the studio.*

KATE: *I'm sorry – I should have texted you to let you know. I didn't want to bother you when you were with Brenda. I lost track of time but will be home right away.*

DRAKE: *Don't hurry. Come when you're ready. Sophie and I are having fun together. Elaine told me we're going to their place for a barbecue.*

KATE: Yes, I agreed already. I hope you don't mind. I'll clean up and be home soon.

DRAKE: I don't mind at all. I love you.

KATE: I love you.

I smiled and turned off my cell, then started to clean up. On my way to the building's trash chute, which disposed of any materials that were toxic or flammable such as turpentine, I ran into a man coming out of the disposal room. Tall, dark with longish hair in a man bun, he looked every inch the artist. Black t-shirt, worn jeans, black boots, and a kerchief around his head, he fit right in to my ideas of the bohemian artist.

"Oh, hello," he said and stopped when I grabbed the door handle to the garbage room. "You're the new tenant in studio 8."

"I am," I said and turned to face him. "I'm Kate."

"Sean," he said and extended his hand, then thought better of it since it was stained with paint. "I'm in studio 6, just down from you. What kind of art do you do?"

"Wildlife," I said. "I just started painting a series based on a trip to Africa."

"Cool," he said and smiled. "I do urban animals."

"Really?" I said and smiled back. "I'd love to see your work."

"Come on over. I'm working on one now."

"I will."

I waited for him to throw out his handful of rags that smelled like turpentine and then followed him down the hall to the studios. We entered his studio and I saw his paintings on the wall. Very impressionistic animals you'd find in the city – crows, sea birds, cats in alleys, dogs roaming garbage bins in a slum that looked like it came from some South American shanty town. He was talented and definitely had a point of view.

"These are great," I said, moving from one to the next. "This looks like it's in Mexico City or some slum in South America."

"Bogota, Columbia. The slum is called Ciudad Bolívar."

"You spent time there?"

"I went on a gap year before college. A friend and I travelled across the USA and down to Tierra del Fuego at the tip of Argentina."

I walked around his studio and examined each painting, and then his studio, interested in what other residents of the building did and how they arranged their spaces. He had an old purple sofa against one wall, but the rest of the space was dedicated to storing canvases and paints, brushes and other supplies.

He leaned against the wall beside me as I looked at a painting of a fox near an upended trash can.

"You want to go for drinks when you're done? There's a great little hole in the wall bar that serves Tapas down the street."

I smiled and held up my wedding ring. "Married. Baby. Sorry."

"My loss. If you ever change your mind, let me know."

"Change my mind about what?" I said with a laugh.

"Marriage," he said, grinning widely. "Fidelity. Monogamy."

"Not likely, but I appreciate the sentiment."

"Well, that's something at least."

I raised my eyebrows, amazed he felt so free to try to pick me up after we only knew each other for ten minutes.

"Can I come and see your etchings?" he said, still grinning.

"Sure," I replied and went to the door. "I paint though. Oil. No etchings."

He followed me down the hallway to my studio and for a moment, in the back of my mind, I was a bit nervous that he might get the wrong idea and make another attempt to pick me up. I opened my studio door and let him in. I glanced around the studio, wondering what someone else would think about my space and what it said about me.

"Nice," he said and went to my easel, checking out the painting. "Did you do this from memory or from a photo?"

I went to the collection of photos I used to compose the piece and showed him. "I was on an art safari in Kenya."

"Cool," and then he checked out the rest of my space. Finally, as I was packing up my things, he came over to me, standing just a bit too close for my liking. I took a step back, my bag on my shoulder.

"Like I say, if you ever change your mind..."

"Not likely," I said and then opened the door. "I have to go. Meeting the husband and baby at my parents for a barbecue, so..."

He walked beside me and I swear he brushed up against me on purpose. What a flirt...

"See you around," he said and then he smiled again, walking down the hallway backwards to his studio.

"Nice to meet you," I replied and then scurried out of the building, glad to be away from him. It wasn't that I was at all tempted, but I didn't want him to get the wrong idea.

I arrived back at the house and found Drake and Sophie sitting on the sofa, watching television. Sophie was drinking her afternoon bottle and was playing with a stuffed toy, her eyes crinkling at the corners when she saw me. Drake was watching the news. On the screen, I saw a reporter standing in front of the district courthouse in Manhattan. On the banner below it read *Murder Trial of Yonkers Billionaire Takes Twist.*

"What's that?" I asked, sitting on the sofa beside Drake and Sophie.

"Apparently, Lisa's boyfriend was involved in another suspicious death before he met her. It involved his girlfriend's younger sister, who died while intoxicated. Seems the police are exhuming the body to do another autopsy."

"They suspect him of having murdered her?"

"Yeah, he was quite a troubled kid, I guess. Neighbors said he was always strange. They always say that after the fact, but in truth, most murderers blend in except for the most psychotic."

"Trust Lisa to get mixed up with a serial killer in the making."

"She knew how to pick 'em," Drake said with a sigh. "This just means there'll be more gossip about me at the hospital. I was mentioned as one of Lisa's BDSM partners."

"Did they give you a new name at least?"

"Former neurosurgeon at NYP now living in California, Dr. Drake Morgan, whose wife was attacked by Lisa. I was hoping things would slowly die down with the case, but I guess not. They're trying him separately from Lisa since he was the one who actually did the killing."

"Do you suppose he killed the little sister and made it look like an accident?"

"Could be. His father is a veterinarian. They have access to drugs."

"How awful."

We sat in silence and watched the news for a few moments. Sophie reached for me, so I took her from Drake's arms and held her while Drake got up to make a cup of coffee.

"Do you want one?"

I nodded. "I'll need one if you're going to keep me up late tonight," I said, my eyes narrow.

"Count on it, Mrs. Morgan," Drake said with a delicious smile. "I have so many plans for you..."

That made my heart race and my flesh respond.

It would heighten my arousal to have to wait all evening, eating dinner with my father and Elaine and then returning home to an entire night with my handsome and very sensual and lusty husband.

I took in a deep breath and tried to be patient but it was hard.

CHAPTER 6

DRAKE

As we drove along the highway that bordered the coast on our way to Ethan's, I held Kate's hand.

"How are you, Mrs. Morgan?" I kissed her knuckles. "Excited about tonight?"

"I am," she said and squeezed my hand. "I've been thinking about it all day."

"Me, too," I said, a surge of lust right to my dick at the thought of having Kate all to myself for the night. "We're lucky that Elaine is such a willing grandmother."

"I know," she replied and watched out the window at the passing scenery. The area was beautiful, with tree-lined streets at the edge of the cliff overlooking the bay.

We pulled up in the driveway and I parked the car, going around to Sophie's door to remove her car seat while Kate gathered up her diaper bag. We went into the house and were greeted by a smiling Ethan in his wheelchair. He zoomed around, the joystick in one hand, a bottle of beer in the other. He seemed in really great spirits.

"Come in, come in," he said, waving to the living room. "We're going to sit on the deck and watch the ocean for a while. The ribs are on the barbecue and are cooking low and slow, Cajun style. They've been on all day."

"Sounds fantastic," I said and carried Sophie inside. While I took her out of her car seat, Kate went into the kitchen to speak with Elaine and so Ethan and I went to the deck. They had a playpen set up for Sophie filled with toys, so I put her into it and she was happy to play for a while. I sat on a lawn chair beside Ethan, who handed me a bottle of beer from a cooler.

"So, tell me about Liam," Ethan said, eyeing me from under the brim of his Yankees baseball cap.

"I want to try for joint custody," I said. "I don't want him living with his grandmother instead of me while Maureen is in Indonesia. I don't want him to grow up without at least one parent in the home. No offense meant against Brenda, but I am his father."

Ethan nodded and took a drink of his beer. "Maureen's not happy about that, I take it?"

I shook my head. "She thinks I'll be a bad influence because of the trial and my past."

Ethan didn't say anything for a moment and I wondered if he felt she had a point.

"I have to tell you that, as a former judge, I might be concerned on first reading of your case that she might be right. I have the benefit of knowing you, and I know the opposite is true. If anyone would be a good – a great – influence on Liam, it would be you. But you're going to have to overcome a judge's natural prejudice against you."

"I understand," I said, trying to see it from a judge's point of view. "I have two strikes against me already. I don't need any more."

Ethan nodded. "The key will be to marshal a whole lot of positive character witnesses for you, people who can counter those black marks. If I were your lawyer, that's what I'd recommend. You have a stellar record at NYP both as a world-class neurosurgeon and as a professor of neurosurgery. You have a history of volunteer work with Doctors Without Borders in Africa. You have a charitable foundation you started in honor of your father that does good works around the world. You're independently wealthy, practicing medicine when you really don't have to work at all. All those things will be weighed against the two black marks. It's more important what you have been doing in the last five years of your life, rather than in the previous ten when you were younger."

I watched the surf, my mind on how a lawyer would represent me in front of a judge. What he or she would say.

"Do you know any good lawyers out here?"

"I'll check around with a few judges I know. They can suggest a few who know how to finesse a case like yours."

"I appreciate it. I hate that I have a case that needs finessing but I guess I do."

"Don't worry about it. You deserve to be Liam's guardian, considering you saved the boy's life. That'll be worth a whole lot in the mind of a judge. At least, it would with me if I had your case in front of me."

We sat silent for a moment and listened to the sound of the ocean washing onto the beach.

"I wish Maureen were staying," I said finally. "I hate to think how this will hurt Liam. I *know* how it will hurt Liam. He's even younger than I was when my mother left me."

Ethan reached out and patted me on the arm. "The judge will take it all into consideration and I have to admit that he'll be sympathetic to you, given Maureen is practically abandoning the boy. Her objections to you having custody will be seen with a very jaundiced eye."

"I don't want to do anything to hurt her," I said, truthfully. "I understand she's sick. People do things that aren't in their own best interest when they are depressed. My mother was depressed after my brother died and she never got over it. I just hope that Maureen gets over it and comes back. She's choosing between Chris and Liam. I hate Chris for making her choose him over Liam. Even though she says it's only for six months, why couldn't she just suck it up for six months while Chris is away?"

"Depression is hard to understand unless you've been there yourself."

I turned to look at Ethan, surprised. "You have?"

Ethan nodded. "After Kate's mother died, I was alone and was at a point in my career when I had to put in long hours. Luckily, Elaine came along and helped me through it. As to your mother, a lot of couples break up when a child dies but it's usually the mother who takes custody during a divorce. It's rarely the father. Even today, it's still uncommon. Regardless, whatever cracks existed in their relationship are magnified and sometimes, the parents aren't strong enough to do what it takes to stay together."

I exhaled, sick about Liam having to say goodbye to his mother for even six months. Who knew whether they'd return at the end of that time? Maybe Chris would want to stay there. Would Maureen want to stay with him? Would Liam ever be healthy enough to go and live with them in Indonesia? Sure, they could afford the best quality medical care that money could buy in Indonesia, but it wasn't the same as medical care Liam could get in the states.

"Liam really can't go somewhere like Indonesia to live until he has the all clear from his doctors, but he'll always be at risk due to his medications to suppress rejection of his transplant. Even though we were a perfect match, he'll always be on a low dose of steroids. That puts him at risk of infections and diseases that he might otherwise avoid."

"Maureen will have to make a hard decision at some point. Hopefully, she'll get over her depression and come to her senses about what really matters."

"Hopefully," I replied.

"Speaking of mothers, have you ever tried to contact yours?"

I didn't say anything for a moment. I'd always been curious about my mother's life after she left me, but I had to admit there was a part of me that felt abandoned and angry at her for leaving. I hadn't done any research into her life and what happened to her after she left. It was always a sore point with my father and we avoided talking about it like the plague.

"No, I haven't. I should, now that I'm out here, but it's been twenty-eight years since I saw her."

"You should look her up. You never know what wounds might be healed if you do."

I glanced at him and he nodded meaningfully before taking another drink from his beer.

"I wanted to ask you about the case," Ethan added. "When will you have to testify?"

"I haven't heard yet from the prosecutor. He wants me to come back to Manhattan to go over some details in the case and talk about my testimony. My lawyer will let me know when they need me. Until then, I don't even want to have to think of it and how close we came to Kate and Sophie dying."

"You'll do fine," Ethan said and held up his beer. "Just tell the absolute total truth and you won't have any problems. Don't hold back any details out of embarrassment. They always come out in the end."

"I won't, but honestly, my actual experiences with Lisa were not very memorable. I do remember pretty much everything from our time at NYU, but our encounters back when she was with Derek Richardson are a blur."

Ethan shook his head. "Like I say, just tell the truth the best you can remember. You won't have anything to worry about."

"I hope so. I wanted our time in San Francisco to be worry free for Kate. I knew I'd have to fly back and testify in the trial, but I didn't expect there to be so much national coverage."

"Juicy gossip with lurid details sell copy. It was inevitable that it would become a national story, given the details."

I told Ethan about my run-in with one of the hospital admins and with Christy.

"She actually said she'd warned the nursing staff about you?"

I nodded and we discussed how to handle these kinds of situations at the hospital. I appreciated having Ethan as a confidant because he knew how to handle these kinds of issues after a life-long career in the justice system.

"You know, you don't have to work, Drake. You could stop completely and live off your investment income."

"I love my work," I said, because it was true. "I don't want to think I have to give it up because of what happened. There's nowhere that I could work where my past wouldn't be quickly discovered and discussed in the staff lunchroom. I have to just face things and buck up, as my father would say."

"It's true," Ethan said and held up his beer. "You're still young and have years ahead of you. You could quit for a couple of years, spend time volunteering, or doing nothing. You could return to practice once all this blows over and becomes nothing more than a bad memory."

"I doubt it will ever go away completely. People will always know I'm the Doctor Dangerous whose ex-lover tried to kill my pregnant wife and who killed an old friend of mine."

"It'll get better with time. You could go up to Canada. Or you could move to Europe or Africa and work there. There's probably a lot of hospitals who would be totally pleased to have a highly skilled young neurosurgeon on staff."

I sighed and took another sip of my beer. "Thanks for the vote of confidence. I'll play it by ear. If things get too bad at the hospital, I'll consider taking a year or two off. I don't know what I'd do with myself in the meantime."

"Live."

I shrugged. "I've always worked, since I started medical school. I've never taken more than two weeks off."

"Now's as good a time as any to learn how to relax. You could write a text book."

I'd never thought about it, but I could write about robotic surgery.

"I'll see how things go, but thanks for listening."

"My pleasure," Ethan said and smiled.

When Kate came out onto the deck, she bent down and kissed me.

"What have you two been talking about?"

"Stuff and things," Ethan said. "The stock market and the price of wheat in China. That kind of thing."

"I don't believe you for a moment," Kate said with a laugh. "What do you know about wheat prices in China?"

"That's code for private man stuff," Ethan replied.

"Oh," Kate said and gave me a look of surprise. "Forgive me for intruding on your father-son *tête-à-tête*. Can I get either of you a refill?"

"As a matter of fact, I think we'll crack the bottle of wine, if you don't mind. Drake? Can you do the honors? I'm not as handy with a bottle opener as I used to be."

"I'd love to." I smiled and stood up, giving Kate a quick kiss before going into the house. She squeezed me, smiling up into my eyes, her expression suggesting so much more would happen between us in a few hours, once we finished dinner and were alone back at the house. I felt a surge of emotion at the thought of how eager she was and hoped it would wash away all the negative thoughts about Maureen and Liam and the trial in Manhattan.

I needed some Kate time.

Badly.

CHAPTER 7

KATE

We had a lovely dinner with my parents at their house and after dinner, I offered to give Sophie a bath before we put her down, but Elaine was insistent that Drake and I go home as soon as possible to start our romantic night alone.

"I want to give her a bath," Elaine said and took Sophie from my arms. "I bought some bath toys specifically for tonight, so you have to let me do it."

"Okay," I said and laughed, pleased to see Elaine so into looking after Sophie. "If you insist."

"She'll be fine," Elaine said.

"She wakes up most nights and wants to sleep with us," I added, feeling now anxious about Elaine having to deal with Sophie if she was upset it wasn't me picking her up in the middle of the night. "She always has a bottle at that point. I hope you won't have any trouble with her."

"We'll manage. I'm sure she'll be happy to go back down with her bottle. Worse comes to worst, I'll bring her into bed with Ethan and me and she'll sleep with us."

"Are you sure?" I chewed my bottom lip, worried now that this was a mistake and I should be taking Sophie home with me.

"We'll do fine," my father said, waving at me from his wheelchair. "I get up every night for a trip to the bathroom, so it won't be any different from our usual routine. Go. You two have a nice night alone."

"If you're certain..."

I looked them both in the eye to make sure they were truly fine with the prospect of Sophie waking up in the middle of the night.

"We'll keep her up extra late and she'll sleep right through. You watch."

Drake took my hand and pulled me towards the door. "Come on, Mrs. Morgan. Listen to what Nurse Elaine says and let's go. Sophie is with her grandparents and will be fine."

"Okay," I said and smiled, waving at them as I left the house. "Call me if you have real problems. I can come by and pick her up, even in the middle of the night."

"You'll do no such thing," my father said. "We'll be fine. We may be a pair of old codgers, but we know how to take care of children."

"Speak for yourself about the old codger thing," Elaine said with a laugh. "I'm young enough to be able to stay up all night if she's fussy. You go. I won't hear another word about it."

Drake took my hand and pulled me out of the house, leading me to the car. I felt a pull at my heart that I was leaving Sophie, but she waved bye-bye happily from the door, apparently not caring that Drake and I were leaving her in the arms of Elaine.

"She doesn't seem at all upset," I said as we drove off.

"Elaine's been looking after her since she was born. She knows Elaine and feels safe and happy with her. It's wonderful and it means she'll probably go down for the night easily. You don't need to worry."

I sighed and squeezed Drake's hand. "I know. It's just this is the first time since she came back from the NICU that we've been apart. It's natural for me to feel nervous."

"I know," Drake said and kissed my hand. "I'll try to take your mind off it."

That send a surge of desire through my body and almost – *almost* – made me forget for a moment about leaving Sophie.

"I'm sure you will."

ONCE WE WERE BACK at our house, before we even got through the door, Drake grabbed me and pushed me up against the wall.

"I've been thinking about this evening for days," he said, his lips warm against my throat. "I wasn't sure I could stand to go to your parent's place and have to sit through dinner and small talk before getting you here, alone."

He kissed me, devouring my mouth like a desperate man, his hands roving down my body to my breast and hip, pulling me against him so I could feel his erection.

When the kiss ended, I was breathless, panting, my body already wet and swollen.

Then he pulled me into the kitchen and went to the refrigerator. I leaned against the kitchen island and watched as he took out a bottle of Anisovaya.

"Let's have a shot together," he said and brought over two very special etched crystal shot glasses he found in his father's possessions.

"We haven't had any Anisovaya for so long," I said, not wanting to drink alcohol while I was nursing. Now that Sophie was fully weaned, I could drink again without concern.

We stood at the island and Drake poured us both a shot. Then, he held his glass up and waited while I took mine.

"To us," he said. "To love."

"To us," I repeated. "To love."

We both downed the Anisovaya and I smiled as the liquid burned down my throat in a way that never failed to arouse me. I'd associated the slight taste of anise and vodka with pleasure and my body responded, a warmth spreading through me at the prospect of a night alone with Drake. Before I could speak, Drake grabbed me and kissed me again, and I knew it was because he wanted to taste the Anisovaya on my tongue.

It brought back so many good memories of our time together after we first met and he introduced me to D/s.

Drake took my glass from my hand and placed it on the counter. Then he pulled me into his arms and kissed the top of my head.

I knew what that meant.

It worked like magic, and my body responded, my flesh swelling at the prospect of him going all Dom on me. For the first time in a very long time...

"I'm yours," I said, my throat all choked.

"You're mine," he replied, his voice thick with desire. "Every inch of you. And you're going to take every inch of me."

"I love all your inches," I said, unable to stop from smiling, closing my eyes to imagine what he'd do to me. Knowing it would be extremely pleasurable, whatever it was.

"They're all yours."

I thrilled to feel him take control, his hands demanding, possessive of my body, in need to feel my skin against his. He pulled down one shoulder of my dress and kissed the skin over my collarbone, then ran his tongue up my neck to my jaw and back to my mouth, which he kissed once more.

I surrendered to his lust, soaking up every sensation.

When he pulled away after breaking our kiss, he stroked my hair, his gaze moving over my face.

"Oh, Miss Bennet," he said, his voice husky with desire. "I have so many plans for you."

"You do?" I asked, closing my eyes while he nibbled my shoulder. I was trying to play coy but wasn't very convincing. "What plans could you possibly have for me, Dr. Morgan?"

"So many plans..."

He ran his hand up the back of my buttock to my waist and then around to one breast, which he cupped, squeezing gently, tweaking my nipple between his finger and thumb. It made me gasp, and was perhaps the first time since I weaned Sophie that I felt like my breasts were mine once more.

Mine to feel free to enjoy without worry about any accidents. There had been so many since Sophie was born and while Drake and I laughed them off, I was pleased to be able to enjoy them sexually once more.

Drake seemed impatient to have me naked and began pulling my dress up over my head, and soon, I was standing practically naked in the kitchen, the overhead lights shining down on me, my reflection in the picture window against the darkened sky.

"Someone could see us," I said hesitantly, for stretched out in front of our house was the sandy dunes and beach.

"Someone would get quite a show. Stop thinking and just enjoy, Kate."

I turned back and closed my eyes, trying to give over control to him, so that he'd decide what we did, when and how. It was hard after so long without any D/s between us, but in a way, it was a relief.

I stopped thinking. I stopped planning and worrying.

I just felt.

I felt his tongue on my skin, his lips moving down my neck to my bare shoulder, his fingers stroking my pussy over the thin fabric of my thong. I gasped when his mouth took one nipple and he sucked, my back arching in response to the intense jolt of pleasure.

I moaned when he moved from breast to breast, sucking and nipping at each one. I squirmed with need, wanting to feel his tongue on my clit, which was throbbing now as I anticipated what he'd do next.

He stopped his motions and stepped back and I felt momentarily denied, my eyes opening. I leaned against the island counter, my hair loose and falling over my shoulders, my thighs spread. He just stood and watched me, his eyes moving over my body from my heels to my head and then to my breasts and thong.

"You look ravishing. I'm going to have to ravish you, Ms. Bennet."

"I'm yours," I managed to whisper.

"Turn around," he ordered in a firm voice.

I did, turning so that my back was to him.

"Spread your legs."

I complied, spreading them a few inches.

"More," he said. "Wider."

I did, my feet almost a yard apart, my hands on the counter.

"I love the way you look right now," he said, his voice low and filled with lust.

I smiled to myself, glad that he felt that way. It aroused me even further to know he found me desirable and loved my curves. He came closer and ran his hands down my body, from my shoulders to my waist and then down over my thong to cup each buttock in a hand. He squeezed them, separating them and pushing them back together.

"Your ass is perfect."

He pressed his hips against my butt and I felt his erection through the fabric of his pants. He was hard as rock and ready. He teased me for a while, pressing against me while his hands slid around my waist to cup my breasts from behind.

"I'm just going to enjoy your body for a while," he murmured against my neck while he played with my nipples. "It's been so long since you were all mine and mine alone."

"I'm yours."

He continued to stroke my body all over, like he couldn't get enough of me. The feel of his hands against me like that drove my arousal even higher. I was so ready, I knew that the merest sensation of his tongue on my clit or his cock inside of me would make me come very fast.

I knew that would be his goal – to make me orgasm fast the first time with his mouth or fingers and then for me to come a second time while he fucked me.

"Turn around," he said when he pulled back.

I did, turning and facing him, my breathing shallow, my heart rate faster. My core ached and I was ready for whatever he decided to do.

"Sit up on the counter." He pointed to it.

I hesitated. Behind me was the huge picture window looking out across the bay. Down below our house was a public beach and anyone could be out there, walking their dog or even just out for a run. I'd seen people out later at night, in the dark, and I didn't want to think of people watching us.

Drake's eyes narrowed. "I can see you need a bit of training," he said, half under his breath.

"The window..."

"What about it? They'll see your back and nothing else. Do it."

I took in a deep breath and tried to shut off my mind. Then I hiked myself up onto the counter. Luckily, it was probably one of the most solid pieces of furniture in the entire house and so I didn't have to worry about my weight damaging it.

So there I was, naked except for my thong and heels, sitting on the marble counter.

"Spread your legs wide," Drake ordered. He stood across from me, still fully dressed, his shirt open, his erection straining at the fabric of his shorts.

I did. The thong split my pussy lips, digging into me and I reached down to adjust the fabric, but Drake held out his hand.

"Stop," he said. "I like the way you look."

I took my hand away. Drake stepped forward, his gaze on my pussy, and he pulled the fabric even farther to one side, exposing my flesh. My core throbbed, an ache building deep inside of me that needed release. His fingers, his tongue, his cock. A sex toy – anything.

"Nice and *wet*," Drake said in a deep husky voice. He stepped even closer and reached out, running a finger over my slit, down over my clit. I gasped, closing my eyes from the sensation. Then he slipped the finger inside of me and stroked upward. It was followed by another finger and he continued to stroke, his thumb to the side of my clit. "I'm going to fuck you later, but now, I'm going to make you come like this."

I opened my eye and met his. I knew he would make me orgasm if he continued to stroke me like that. His gaze moved between my face and his fingers deep inside me, his thumb stroking lazily over my clit.

"You're so fucking beautiful," Drake said, his voice lusty. "I love watching you come, Katherine. I love making you come."

I couldn't stop myself from moving with his fingers, needing more stimulation, wanting the sweet release of an orgasm.

"That's it," he said, pleased with me. "Fuck my fingers. Show me how much you need it."

I did, moving my hips forward while he stroked inside me. I felt wanton, lusty, and it felt so good. My body was desirable to him and it made me feel like a woman again, and not only a mother, to have him watching me like that, have him touching me like that.

I felt the sweet buildup of pleasure peak and then I came, shuddering, my body clenching around his fingers.

"Keep watching me," he ordered and it was practically impossible. I managed to keep my eyes open while he fucked me with his fingers, his thumb still on my clit while I came.

"Oh, God," I moaned, my body spasming while the pleasure seared through me.

"So good," he said, his fingers deep inside of me. He moved closer and sucked on one of my nipples and that made me clench even harder, my body tightening around his fingers. "So fucking good."

I panted, recovering while my orgasm waned. Drake kept his fingers inside of me and then pulled me closer for a kiss, his mouth devouring mine. When he pulled back, he finally removed his fingers and licked them, his eyes not leaving mine.

He lifted me off the counter and I stood up, my legs weak.

"On your knees," he commanded. I knelt in front of him and waited for his next order. "Unzip me."

I did, unfastening his belt and then unzipping him. I could see the thick outline of his cock, a wet spot where his fluid leaked out.

"Take them off."

I complied, pulling his shorts down over his thighs and to the floor. He stepped out of them and stood in his boxer briefs.

"Put your mouth on me."

I held his hips in my hands and leaned forward, my mouth on his shaft. I moved it over his length from the base to the tip, stopping to mouth the head, licking it, tasting his saltiness.

"Take them off," he ordered and I complied, slipping his boxer briefs down over his thighs and down to the floor. His cock sprung loose and bobbed in front of my face. I tried to hold back a smile, because he was so ready, dripping.

"What are you smiling about? You're going to take it – all of it – down your throat."

I glanced up at him and his eyes were narrow, like he was angry with me, but I knew he wasn't. He was struggling not to smile as well.

"Sorry," I said. Then I did what he said and took him in my mouth, slowly sucking his length into my throat, as far as I could take him until I gagged.

"You're out of practice," he observed. "I guess I'm going to have to train you again. Now, I'm going to fuck your mouth for a while. Then I'm going to fuck you until you come on my cock."

I couldn't respond with his very thick cock stretching my mouth wide. Instead, I sucked on the head, my tongue running around the rim of flesh, then I held still while he slowly and lazily fucked my mouth. I cupped his balls with one hand while I sucked him, my eyes open and gazing up into his eyes. I saw such lust in them I wondered if he wouldn't just finish in my mouth, but he didn't. When he got close, he stopped and pulled out. I'd only come once and once was never enough for Drake.

I had to have two orgasms – at a minimum – to each one of his. He always said one of my orgasms was for him and the other was for me. No matter how I tried to make the math work, I never could.

"I'm selfish. The first orgasm you have is always mine because I give it to you and it's mine alone."

"But they're both mine," I said, smiling at him.

"You don't understand," was his simple reply.

Now, he lifted me up and turned me around so that we faced the kitchen island, and we could see our reflections in the picture window.

"Drake, people could see..."

"Let them watch. They'll be jealous."

I smiled to myself and closed my eyes while his hands squeezed my breasts, his fingers tweaking my nipples. Then he stroked my clit, his erection pressed between my buttocks. Soon, I was moving my hips against his hand, needing the sensation.

"You're ready again," he said, nibbling on my shoulder. "Insatiable aren't you, Katherine?"

"I'm always hungry for you," I replied.

"Good, because I'm going to fuck you – hard." He entered me in one smooth push right to the root, and I could feel his balls slap against my pussy as he began thrusting. In the reflection, I could see my breasts shaking with each thrust and watched as Drake grit his teeth and pumped hard, one hand on my hip, the other slipping around to stroke my clit.

He knew my body so well that soon, I was at the edge of my second orgasm, the sweetness cresting and threatening to overflow.

"I'm going to--"

"Come for me..."

I did, the pleasure spiking, my body tensing, my flesh convulsing around his cock as he thrust inside me.

"Oh, God, oh God..."

Drake thrust harder and soon he too orgasmed, his face contorted in pleasure, his hands gripping my hips and pulling me against him with each thrust.

"Fuck," he groaned, breathing in through his teeth.

When he was finished, he leaned over me, his hands on either side of mine on the marble surface.

"I needed that," he murmured in my ear.

"I did, too." I smiled when he kissed and playfully bit my shoulder.

"You came so fast both times. I've been depriving you, I see."

"You have been. You're very mean."

We laughed, because of course, Drake would never deprive me of pleasure. It was me who was always too tired for sex.

I hoped that would change, now that Sophie slept most of the night through plus had a nice nap during the day. I didn't feel nearly as exhausted as I had when she was younger.

I felt Drake slip out of my body and immediately grabbed a paper towel from the counter and placed it between my thighs.

"Gotta run," I said and ran to the bathroom to clean up.

Drake followed me and watched as I washed up.

"Let's have a shower," he said, as he turned on the water. When it was the right temperature, he opened the glass door and led me in. Then, he washed me, taking his time, his eyes on mine the entire time.

"It's nice to have you all to myself," he said in a deep warm voice. "I miss you."

"I miss you," I said softly. It was so nice standing there in Drake's arms as the water flowed over us, the warmth comforting. I could have stood there for an hour, enjoying the moment with Drake that happened all too infrequently.

When we went to bed later, after a drink of hot tea, watching the stars twinkle over the ocean, I felt like my life was finally back to normal. While I often fell asleep within seconds of my head hitting the pillow, that night I lay awake for a while, Drake's arm thrown around my waist, our hands clasped, and tried to appreciate what I had.

CHAPTER 8

DRAKE

I SPENT most of the next afternoon visiting with Brenda to talk about Liam while he was still at school. We discussed Maureen's mental health since Chris decided to return to his job in Kuala Lumpur. She thought Maureen was depressed and needed counseling if she was willing to leave Liam behind for six months at a time. I had to agree. For a mother to decide to leave their child behind, she had to be depressed and unable to face losing Chris.

I couldn't imagine having to choose between Kate and Sophie.

I couldn't imagine it.

I would do everything in my power to not have to choose, but you can only control your own actions. You can't control the other person and I guess Maureen couldn't convince Chris to stay in the USA.

I would have stayed with Liam, had I been Maureen.

If Chris was so selfish that he would rather lose contact with Liam than stay and work at another job, he'd in effect bailed on Liam.

Then Maureen did as well. It was horrible.

When Liam came home from school, I spent some time with him, sitting on the floor in his bedroom while he played with his video game, listening to him talk about school and how he liked being able to go with the other kids. He'd missed most of his first grade due to treatment and was a year behind, but he didn't care. He wanted to go to school. He loved being in remission and being able to ride his bike around the neighborhood, or play soccer with the other boys in the playground.

It would have been a shame to take him away from his life in California after finally getting healthy enough to go to school and be 'a normal boy.'

"Thanks for coming by, Drake," Brenda said when I went to the door to go home. "We'll get this figured out. Maybe if Maureen is away from Liam for a while, she'll realize that she can't be happy with him here, separated from her."

"I hope she comes to that realization before she goes. You know and I know it will be really hard on Liam if she doesn't come back and decides to stay."

Brenda shook her head sadly. "I don't know what happened to her, but she must really be broken about Chris's decision to go back to Indonesia. I hope she comes to her senses."

"Me as well. See you later. Call me any time you need to talk. And please, I'd like to spend more time with Liam. I'll be talking to my lawyer about joint custody and we'll get going on it as soon as possible."

"I hope it works out," she said but didn't look all that positive about the prospects. "You'll have to be prepared in case your personal history makes a judge hesitate to give you joint custody. Even given the circumstances."

"I know," I said. "I'm trying to be realistic about it."

I waved goodbye and went back home, feeling good about seeing Liam, but torn about what I was facing with getting joint custody. I knew it would be an uphill battle.

When I got back home, it was almost time for dinner and Kate was standing at the stove, stirring a pot of Italian tomato sauce. In a frying pan next to it, about a dozen meatballs sizzled. Sophie sat in her high chair and played with her toys. She gave me a big smile when I went to her and kissed the top of her head.

"How did it go?" Kate asked when I went to her and slipped my arms around her.

She turned around in my arms and held my face in her hands, giving me a quick kiss.

"Good. I saw Liam, had a nice visit with him. Brenda and I had a good talk about Maureen and Chris. Not much to report other than that. We'll have to just give it a try and hope the judge we get is reasonable about my past."

"He or she would be a fool not to grant you joint custody, especially considering Maureen is planning to go to Indonesia for at least six months."

"You're biased," I said and kissed her.

"I am."

Two DAYS. Forty-eight hours of family bliss with my beautiful wife and baby.

That's all I had before getting a call to cover the shift of one of the other neuros who had a family crisis and couldn't come in to work. I'd promised my supervisor that I'd be as flexible as possible, covering shifts when needed because I wanted to work and would be happy to be the grunt doc at the hospital.

When I got the text, Kate was sitting with Sophie on the beach down from our house, digging in the sand. I stood on the deck and watched them while I decided what to do. Technically, I was due five days off because that was my shift – five on and five off. But I had agreed to be the resident neurosurgery float who would come in and cover a shift if necessary, so that's what I had to do.

Kate was supposed to go to her studio after lunch and work on her painting, while Sophie and I were going to spend the afternoon together, walking the beach and doing baby daddy things.

Now, I would have to screw everything up.

I felt bad that I would be leaving Kate after being away the previous day all afternoon. She'd happily forgone going to the studio so I could visit with Brenda. I texted Elaine to see if she could sit for us so that Kate could go to the studio as planned.

DRAKE: *I was supposed to be home with Sophie to let Kate go to the studio and get some work done on her painting, but I was called in to cover a shift and I can't say no. Would you be able to come and sit with Sophie so Kate can still go to the studio?*

I sent the text and waited. Elaine was usually on top of things so I got a response within a couple of minutes.

ELAINE: *I'd love to come by. I'll see if Ethan will join me so we can both play with her.*

DRAKE: *Kate could drop Sophie off at your place if that would be easier for Ethan.*

ELAINE: *No, it's better that Sophie is at her house. Besides, it gets Ethan out of the house, which is good for him. He gets a bit down when he stays in the house too long. I'm sure he'd love to be able to come to your place. I'll text you right back.*

I waited while she talked to Ethan and sure enough, in a couple of minutes, she replied.

ELAINE: *Ethan has a teleconference at 3 so maybe it's best if you drop Sophie off here. Sorry! I forgot about it...*

DRAKE: *No, that's perfectly fine. I'm sure Kate will be just as happy to leave Sophie with you. Thanks again for all your help, I just hate to disappoint Kate when she's so eager to get to work on her painting.*

ELAINE: *We're always happy to sit with Sophie. Never hesitate to ask.*

DRAKE: *Thanks again. Talk later.*

It was great of Elaine to be so willing to look after Sophie on a moment's notice but I figured that she never had her own kids and probably saw Sophie as her only chance to mother a child. Whatever her motivation, I was glad. I knew how much Kate was looking forward to her trip to the studio that day and wanted her to feel able to go even if I had to take an extra shift at the hospital.

I put my cell down and took my coffee out to the beach where Kate and Sophie were sitting under a sun umbrella.

"Hey there, pretty ladies," I said and plopped down beside them. "What are you making?"

"A sandcastle. You can't tell by looking at it, because each time I put a pail of sand there for a turret, Sophie demolishes it."

"That's my girl," I said and patted Sophie's head affectionately. Then I turned to Kate. "Just to let you know, I got a text that I'm needed to cover a shift at three."

Kate's face changed and I knew she was disappointed. Before she could respond, I added: "I talked to Elaine and you can drop Sophie off at their place before you go to the studio. I didn't want to ruin your plans at least."

"Aww," Kate said with a frown. "That's too bad. I had hopes of us spending five whole days together." She pouted.

"I know," I said and stroked her cheek. "Me, too. But duty calls. It's because I agreed to be really flexible and cover shifts that I was hired in the first place. I don't want to bite the hand that feeds me..."

"Drake, you don't need to ever worry about money," Kate said. "If you wanted, you wouldn't have to work at all."

"I'm a neurosurgeon," I said and shrugged. "What would I be if I didn't cut into people's brains?"

"You'd be a philanthropist and a bass player and a wonderful human being. Isn't that right, Sophie?" Kate bent down and peered at Sophie's face under the brim of her floppy sunhat.

Sophie smiled up at Kate and proceeded to slap her shovel against Kate's latest attempt at a sandcastle.

"My cheering section," I said with a sigh. "We still have two days after today. Hopefully, Wallace will be back to do his shifts tomorrow, although I doubt it. I don't want to have to miss two days with you but we may only have one."

"Can't someone else cover for him?"

I shrugged. "I either say yes or no, and if I say no too many times, they'll find someone else."

"It's not like neurosurgeons with loads of experience are a dime a dozen, Drake."

"I know," I replied, helping build up the sand around the single turret Kate had managed to construct before Sophie could destroy it. "But I signed a contract. I have to live up to my end."

Kate sighed audibly, which made me feel good that she wanted us to spend time together as a family – and as a couple.

"It's really not so bad. We've had a nice two days together, haven't we?"

She smiled. "We have. But I need more Drake," she said, climbing over to where I sat and snuggling into my arms. "I don't get nearly enough Drake."

"Drake is all yours," I said. "Hopefully, tomorrow and the day after. I promise you lots more Drake. Six feet two inches and even more inches of Drake. Tomorrow, okay?"

We kissed and she wrapped her arms around my neck. Beside us, Sophie pounded the lone turret until it fell onto nothing.

I CHANGED into a clean set of scrubs and then kissed both Kate and Sophie goodbye before driving off for my shift at the hospital. My shift was busy, and almost immediately, we were inundated with several head injuries coming from a multiple car accident on the free-way. After we were finished triage and I took my patient to the OR, I spent the next two hours doing delicate surgery to relieve pressure on the man's brain. An elderly man in his eighties, he and his wife had been traveling north when a drunk or drugged driver crashed into them and sent them careening into the path of a semi-trailer. There were five cars involved and several traumas due to the high speeds involved.

When the last of the surgeries was finished, we gathered in the staff room and had a break, trying to decompress during whatever down time we had before the next cases came in.

"Your dad was a trauma surgeon in Philadelphia, right?" Pete, one of the trauma surgeons said. "I remember him. He did a lot of work with Doctors Without Borders, right? Died in a plane crash in Ethiopia? He was legendary. He developed these crazy good surgical clamps that we use today."

I nodded and we discussed my father.

"He was really good with tools," I said. "He had his old Lada that he bought from someone who immigrated from the Soviet Union and used to tinker on it every weekend. He always had trouble with that car, but he made it run. He always said that if he couldn't have been a surgeon, he would have been a mechanic."

"He was in Vietnam, right?" Pete asked.

I nodded. "He was."

Our discussion made me melancholic and I missed my father in a way I hadn't for a long time. The truth was that he was always in the back of my mind, but there were few opportunities to discuss him in any depth. Doing so brought out a deep ache in my chest. I was lucky to have Ethan in my life as a father-substitute, but it wasn't the same.

It made me even more determined to apply for joint custody of Liam. I wanted to make sure he knew and felt that I was a father to him. Chris had been a father to him all this time and I knew he was a good father, but I suspected that finding out Liam wasn't his had put a damper on his feelings for the boy. It was cruel if true. Liam didn't know anything different other than Chris was the only father he had known his entire life. I was still just a stranger, becoming more familiar to him as time passed. But I knew I wasn't a father – not yet.

I promised myself that I would become a great father.

So, it was all the harder to encounter the next case that took me from the staff room.

A young boy in a coma, victim of child abuse, his little body battered. He was brought in by EMS just before nine in the evening. Parents had called 9-1-1 with claims that the boy had fallen down stairs and was unresponsive.

When I saw his little body, I knew different.

He was maybe four years old and when we scanned him for trauma, we saw old broken bones that had never been set. He had been abused repeatedly.

"Oh, God." The three of us on the team looking after the boy sat in front of the monitor and studied the damage, imagining the abuse inflicted on such a small child.

"It makes me want to puke," Pete said from the chair beside me. "It's really too bad that any fucking moron can have kids while so many really great people can't."

"I know," I said, a choke in my throat, glad that if this poor child survived, he would be taken from his abusive family and put in foster care, with strangers or maybe other family members. Even if it were for the best that his abusive parents lose custody, it was the only one he had known and it would be hard for the boy to grow up knowing that his parents almost killed him.

If I was skilled enough, the boy would survive.

"You have some pediatrics background, right?" Pete said, turning to me. "This is yours."

"Yes," I said. "This one's mine. I better go scrub in." I stood up and made my way to the OR where they were prepping him for surgery.

SEVERAL HOURS LATER, after doing everything I could to save the boy's life, I left the OR and went to speak to the family – such as they were. The mother and father had been taken into custody and now, a grandmother sat with another daughter and waited for me. I had to break the news that the boy might not survive the night, despite my best efforts.

I sat down with them in the small waiting room and removed my surgical cap.

"He's very sick," I said, making eye contact with them both. "He has a serious brain injury plus multiple broken bones. He had some internal hemorrhaging and we had to remove his spleen. If he survives the next few hours, he has a chance but we won't know until we do some more tests."

The grandmother covered her mouth with a hand and she and the other woman embraced.

"His scans suggest that he's been abused over a long period of time," I said. "We saw old fractures that suggest he's been abused repeatedly. Were you aware of him being treated for broken bones?"

"I had no idea. I knew that something was wrong between my daughter and her boyfriend," she said. "But we had a falling out over it and I haven't been by for months."

"I'd say this has been several years, by the way the bones have healed."

"Oh, God," she said and closed her eyes. "I had no idea..."

"I'll keep you updated on any change in his status," I said and stood up, feeling bad for the woman who was obviously traumatized by the thought her grandchild had been abused under her nose and she had done nothing about it. I knew enough about the issue to understand that most people learned abuse in their families. If the father had been the culprit, he was likely abused in his childhood and so on. Child abuse was largely a multi-generational issue.

I knew that the child welfare system was overworked and under-funded and never seemed to be able to keep completely on top of some cases. I hoped little Nathan wasn't one of those cases, but I had a bad feeling that he had never come to the attention of the authorities and so the abuse had gone on for years and had accelerated recently, probably due to some stress in the family system.

I spoke with Dora, the social worker on shift, who stayed late so she could meet with the family to discuss the child's future – if he survived.

"We'll check on the grandmother and see if she can safely care for him if and when he is discharged. If there are adequate supports, it's best he goes with his family than being placed in foster care."

"As long as his grandmother's safe," I said, uncertain myself if she was.

"We'll make sure," Dora said and nodded. "This one is hard to deal with."

"I know," I said softly. "I have a son a few years older than him," I said and thought about Liam. "I can't imagine anyone harming a child. It's unthinkable."

"Sadly, it's all too common," Dora said with a sigh. "Talk to you later. I'll let you know what happens with him."

"Thanks."

When I finally left the hospital and arrived home, I popped my head into the bedroom to see that Sophie and Kate were asleep in our bed, Sophie snuggled up to Kate, her pacifier in her mouth.

I had a quick shower and then slipped into bed, trying my best not to wake them, a choke in my throat at the memory of the small boy whose life I saved, wondering what kind of life he'd have. It made me even more determined to get joint custody of Liam so I could make sure that he had a father there all the time – a father who loved him. I did love Liam with a fierce love I was surprised to feel considering that he had lived most of his life not even aware of my existence.

But I did. I lay beside Kate and Sophie, my arm draped around them, thinking of little Nathan. Then, I thought of Liam, and how his life would change with his mother gone to Indonesia for six months. I had to cover my eyes and bite back tears.

How could he feel anything but abandoned?

There were only a few things I knew in life with complete and utter certainty: I loved Kate and Sophie with all my heart. Another thing I also knew.

I wouldn't abandon Liam.

I'd fight to the bitter end to get joint custody so he could live with me.

I pulled Kate and Sophie closer to me and tried to sleep, but it evaded me and I drifted in and out of consciousness, images of Liam's smiling face interspersed with Nathan's battered little body haunting my dreams.

CHAPTER 9

KATE

I woke early to find Sophie sitting up in the bed, playing with a toy we'd brought in with us when I went to get her at around 2:30 a.m. Drake wasn't in bed, but I could tell he had been because his pillow was propped up the way he always left it and his dirty scrubs hung out of the laundry hamper just outside our en-suite bathroom.

He must have woken up early. Then I caught a whiff of bacon cooking and realized he'd got up to make breakfast. I smiled and turned to Sophie.

"Daddy's up and made us bacon," I said to her. She smiled at me around her pacifier and shook her toy – one of the minions from Despicable Me – Stuart. The toy Liam had given her that first time they met. It was Sophie's favorite and I had to wash it repeatedly so she could keep it in her crib.

I got up and quickly pulled on a sundress, then I took her and Stuart to her bedroom for a quick diaper change. When we were done, we went to the kitchen where Drake stood at the stove, dressed only in his boxer briefs, his hair still wet from his shower.

"Good morning, early bird," I said to him, going up behind him with Sophie in my arms.

He turned and smiled at us, then leaned down, kissing me and then Sophie.

"Good morning, my two girls," he said and stroked my cheek and then Sophie's. "What a nice way to start the day."

"You should be sleeping," I scolded while I put Sophie in her chair. "You worked last night."

"I couldn't sleep in," Drake said, his voice sounding weary. "Had a bad night."

"Oh, I'm sorry," I said and went over to him after I had her secured in her chair and some Cheerios on her tray. I put my arms around his waist and hugged him from behind. "What happened? Do you want to talk about it?"

He shook his head and didn't say anything, so I knew he was really upset. It must have been bad, whatever it was and my heart clenched for him. Drake was always so positive and quick with a smile and laugh. To find him like this meant something had really upset him.

"Okay," I said softly, hugging him harder. He squeezed my hands, which were clasped around his waist. "If you want to talk about it, you know you always can with me."

"I know," he managed, his voice low.

I let him cook away without trying to make small talk, because I could tell his mind was elsewhere. Instead, I busied myself getting Sophie's breakfast ready and after pouring myself a cup of coffee, I sat beside her and fed her. Drake would talk when he felt up to it. I had to give him the space to do so.

"How do you want your eggs?" he said after a while. "Fried or scrambled?"

"Scrambled," I said and he nodded. I watched him whip the eggs in the bowl before cooking them, while I fed Sophie, the silence broken by the sound of news on the television in the family room beside the kitchen. He was efficient in the kitchen, moving from the frying pan where the eggs cooked, to the toaster and the pan with the bacon like an old short order cook.

He plated our breakfasts and then placed them on the island countertop in front of me.

"There you are, Mrs. Morgan. Just the way you like them."

He smiled at me, and I could see that he recovered by the way his eyes crinkled at the corners the way I loved.

"Thank you, Doctor Morgan," I said with a smile. "Or should I say, Chef Morgan?"

"Ha!" he replied and came around to where I sat, pulling out the stool and sitting beside me. "Not likely. More like Grill Cook Drake."

He bent over and kissed me and together, we dug into our plates.

"Sadly, I have to go in again tonight, but I switched shifts on Friday so I'll have two days off in a row."

"That's too bad," I said and brushed hair out of Drake's eyes.

"No, it's really okay," he replied and glanced away. "I want to work tonight. I have a patient..."

Then he said nothing more and I knew he wanted to go in to check on a patient he worked on last night.

It must have been that patient that upset him so much.

"I understand," I said and turned back to my plate. We ate for a few moments and finally, he sighed.

"A boy, Nathan, about four years old."

"That must have been hard," I said softly.

"Yes. It was."

I nodded in understanding. "You want to be able to check on him, and working tonight will let you."

"Yes," he said. But that was it. He didn't say any more so I knew it must have been a bad case. The boy must have been near death or maybe still was. A car accident, a bike accident, a brain injury from a fall at a playground – Drake had seen so many since he started working at the hospital ER. Usually, Drake took on cases that were a whole different kind – brain tumors, epilepsy, spasms. Trauma cases were a whole different world. He wasn't used to it yet and having a small patient nearly the same age as Liam would just be all the harder.

Finally, after another few moments of silence, Drake turned to me.

"How are you? How was your time at the studio?"

I smiled at him. "Great. I got two solid hours in on my waterhole piece."

"That's fantastic," Drake said and stroked my cheek, brushing a strand of hair back from my cheek. "I'm so glad you're getting to do what you love."

"Me, too," I said and squeezed his hand. "Do you want to keep working at the hospital? You seem to have been really affected by your patient."

"No, it's fine." Drake turned back to his plate and picked up a piece of crisp bacon, crunching on it. "I actually enjoy the excitement, but this was just a really hard case. Child abuse. I'm used to accidental injury not intentional."

"Oh, Drake, I'm so sorry," I said and reached out, squeezing his arm. "That must be unimaginable to deal with."

He nodded and stared out at the ocean outside our window. When he said no more, I didn't either, letting him take his time. He'd tell me more when he felt able.

"Can you get Elaine to come by or can you drop Sophie off at their place and go to the studio again today?" Drake asked, not looking at me. "I hate that you might lose a day there while you're working on a piece."

"Yes, Elaine said I could drop Sophie off again today if I wanted."

"Good," Drake said. He turned to me and smiled finally. "I like to think of you in your studio, absorbed in a painting, losing track of time."

I smiled back and then stood up and went to him, slipping my arms around him, our foreheads pressed together.

"I love being there. Even two hours a day feels like a complete and total indulgence. It makes me happy to come back here and spend time with you and Sophie. I feel so blessed."

"We are blessed," Drake said and kissed me warmly.

"We are."

I sat back in my place and gave Sophie a tiny piece of my toast, which she happily shoved in her mouth.

When we were finished, I stood up and took Drake's plate. "You go back to bed. I'll clean up. You'll need your sleep if you're going to function tonight."

"Thanks," Drake said and yawned. "I need another few hours. I'll set the alarm for one o'clock. That'll give me some time with the two of you before I go back."

"Whatever you need," I said and carried our plates to the sink. Drake came over and pulled me into his arms.

"Thank you for being so understanding," he said, his voice low and full of emotion. "I'm just processing everything. It's taking me a while to adjust to this kind of case."

"You don't have to thank me," I said, my own emotions swelling. Drake was such a loving man, a caring man. His patients were lucky to have him.

Sophie and I were lucky to have him.

We kissed once more, a nice warm kiss, and then he left me and went to Sophie, kissing her on the cheek before returning to the bedroom so he could sleep for a few more hours.

On my part, I quickly finished tidying up the kitchen and then I took Sophie to her room and got her dressed in a romper so we could go for our usual walk and let Drake fall back to sleep. I put her in her stroller, tied her sunhat under her chin and together, we went for a walk along the walkway that bordered the ocean. It had been packed down and was used by the city workers who cleared off the beaches each day so it was good to walk on with a stroller. We found a nice spot and I took Sophie out and put her onto the sand with her pails and shovels and then we sat for a while, the surf lapping at the beach a few feet away.

110

About fifteen minutes later, my cell rang. I checked the call display but the name was blocked so I didn't answer and let it go to voicemail. When it dinged to indicate a voice message, I listened.

Hello, Kate. Allow me to introduce myself. My name is Kent Reynolds. I wanted to contact you before I contacted Drake, your husband, who is my half-brother. Our mother, Louise, is very sick and may not survive. We wanted to contact Drake and give him the chance to come and see her if he wants. We understand that this is completely out of the blue and that they have had no contact since soon after she left Manhattan when he was a boy. We thought it would be best to contact you first, for you would know if this was something Drake would even want to do. If he doesn't, we understand, although we would be happy to meet him. Family is the most important thing in the world and it's often only too late that we realize that. Please call me back at the following number. Cheers, Kent

Then he listed a phone number.

I sat for a moment and tried to absorb what I had just heard. Drake had talked only rarely about his mother and most of the time, it was with considerable pain in his voice. He had grown up with a series of housekeepers and nannies who provided good care for him, so that he was never alone when Liam was busy working in the ER as a trauma surgeon or on one of his jaunts to Africa. But he had been very lonely and of course, he never had a real mother after he was ten. Liam certainly didn't take over that role and never remarried, preferring to have temporary liaisons with women but never getting serious again.

As a result, Drake was very self-contained as a person. He looked after himself from then on emotionally. He became very intellectual, and kept his emotions in check by focusing on his studies and had graduated high school early and attended college early. A high achiever, he overcompensated in life by being the best at everything.

I couldn't imagine not having a mother. Losing my mother when I was an adult was hard enough. I couldn't imagine how hard it must have been for Drake as a ten-year-old. What happened at Christmas? On birthdays? When Drake had a broken heart or injured ego? There was no one to kiss him better.

He met and married Maureen, but he had never really opened up to her, and theirs had been a distant marriage after the first year or two.

Drake had opened up with me and with Sophie. I could see the change in him. He was still an achiever but he devoted his every waking moment, when he wasn't at work, to us – to Sophie and me. He always wanted to be with us when he wasn't at the hospital.

How would he react to the news that his half-brother had tracked him down and wanted to meet him? How would he feel to know his mother was dying?

I called Kent's cell right away. Once we got our introductions out of the way, I got right to the meat of things.

"Does Drake's mother want to meet with Drake? I think that will have a bearing on his decision."

"She's got early-onset Alzheimer's. She's confused at this point so, no, she's not aware of this. My siblings and I got together and thought it would be a good idea to contact Drake and give him the chance."

"Oh, that's too bad. We didn't really know anything about your mother. How many half-siblings are there?"

"Four, including myself. Then, there's Amanda, my little sister, and my two younger brothers, Craig and Andrew. The four of us have seven kids between us so he has nieces and nephews as well."

"I'm sorry to be so forthright, but is your mother dying because of the Alzheimer's?"

"No. She got septicemia after a virus and the doctors said she may not survive. She's been living in a nursing home for dementia patients and she must have picked up an antibiotic-resistant bacteria. They tried everything but she's very sick. She's at UCSF right now."

"Oh, God."

"I debated contacting Drake earlier, but I didn't want to just call up and talk to him out of the blue so we tracked down someone at New York Presbyterian and he filled me in on you and that you'd moved to California. Luckily, he gave me your number because I would never have found you."

"Drake's sleeping right now, but I'll talk to him about this as soon as he gets up. He works the evening shift and so I don't think he'll be able to come by right now or even later today. He's working tonight, but as soon as he gets off work and has rested tomorrow, I'm pretty sure he'll want to come and at least see her once. And meet you and your brothers and sister, too."

"That's good. I hear he's working at UCSF as a neurosurgeon?"

"Yes," I said. "He's a visiting neurosurgeon providing coverage in the ER for the trauma team."

"Look, tell Drake that if he doesn't want to see her, we all understand but we want to meet him and establish a connection. Life's too short."

"I agree. I'm sure he'll want to see her. How bad is she?"

"Pretty bad. She really doesn't recognize us anymore and is non-verbal. She might not understand who he is, but I wanted him to make that choice himself. Besides, for as long as I knew about him, I wanted to meet Drake. The others did as well."

"I'm sure he'll want to meet you. He'll call or text you with his answer."

"Thanks. Tell him I'm sorry that we didn't connect before this, but we thought he'd want to know about mom."

"I will. Goodbye and I'm really sorry about your mom."

"Thanks."

We ended the call and I sat beside Sophie and watched her playing, a lump in my throat, my eyes filling with tears at the prospect of telling Drake that his mother was very sick and could be dying.

He'd want to know. I was sure he'd want to go and see her once before she died. I was almost certain he'd want to meet his half-siblings. He had brothers and a sister? And seven nieces and nephews? And they all lived nearby. I knew Drake would want to become family with them, despite the years they'd been apart. Drake had been deprived of a family all his life but now, he had a wife, two children and would soon have brothers and a sister.

That made me tear up even more, imagining him meeting them and finally feeling like he was part of the kind of large family he always dreamed of while growing up.

"Did you hear that, Sophie?" I said through tears. "You have a grandma and uncles and aunts. And cousins."

Sophie smiled up at me, chewing on her pacifier, a toy in her hand.

When we'd been gone for about an hour, I packed us up and we walked back to the house, entering just before eleven. The house was quiet and so I took Sophie out of her stroller and took her into her bedroom to remove her clothes and give her a bath. She was splashing in the water happily when the door opened and Drake peeked his head inside.

"How are my girls doing?"

He came inside and knelt beside the tub, kissing my cheek and reaching out to stroke Sophie's wet rosy cheek.

"We're fine. How did you sleep?"

Drake stretched his arms over his head and smiled. "Fantastic. I feel great. Ready to face the night."

He seemed so happy, I hated the thought of bringing up the whole business of his mother, but I had to.

"I got a call while I was out," I said while Drake sat on the edge of the tub and played with Sophie.

"Oh, yeah? From who?" he asked, peering at me, his smile fading.

"From your half-brother, Kent."

He frowned, and I could tell he was confused. "My half-brother Kent?"

I nodded. "Your mother remarried and had four children. Three boys and a girl. There's Kent, the oldest, then Craig and Andrew and Amanda, your half-sister. Kent called, wanting to get in touch with you. Your mother is very sick and may not survive. She's early-onset Alzheimer's and has contracted septicemia due to an infection with an antibiotic resistant bacteria."

"Oh, God," Drake said, his face falling before my eyes. Gone was the happy Drake, the well-rested Drake, ready to face his day of work and family. "Is she dying?"

"She's very sick. Kent wanted to give you the chance to come down and see her in case she dies. He and the others want to meet you, get to know you and they thought it should be now, while there is still time."

Drake stared off into the distance for a moment.

"Kent said he wasn't sure if she'd even understand who you are, so it's fine if you don't want to go. She barely recognizes them now and doesn't really talk."

"I have to go and see her," Drake said finally. He looked in my eyes, and I could tell he was steeling himself for the ordeal. How could it be anything but heartbreaking? To see her after all these years?

"If she doesn't or can't remember you, is it really worth going?" I asked, wanting to give Drake an out, just in case he really didn't want to go to see her.

"I want to see her," he said, his voice throaty, emotional. "She's my mother, even if she abandoned me." He nodded, more to himself than to me. "Besides, I really do want to meet my brothers and sister."

"I'm so sorry about this, Drake. It's too bad you couldn't have contacted her before this happened."

"I can see her now. She may not recognize me, but I need to see her."

I picked Sophie up out of the tub and wrapped her in a huge soft towel, drying off her hair with the corner. She was all clean and smelling like the soap we used on her hair, her cheeks rosy.

"Let me have her," Drake said and held out his arms. I handed her to him and he held her close, kissing her head and cheeks, smiling at her as he stroked her cheek. He looked up at me, his eyes filled with tears.

"I have to go and see her."

I nodded. "I know."

CHAPTER 10

DRAKE

I WENT to the hospital to see my mother for the first time in twenty-eight years.

Before I went, I sat in my office and called Kent, figuring I should let him know I was on my way to the hospital so the family could be prepared. Kate stood beside me, her hand on my shoulder, and listened when I put the call on speakerphone. Kent answered and we spoke briefly, introducing ourselves and then he talked about finding out they had a half-brother.

"Craig and Andrew aren't able to get here right now and will wait and see whether they need to come if she gets worse. Craig's in the Navy and is currently deployed. Andrew's in Texas and is working a big project. Amanda and I live in San Francisco so we're the two who have been watching over mom. We never knew anything about you until she started to lose her memory. Then, it was like she wanted to tell everyone about you before she forgot entirely," Kent said, his voice soft. "She finally told us that we had a half-brother from her first marriage and that she lost a son to leukemia. She said her marriage broke down and she went through a serious depression and left Manhattan, determined to kill herself by jumping off the Golden Gate bridge. But instead, she met my father, Herb, at the local Mission where he was the manager and that saved her life."

"I knew she was depressed. She felt she couldn't care for me and that's why she left."

"It must have been hard on you," Kent said and that brought out a wave of emotion in me. "I couldn't imagine my mother leaving me or my wife leaving our son."

"I survived," I said. "No doubt it affected me for a long time. My own first marriage failed."

"I'm sorry to hear that, but it's understandable. We all wanted to meet you, once we learned about you. I did some sleuthing, hired a private detective in Manhattan to find out what he could about you and he gave us your contact information. He compiled a dossier on you and that's when we learned about the troubles you had with the attack on your wife."

"Yeah, sadly, it's become national news and fodder for the gossip magazines."

Kate squeezed my shoulder and I took her hand in mine.

"We didn't want to bother you in the middle of the trial. But then I spoke with someone at NYP and learned that you came out to San Francisco. When Mom got sick, and when she started to fail, we thought we should contact you right away."

"I'm so glad you did," I said, a lump in my throat. "I would have been really sad to find out about you only after she died."

"She probably won't recognize you or anything," Kent said. "But I thought you should see her at least once before she dies."

We spoke about her failing health and I indicated that I wanted to go to the hospital as soon as possible.

"I won't be there until later due to work," Kent said, "but my dad Herb will be there with my sister Amanda. I'll call them and let them know you're on your way."

"Thanks," I said and rubbed my forehead. "I really appreciate this, Kent."

"Hey, I'm happy you'll get a chance to see her and look forward to meeting you."

"Me as well."

We ended the call and I turned to look at Kate, my eyes filled with tears.

"I guess I'll go," I said and pulled her onto my lap, our arms around each other. She pressed her forehead to mine and rubbed my back.

"I'm so sorry, Drake. Like you need this on top of everything else."

"No," I said and shook my head. "This is good. You know I've always wondered about her and what she did with her life after she left. I had no idea that she was planning to kill herself. I'm glad she met her husband and had a happy life."

"Still, it's upsetting."

I nodded but in truth, I was happy to see her despite everything. Kate and I kissed and I stood up, letting her out of my arms with reluctance.

"I'll go and stay for a while," I said. "I'll text you when I can but I'll probably just go right to work afterwards."

Kate kissed me and then I left, hopping into my car after collecting up my things. I drove off, on my way to the hospital.

I MET Herb Reynolds at the hospital, along with his youngest daughter, my half-sister, Amanda.

Herb was a man in his late sixties, balding, with a bit of a comfortable paunch. His dark brown eyes were bleary and he looked as if he'd slept at the hospital. Amanda was about Kate's age, pretty with dark hair and dark eyes like her father.

We all shook hands, introducing ourselves and then he just stood there, giving me the once over. Finally, he shook his head.

"You look so much like her," he said, his voice emotional. "Like when I met her back when she first showed up at the Mission."

"My father told me I had her coloring," I replied. "The fair skin and dark hair."

"Yes," he said. "I could tell she was troubled right away. She had this distant look in her eyes. We worked together for a while and then started to date."

"You volunteered at the Mission?"

"Yes," he said. "It's a family tradition."

We talked for a while as we stood outside my mother's room. The nurses were in to administer some meds and so we talked while we waited but I caught sight of her through the window. She looked extremely frail, with longish grey hair, a nebulizer mask on her face to administer the medicine to make her breathe more easily. An IV was in place and there were several bags hung on the IV pole, including what looked like antibiotics and liquids for hydration.

"She's been in a nursing home because of her dementia. I kept her home as long as I could, but I work as a partner at a tax consulting firm. I had to choose between continuing at my job or quitting to care for her. I took as much time off as I could, using all my vacation time for the year, and then I took a six-month leave of absence, but in the end, I had to put her in care."

"Alzheimer's patients require a lot of care at the end," I said, my voice choking up. "I'm familiar with the rapid decline because I've had to care for a few patients over the years since I started practicing."

When the nurses were done, they let us go inside and I was uncertain how she'd respond, if at all, to seeing me.

We went into the room and Herb went to the bedside and took her hand.

"Louise," he said, bending down and talking to her in a loud voice. "We have a visitor here today. It's Drake Morgan, your son."

She looked up at his face, frowning, and made some incoherent mumbles. It was clear she was distressed, and breathing hard, her hand and arm shaking as she held Herb's hand. Not once did she turn to look at me, and I realized that she probably didn't understand what Herb had said.

"Mom," Amanda said and leaned over to kiss her cheek. "Your other son from your first marriage is here. We found him and he's here to say hello to you."

Amanda ushered me closer and both Herb and she stepped away from the bedside. I went to her, dressed in my scrubs, and took her hand. She probably thought I was another doctor to check on her – if she thought anything at all.

I took her hand in mine and smiled down at her, my eyes filling with tears as I realized how frail she was. She had been a taller woman from what I knew of her, maybe about five feet eight inches, but she seemed to have shrunk down, her hair grey and straggly, her cheeks gaunt. But her blue eyes were bright.

"It's me, Drake," I said softly. "Your son. From your marriage to Liam Morgan when you lived in Manhattan."

I couldn't see any recognition or understanding in her eyes. Instead, she gripped my hand and mumbled something I couldn't make out. I leaned down closer and tried to hear what she was saying, but it was muffled by the nebulizer mask. There was still medicine to be administered so I'd wait until it was finished. Perhaps then I'd be able to understand what she said.

I glanced up at Amanda and Herb, who were both smiling sadly, as they watched Louise hold my hand.

"She can't recognize me," I said. I turned back to my mother. "How could she? I haven't seen her for twenty-eight years."

"She probably doesn't understand what you're saying," Amanda said.

"Sometimes, Alzheimer patients have deep memories, but all their recent memories get progressively destroyed. She may remember having a son named Drake, but may not be able to comprehend that I'm him, but grown up."

I watched her breathing, which was strained, and knew her pneumonia was the cause. I checked the bag of antibiotics and saw that they were giving her some of the strongest available. If she had a drug-resistant bacterial infection, it would be useless. She'd get progressively worse, her oxygen would go down and she'd die from septicemia, her organs shutting down, one by one.

"I can't stand to watch her struggle," Amanda said, tears running down her face.

"They'll give her medicine for her pain and that tends to calm their breathing," I said, wanting to assure Amanda that she wouldn't struggle at the end. "She'll go to sleep and that will be how she dies. But if the antibiotics work, she should start breathing easier soon."

Amanda nodded and took our mother's other hand. We stood together like that, both of us holding one of her hands while she struggled to breathe.

Herb excused himself and left the room to get a cup of coffee, and Amanda told me stories of her mother and how she used to take them to the beach and to the fair each year. It seemed she had been a very loving mother. I felt glad that even if she couldn't be a mother to me, at least she became one to her children from her second marriage. It was possible for a person to make a new life after leaving the ruins of an old one.

Part of me wished she could have recovered while she was living with my father, but neither of them could deal with the loss of my brother and they grew so distant, my father couldn't help her when she became seriously depressed.

I was glad she met Herb. I let go of all my resentment towards her for leaving me and forgave her, and it felt as if a huge burden of guilt and shame fell off my shoulders. It wasn't because of me that she left us. It was because of her inability to deal with the death of my brother.

Tears spilled over my cheeks while I held her hand, not caring anymore if Amanda saw me, because she was crying as well.

"I'm glad you came," Amanda said, wiping her eyes with a tissue. "Even if she doesn't remember you, it's important that you got to see her before she dies."

She handed me the box of tissues and I wiped my eyes. "Me, too. It's hard, but I would have regretted it the rest of my life if I hadn't."

I spent another fifteen minutes with my mother, and soon, Kent showed up. I let go of my mother's hand to introduce myself.

"Drake," he said and came over, opening his arms to me. I was surprised at the show of affection, considering we'd never met, but I welcomed it. We hugged briefly and then he looked me over. "You look like her when she was young," he said. "I saw pictures of your father when I was doing research, and you look like him, too. But definitely like mom."

I nodded. Kent was pretty much a dead-ringer for a younger Herb with dark hair and brown eyes. I glanced between Kent and Amanda, my brother and sister, and felt thankful that Kent had taken the chance to find me.

"Thank you for tracking me down and calling."

"My pleasure," he said and then went over to our mother and bent down to kiss her. "Mom, how are you? It's me, Kent."

She grasped his hand and seemed to try to lift up to speak to him, but of course, the nebulizer was still on her face. I checked and the medicine was gone so I removed it for him. She tried to speak, but it was gibberish.

"She doesn't make any sense," Kent said sadly.

"Once her oxygen goes down, she might be more confused than normal."

I slipped her oxygen cannula over her head and threaded it under her nose. She probably thought I was just another doctor come to see her, instead of her son. I smiled at her, but there was nothing in her eyes that said she knew what was going on around her.

"I have to go," I said and pointed to my watch. "I start my shift in fifteen and I have to get ready."

"Good to meet you," Kent said and beside him, Amanda nodded.

"Yes," she said, and came to give me another hug. "I'm so glad Kent decided to find you. Come by and see her anytime you want. If she starts to decline really fast, we can text you if you want."

"Please do," I said and then I went over to my mother and took her hand once more. "I'm going now, mother, but I'll be back to see you on my break. Try to relax." I squeezed her hand and looked in her eyes. "I love you." But I saw no response. Just confusion.

"See you later," I said to them and left, needing to get out of the room as quickly as possible or I was going to start tearing up again.

I made my way to the nursing station and asked to read my mother's chart. I checked it over quickly, noting what meds they were giving her and how she had been since she was admitted. I thanked the nurses and then took the stairs to the ER wing where my office was. I needed a change of scrubs and to get my mind in the proper state for my shift.

After my shower, I went to the ward and checked on my patients from the previous shift who were still in the hospital. First on my rounds was little Nathan, who had made it through the night but was still sedated. I was thankful that he was doing so well. It was one bright spot on an otherwise depressing afternoon.

Once I'd finished seeing my patients from the previous night, I went back to the ER and looked over the roster of patients waiting to be given tests or consults, but I couldn't shake the sense of grief about my mother during the first few hours I was there, despite being kept very busy and relieved that Nathan had survived. Every time I had a five-minute break between patients, as I was washing my hands after leaving a case, while I was waiting for results to come back from the lab, I thought about my mother and what I had learned of her from my new brother and sister.

It was a very long night.

Before I left, as we were sitting around in the staff lounge, decompressing after a long shift, one of the attending physicians was talking about a patient who came in with the police in a very dissociated state.

"We had to restrain him," Lou said, a cup of coffee in his hand. "He threw a punch and just missed me, luckily, or I'd probably be a patient. He was huge."

We all nodded in understanding, for most doctors and nurses had seen similar cases in their time practicing medicine.

"Better keep Drake away from those restraints," Christy said with a snort.

There was a very awkward silence in the room and several of the staff glanced over at me.

I froze, cup of coffee in hand, and wondered how to handle this. Christy hadn't said anything to me since that encounter in the parking lot when she chased me out of the build to warn me about my behavior.

At first, I said nothing, because what could I say? That it was none of her business? It was public knowledge. I couldn't deny it.

"Don't worry yourself, Christy," I said dryly. "I wouldn't be using them on you, anyway."

I stood and finished my coffee, crumpling the cup and throwing it into the trash can.

Nick, one of the staff physicians, let out a guffaw of laughter. He held up his cup of coffee to me in a toast and took a drink.

I glanced at Christy, who crossed her arms and harrumphed.

Then I left the room.

I went right to my office and sent off an email to my supervisor, tendering my letter of resignation. I read it over once, changed some wording, and then sent off the email, hoping that I wasn't making a mistake

When I was done, I went back to the medical ward to see my mother.

CHAPTER 11

KATE

DRAKE DIDN'T ARRIVE BACK HOME until after eight in the morning.

I woke up at six thirty, surprised that Sophie was still asleep. At first, I had a bit of a panic attack, because she had been waking up every night at around three a.m. and coming into bed with me, but she slept through the night. I lay in the bed all alone, and worried first about Sophie, until I heard her babbling softly to herself over the baby monitor, and then I thought about Drake.

Where was he?

I realized that he was probably at the hospital visiting his mother. I sat up in bed and grabbed my bag, removing my cell to check for a text from him. Sure enough, there it was.

DRAKE: *Staying for a while at the hospital to watch my mom. Will be home for breakfast, unless things take a turn for the worse. If so, I'll let you know and will probably have breakfast at the hospital. Love you.*

I covered my mouth as a surge of emotion went through me, imagining Drake at his mother's bedside, holding her hand. I had done the same when my mother passed away, so I knew how he must feel, except I knew my mother was dying. She'd been dying for weeks when she finally passed. For Drake, her sickness was sudden and shocking. It had to be even more traumatic, being so unprepared to see his mother again after all that time and then to find out she might be dying.

My heart squeezed for him.

KATE: *Take as much time as you need. Sophie and I are fine. I hope your mother isn't suffering. Give her a kiss and hug for me. I love you.*

Then I got up and went into the bathroom for a quick pee before going in to get Sophie ready for the day. When I got inside her room, I saw she was sitting up playing with the toy attached to the side of her crib, flipping the roller that made a jingling sound and sucking on her pacifier. She grinned around it when she saw me and held out her arms.

"Good morning, sunshine," I said and picked her up, kissing her chubby cheeks one after the other. "You slept all night."

I took her over to the change table and changed her, then dressed her in a playsuit. As I was on my way to the kitchen with Sophie so we could have our breakfasts, my cell rang. I grabbed it from my bag in the bedroom and checked the call display. It was my father so I put it on speakerphone. I wanted to keep working while I talked.

I'd called my father and Elaine the afternoon before to let them know that Drake's brother had contacted him about his mother. I didn't really feel like being alone, so I'd skipped going to the studio and went to their place instead, having dinner with them so I wouldn't miss Drake so much.

"Hello," I said, wondering whether it was him or Elaine.

"Good morning, sweetheart," he said in his usual ebullient voice. "How're my two girls? How's Drake holding up?"

"Sophie and I are wonderful, but Drake is at the hospital seeing his mom."

"Oh, that's too bad. She must be very sick for him to stay."

"She is," I said. "He'll be home soon for breakfast unless she's going downhill."

"What are your plans for the day?"

"Sophie and I will spend the morning on the beach and then probably just stay at home while Drake sleeps."

"You know that you're always welcome to come over any time you want. We love to see you and Sophie."

"Thanks, daddy. I know."

"Do you want us to sit with Sophie while you go to the studio today?"

"I'll think about it. I'll wait and see how things are with Drake's mom first. If she's really bad, I might drop Sophie off with you while I go up with Drake and see her."

"That's fine with us," he replied. "Whatever you need, sweetheart. Let us know."

"I will," I said and ended the call. "Well," I said to Sophie, who sat in her highchair, her mouth stuffed with Cheerios. "Looks like we'll have a busy day."

WE TOOK our usual walk along the beach and played in the sand. I was surprised to find that Drake was home when we got back. The car was in the driveway and the patio doors were open to let in the breeze. Drake was in the shower, and so I put Sophie in her play chair and put some fresh coffee on to brew. When Drake came out of the bathroom, bare-chested and wearing a pair of Bermuda shorts, toweling his hair off, I went to him and slipped my arms around his waist.

"Welcome home," I said and we kissed. "How are you? How's your mother?"

"She's doing a little better," Drake said, his arms around me. "I spent the past few hours with her because she couldn't sleep."

"Did you get to talk to her?" I asked, not sure if she was able to understand who Drake was. "Is she aware of who you are?"

"I talked with her, but I have no idea if she knows who I am. I decided I'd tell her all about my life after she left, and my family. How dad was, and how he died, although I'm sure she knew."

"So, she didn't respond? Not at all?" I said, my heart sinking for Drake when I saw him shake his head.

"Sadly, no."

"That's so sad. How are you?"

He shrugged and took in a ragged breath. "It's been hard, but I'm glad that Kent and Amanda were there so I got to meet them both."

"What are they like?" I asked, curious to learn more about Drake's half-siblings.

He led me to the sofa, where we sat together. As usual, he pulled me onto his lap and we sat like that, my arms around him, his arms around me.

"They seemed nice, from what I could tell. I didn't get a chance to talk to them very much, but they did tell me some stories from their childhoods. Gave me an idea of what kind of mother she was to them."

"And?" I asked, wanting to encourage him to talk.

"She seems like she was a devoted mother. They love her. They felt loved."

He said it with no emotion in his voice and it made me feel sick that Drake had been denied that love.

She couldn't give it to him. That's why she left.

"She met her current husband and he saved her life. She turned things around, they got married and she had her children."

Drake turned to look in my eyes. I could see sadness in his.

"You have a family," I said and stroked his cheek. "Half-brothers and a half-sister, nephews and nieces. And a step-father."

He smiled finally. "I do. I never thought I'd have a family. After my father died, your father and the O'Rileys were the only family I had. Until you." He kissed me, his fingers tangling in my hair. "If I didn't have you, I'd still be keeping my distance from some new submissive, never getting emotionally close to any of them. Using them for sexual release and nothing more."

"You do have us," I said and kissed him again.

"I want you," he said, his voice low. The tone of his voice sent a thrill through me.

"We have five days off. Maybe Elaine and my dad can take her for an overnight again."

He nodded and then narrowed his eyes. "We could put Sophie in her playpen and fuck in the next room, with the baby monitor on loud."

I laughed. "You think you could concentrate with her babbling in the background? I couldn't."

He smiled. "I guess not. When does she normally go down for a nap?"

"Around four."

"Damn," he said. "I'll be at work. Although, I did send in my letter of resignation."

"What?"

Drake nodded. "We had a belligerent patient who was brought in by the police. They had to use restraints to treat him. One of the nursing supervisors made a crack about me being tempted to use the restraints."

"Oh, Drake," I said, horrified that someone had made a nasty remark about Drake and his past. "What did you say?"

"I said she didn't need to worry because I wouldn't want to use them on her anyway. Then, I left. I wrote an email tendering my resignation and sent it off. So, I'm going to be a free agent at the end of the month."

"That's terrible," I said and squeezed him, kissing him tenderly. "That nurse should be disciplined. And not in a good way."

I smiled slowly and of course, Drake did as well.

"Speaking of restraints, Ms. Bennet, I think I may have to look in my treat box for those lamb's wool restraints I gave you, so I can torture you with pleasure."

"I look forward to it," I said with a smile, my body already responding to the thought of Drake and I doing a scene. "I guess we'll have more time if you've quit your job."

"We will," Drake said and kissed me.

I felt a swell of love for him, and but it bothered me terribly that he felt he had to quit his position at the hospital.

"Are you sure about this?" I said, frowning when I thought that this woman had so much power over him. "You told me that you really enjoy working in the ER. I hate to think this bully forced you to resign from a job you love."

He shrugged. "I don't have to work, Kate. I certainly don't have to take any shit from some judging nursing supervisor about my past."

"You don't have to work," I replied. "But you love being a neurosurgeon. You told me how much you enjoyed your work. You're lucky you can do what you want. Most people have to work. They don't have options."

"I am lucky, and that's exactly what I'm doing. I don't have to work. I'll be called as a witness for the trial and we'll have to go back to Manhattan for that. Plus, we've been apart a lot because of the shifts. I miss being around Sophie when I work. We haven't spent much time with your dad and Elaine. And there's Liam, and now my mother..."

"It's a lot to deal with," I said, running my hands through his hair, which was rapidly drying. "I'd be happy to have you all to myself. Sophie and I would be more than happy to have you around all the time."

"You need time at the studio," Drake said, and tapped my nose with a finger.

"You can have daddy-daughter time when I do go to the studio."

"See what I mean? It'll be perfect." We kissed again, our arms tightening around each other. "I do have to go in for a shift tonight because I promised I would, but then I have five beautiful days off. Which will be good so I can spend time with my mother."

"How is she?" I asked again. "Do you think she might survive?"

"I do," he said and nodded. "But we won't know for sure until we see how she responds to this last-ditch antibiotic regimen."

"Good. Maybe you'll be able to connect with her, when she's better."

"I think so," Drake said and took in a deep breath. "Right now, she's very confused because of the infection, but if it clears up, she might be more coherent. I want her to know who I am, if it's possible. Kent and Amanda said she was much more aware before the infection so it may be because of that and her low oxygen that she seems so bad. She tried to speak to me, but it was just mumbling."

Drake covered his eyes and I realized how deeply he was affected by seeing his mother again. "Oh, Drake..."

I slipped my arms around him once more and squeezed, kissing his cheek. He wiped his eyes and forced a smile. "It would be really nice for her to see me. To really see me and know who I am."

"You can only try," I said. "If she recovers."

"If she recovers."

We sat like that for a moment and then Drake let out a sigh. "I better get going. I need to go back to sleep for a few hours. I want to go to the hospital to see how she's doing."

"You need to sleep," I said, putting my hands on his shoulders. "You need sleep if you're going to work a shift. You can pop in and see your mother just before your shift."

"You're right," he said and finally we stood up. "I just want to be there."

"I know, but you can't be there for her and be there for your patients if you don't get some sleep. Did you eat something at the hospital before you came home?"

Drake nodded.

"Good. Go and lie down. I'll make sure to wake you up so you'll have enough time to get dressed and go to see your mom before your shift."

"Okay, Mrs. Morgan," Drake said with a guilty smile. "I'll let you be the boss of me just this once."

"Ha," I said and slipped my arms around his waist. "We're the boss of each other."

"We are."

We kissed once more.

"Maybe if your mom improves, Sophie and I can come up and see her. What would you think of that?"

Drake's eyebrows raised. "Would you want to come and meet her?"

"Of course," I said. "I'd want her to see her other grandchild."

"She may not be coherent, even if she recovers."

"We have to hold out hope."

He nodded and stroked my cheek. "We do."

Then, he went to Sophie and kissed her before going to the bedroom for a sleep.

While Drake slept, Sophie and I did our usual routine of driving to the small neighborhood shopping mall. I had a cup of coffee while we sat on the patio and watched the people walk by. When I was done, we stopped and got a few things from the local Whole Foods store for the kitchen, and then returned home. I hoped Drake had enough time for a few good hours of sleep. I wouldn't wake him up until two o'clock. He'd already had a shower and so would only have to dress and then drive to the hospital which was about twenty minutes away. He could pop in to see his mom at that point. If she was well, we'd come up and see him there on his break and meet her.

S. E. LUND

I made a light lunch for Sophie and me and we sat on the patio and ate, watching the ocean below us. It was peaceful. Sophie was happy to babble away in her playpen while I finished reading some news headlines on my tablet.

After lunch, we watched some television and then, when it was almost two o'clock, I went into the bedroom and woke Drake up.

I leaned over Drake, moving the pillow off his head. I brushed hair off his cheek and kissed him.

"Time to wake up, my love."

He blinked awake and then stretched rolling over and pulling me on top of his body. He smiled when I squealed and then tickled me, trapping me beneath him.

"Tomorrow, Ms. Bennet, I am going to enjoy you."

"I'm going to enjoy you enjoying me."

"It's a date."

We kissed briefly and then Drake sighed. "I'll call you and let you know how my mother is. You can decide whether to come up or not."

"Sounds good," I replied. "I don't want to barge in on family business but I would like to see her."

"It's your family as well."

I nodded and then we heard Sophie from the other room, babbling over the baby monitor.

"Better get up and at 'em," Drake said and together, we got up off the bed. Drake went into the bathroom and I went back to the living room, where Sophie was happily playing in her playpen, her pacifier in her mouth.

138

When Drake was dressed, he came out to the living room where we sat and bent down to kiss us both goodbye. I walked him to the door with Sophie in my arms.

"I wish you didn't have to go to work tonight," I said. "You should be the one who gets to switch shifts considering your mother's so sick."

"There are only so many neurosurgeons to switch with."

I nodded but felt bad for Drake that he had to work despite all the stress he was facing.

"Tomorrow," Drake said and stroked my cheek. "We'll try to relax and enjoy each other but it depends on how my mother is doing."

"We'll play it by ear."

We kissed once more, he kissed Sophie and then he was gone.

CHAPTER 12

DRAKE

I STOPPED in to check on my mother before my shift started.

She was alone in a rare moment when her family was either taking a coffee break or was on their way to the hospital. Her room was quiet and she was laying with her head turned to the window. I wasn't sure if she was asleep so I walked in quietly, just in case.

I sat on the other side of her bed and waited, not wanting to wake her up. Her hands had been restrained with soft fabric restraints. She must have been pulling at her IV. I checked and I could see they'd wrapped her arm where she must have torn out the previous IV. They started another in her other arm and restrained her.

No matter what she had done to me, I still hated to see her that way – incoherent, confused, and panicking. She was still my mother and I did have fond memories of her from long ago. I remembered sitting on her lap when I was very young, listening to her read to me from her favorite children's books – Winnie the Pooh, Lightfoot the Deer and other books she was read as a child. I remembered her caring for me when I was sick and had whatever virus was going around. I remembered her baking special cookies for me and sitting with me after school while I ate them and drank my milk.

It was my father I rarely saw. He was the one away at the hospital for hours and hours. He was the one to hop on a plane and fly to some far-flung African community to do surgery for free. He was the one working late in his garage on his car or in his office, perfecting the design of a new surgical tool.

My mother was always there – until she wasn't.

Then, she was gone from my life without a word. My father told me that she left suddenly but that she had been unhappy for months, perhaps years he finally admitted. He blamed himself and said that instead of turning to her for comfort with his own pain and loss over Liam's death, he turned to his work.

He became a workaholic who failed to see my mother's emotional decline and distance. He had no idea she was suicidal. She put on the best face she could and kept on going through the motions but her heart and mind were no longer with us.

When she left, that was it. My dad sat me down at the kitchen table and said that my mother had gone away and would probably not ever come back.

I felt, as all children do, that she left because of me. That I was a bad boy and that if I had only been better, if I had only tried harder, she would have stayed and loved me more.

So much of my adolescence, teen years and adulthood had been spent looking for a way to work out my deep-seated trauma from her leaving me.

I stopped trusting. *Everyone.*

To adapt, I followed my father's example and worked everything, trying to compensate for my feelings of in achieving more than everyone else. I was the youngest g high school and the youngest – at the time – college stu... medical student. I was the youngest neurosurgeon.

None of it was enough.

My mother stirred on the bed and so I stood up and went to the other side and saw that her eyes were open.

"Hello, mother," I said, despite the fact she didn't know me – or might not remember. "It's me, Drake."

I took her hand and held it in mine, then leaned down and kissed her cheek.

She didn't pull away, but I saw no recognition in her eyes.

"Doctor, doctor, doctor..." was all she managed.

I glanced down to see my scrubs and my stethoscope around my neck. Of course, she would think I was there as a doctor.

"How are you?" I said, deciding not to push the whole Drake business with her, since she clearly didn't recognize me or understand what I'd said to her. "Are you feeling better? You look better."

I checked her pulse and found it was stronger than it had been before. Her O2 was better – still not perfect, but improving with oxygen. She was a bit raspy, her occasional cough wet, but she seemed less agitated than she had earlier in the morning. She must have slept.

I sat like that for probably fifteen more minutes before Herb and Kent arrived. They had coffee cups in hand from the hospital's cafeteria.

"Drake," Kent said and gave me a nod. "I thought you might drop by before your shift. I hope you got some sleep."

"I'm fine. I'm used to working with little sleep."

"You doctors," Herb said. "You're used to torturing yourselves."

He smiled and then, I saw a look pass over his face and I wondered if he only then thought about my background in the BDSM community. Did he know about my past? About the trial? No doubt he wouldn't understand the difference between the SM and BD side of things. There was nothing to be done about it, so I merely smiled back.

"Medical school is hell, being a resident is even more hell, and being a specialist means you never get much of a break, especially if your specialty is rare and in demand."

"I can imagine," he said.

"She seems better," I said. "I didn't check in with the nurses because they were on a report before the shift change, but I will on the way out. How does she seem to you?"

"Better," Herb said and took my place at my mother's side when I stepped away. He bent down and kissed her on the lips and she seemed to recognize him at least and kissed him back.

"That's my girl," Herb said, squeezing her hand. "You remember me, don't you, sugarplum. It's me, your husband Herb."

She whispered something and he bent down to listen. When he stood up, he shook his head sadly and turned to me.

"Can't make anything out, I'm afraid. But she does recognize me. I can tell. She wouldn't let me kiss her otherwise."

I felt so bad for him and couldn't imagine how I'd feel if Kate was to stop knowing who I was. It would break me in two.

"She may, but just can't vocalize it because of the disease."

"I think so," he replied.

I watched them for a moment and then checked my watch. "Well, I better get to the ER. My shift starts soon and I want to check on my patients from yesterday first. I'll drop by on my break and see how she's doing."

"Thanks, Drake" Herb said and came to me, his hand on my shoulder. "I'm so sorry you had to meet your mother again in these circumstances. I wish we had tried sooner to contact you, but just weren't sure if it was a good idea to bring it all up at the time."

"No, that's fine. I understand completely. I'm just so glad that Kent did decide to contact me. It means the world to me to finally see her again. I wasn't sure I would want to, but no matter what happened, she's my mother. I love her."

Tears filled my eyes and Herb put his hand on my arm. "We all do. She's loved."

I forced a smile and then kissed her cheek, even though I was sure she had no idea who I was, and then I left the room, wiping my eyes quickly.

I went to the nursing station before I went to the ER and looked over my mother's chart, to check and see what changes there had been during the time I was away. She had steadily improved, although her condition was still guarded. Satisfied that she was doing as well as could be expected, I left the ward and made my way to the ER, stopping to change into something fresh before my shift. I was happy to be as busy as possible for the next twelve hours, so the time would pass quickly and I wouldn't worry too much about my mother.

Luckily, the cases I had to consult came fast with little time between them and so I didn't look up from my work until it was time for my first break. At seven o'clock, I left the ER and went to the cafeteria, grabbed a sandwich and a drink, and ate on the way to my mother's ward. I didn't stop into the staff lounge. I could only imagine what would greet me if I did – my fellow staffers would no doubt be talking about my resignation. I still hadn't had the chance to talk to my supervisor about it, but expected I would at some point in the evening.

My mother was resting quietly and had been fed, and had eaten a bit of pudding and drank some liquid protein. It was good because if she hadn't, they would have to tube feed her and that would only add to her stress.

I spoke with Amanda for a moment and then said hello to my mother. She was as confused as before, willingly taking my hand, but not being able to say anything sensible. I said goodbye and left after only a few moments, because I didn't want to intrude too much into their lives.

"Please, Drake, feel free to come back and visit any time you want," Amanda said. "Honestly, it's good to have you here. You can check over her chart and let us know how she's doing."

"You don't trust your doctor?" I said, frowning.

"No, it's not that. It's just that doctors tend to sugarcoat the worst news and downplay the best. At least, in my experience. You can tell us straight how she's doing."

I shrugged. "It's really just a matter of personal preference how a physician chooses to communicate with his or her patients. I think she's doing better than yesterday, but she's still sick. She's been rehydrated, and her oxygen sats are better, but she still has an infection. If this new combination of antibiotics is going to work, we should start seeing more profound improvement by tomorrow."

"Thanks for coming by and letting us know," Amanda said. She gave me a quick hug, and I left to go back to the ER.

I did stop by the staff room on my way there, to pick up a fresh cup of coffee, and there were several staff sitting on the two sofas in the seating area. When they saw me, conversation stopped and heads turned.

"Hey, Drake," Nick, one of the staff physicians said. He left the group and came to stand beside me in the alcove where the coffee machine was located. "We heard you've tendered your resignation. I hope it's not because of Christy. She's a busybody of the worst kind."

I turned and had to decide whether I wanted to talk to him about it or just write it off and not say a word. Nick had always been a nice person to me so I didn't want to be rude. It wasn't because of him that I was leaving.

"It's not just Christy," I said and stirred my coffee. "I have a lot going on right now. I need some sanity and the long shifts were taking me away from family. But thanks for the heads-up on Christy."

"No problem," Nick said. "I speak for a number of us. We'll be sad to see you go and especially if Christy's big mouth had anything to do with it."

"It really isn't primarily Christy. My mother's very sick and right now, my priority is to spend time with her in case she doesn't recover."

"Oh, I'm sorry to hear that."

I nodded and put the lid on my coffee. "Thanks. And thanks for the kind words. Now, I've got to get back to the ER."

"Cheers," Nick said and raised his coffee cup.

I smiled and left the staff room, making my way down the hallways to the ER. For the rest of my shift, I tried to focus my entire attention on my cases, and tried hard not to notice any quiet conversations taking place just out of my earshot and the surreptitious glances at me from the nursing staff.

In the end, I was glad I made my decision to quit my position. I could feel the weight of responsibility sliding off my shoulders as the end of my shift neared. I'd be able to spend all my time with Kate and Sophie, and with my mother – at least until she recovered or died.

When my shift was finished, I stopped in to my mother's room and checked on her. It was just after three in the morning and the ward was quiet. She was sleeping, her breathing easier, and for the first time, I felt some hope that she was in fact getting over the infection. If so, it would be wonderful. Even if she was in the later stages of Alzheimer's, I would get a chance to see her, talk to her if not with her, and of course, meet my other brothers.

I left the hospital with a sense of relief, and happy to face five full days off before I'd finish the month off with one last five-day shift cycle.

Then, I would be completely free to spend as much time as I wanted on my family – all of them.

I couldn't wait to get home to my own family, to Kate and Sophie, and as I drove along the highway back to our house, I felt relief that my mother just might survive.

AFTER I PARKED the car in our driveway, and made my way inside, shutting on the alarm system and taking a quick shower, I walked to our bedroom and stood beside the bed. Kate was alone in the bed, so I went to Sophie's room and saw her lying on her back, her eyes open and her pacifier in her mouth. When I saw her eyes, I thought I should step back so she didn't see me, but I was too late and she latched onto me with her baby blues.

She waved her arms excitedly and rolled over, crawling over to the side of the crib.

"Hey, baby," I said and picked her up. "You're awake."

I rocked her, hoping I could put her back into her crib without taking her into our bed, but soon, Kate showed up in the doorway.

"I already tried," Kate said, smiling at me. "I put her in her crib about fifteen minutes ago. I must have fallen asleep."

"I blew it, in other words."

"You know what they say – let sleeping dogs and babies lie. Why don't you bring her into our bed? She'll fall back asleep soon enough.

"Okay," I said, "but I was hoping for alone time with mommy."

Kate laughed lightly. She led the way back down the hall to our bedroom. "You're going to have to wait until tomorrow night for that."

"Are Elaine and Dad going to take her overnight?"

Kate crept into bed and I put Sophie down on the bed between us.

"Yes," Kate said and pulled covers up over us. "They know you'll want to spend time at the hospital and that we need time together."

"Good," I said and kissed Sophie. The three of us snuggled down and soon, Sophie's eyes were closing and she fell asleep. I watched Kate as she snuggled down more deeply in the bed. She fell back asleep quickly but for me, sleep was a long time in coming.

CHAPTER 13

KATE

DRAKE and I woke early in the morning to the sound of Sophie babbling happily between us. She had squirmed out of her covers and was playing with her feet, chewing on her pacifier and muttering baby talk. I turned over and faced her, smiling when she saw me and her little face lit up.

"Hi, baby," I said softly, not wanting to wake up Drake. "Ready to meet the day?"

I managed to creep out of the bed with Sophie in my arms. As I did, Drake woke up and pulled the pillow off his head.

"You two early birds awake already?"

I craned my neck to see the clock radio. It was just after seven o'clock. Sophie's usual time to get up and start our day.

"You sleep in. We can have lunch together."

"Sounds good," Drake said when I bent down with Sophie to give him a kiss. He kissed me and then kissed Sophie on both cheeks.

I left Drake in bed and took Sophie into her bedroom for a diaper change, and then we went to the living room, where she went right into her playpen so I could have a quick pee. When I returned, she was playing happily so I fixed us both breakfast, and then put her in her high chair.

It was while I was cutting up some fruit for Sophie that my cell rang. I checked the number and saw that it was Brenda. She must be calling about Liam.

"Hello," I said, glad to hear from her. "How are you?"

"We're fine," Brenda said. "We thought that it might be nice for Drake and Liam to get together during his five days off. Drake texted me to let me know he'd be off so I'm calling to see if he wants to take Liam this afternoon for a few hours."

"Oh," I said and frowned. "I know Drake would love to spend time with Liam, but I don't know if he can today. I don't know whether he told you, but he recently found out that his mother is very sick, and he's been spending every spare moment up at the hospital visiting her."

"Oh, I'm so sorry to hear that," Brenda said. "His mother? If I remember correctly, he hasn't seen her for years. Am I right?"

"Yes," I said and sat at the island counter to have my breakfast and feed Sophie. "Drake's half-brother contacted me and let me know about their mother. He found out he has three half-brothers and a half-sister. He's met a couple of them and has seen his mother as well."

"You tell Drake it can be another day. I'm sure I can entertain Liam for a day or two, but it would be really nice for them to get together soon since Liam's looking forward to it."

"I'll tell Drake you called and as soon as he's up, he'll call and you two can talk."

"Sounds good," Brenda said in reply.

We said our goodbyes and I ended the call, sighing at the prospect of yet another fight for Drake. He had so much going on right now that I felt it was a good thing he quit his position at the hospital.

Now, maybe he could focus on his mother and Liam.

Sophie and I ate our breakfasts and took our daily walk down the beach, and when we returned, Drake was up and in the shower. I made a pot of coffee and sat in front of the flatscreen so I could watch some news while Sophie played on the floor with her toys. When Drake was finished with his shower, he emerged from the back room dressed in a pair of shorts, his chest bare, his hair still wet.

He bent down and kissed me warmly. "Mrs. Morgan," he said and stroked my cheek. "I am eager to spend the entire night with you tonight."

"Me as well," I said and smiled up at him.

He went over to Sophie and picked her up. "And I'm looking forward to spending most of the day with you, Miss Sophia." He kissed her on her cheeks and sat down beside me with Sophie on his lap. "Maybe your mom can go to her studio and do some painting."

He glanced over at me expectantly.

"I'm okay," I said, not wanting to tie up the day at all with my trip to the studio. That was the lowest priority on my to-do list. "Do you want me to get you a cup of coffee?" I went to the kitchen to refill mine.

"Please," Drake said. "And bring me one of those croissants."

"Coming right up."

I poured him a cup and grabbed a croissant from the container then I sat back down beside him and he put Sophie back onto the floor. She was more interested in crawling around to get her toys at the moment and was happy to be left to herself.

"I got a call from Brenda," I said and proceeded to tell Drake about the conversation.

"I'd like to spend time with Liam," Drake said. "I might take him up with me to the hospital."

I frowned. "Do you think that's wise? Won't it be upsetting to him?"

Drake shook his head. "Liam's seen more sickness and death than most of us have. He spent a lot of time on hospital wards, around other children who were sick and some of whom died. He doesn't understand it the way an adult does, but I think he'd be fine. I'll talk to Brenda and see what she thinks, of course."

"Of course," I said, realizing that Liam wasn't an ordinary child. Having cancer altered them, making them see the world differently than a child who has never been ill. "Whatever you think."

Drake took out his cell and called Brenda. I watched him while he waited, amazed that he could face all this turmoil in his life and still seem positive.

Finally, she answered.

"Hello," he said and smiled. "Yes, I'd like to very much. Maybe we could get some ice cream and go to the beach. Let me talk to your grandma, okay?"

He raised his eyebrows at me and waited. She must have come on the line and Drake said hello and nodded.

"Thank you. Yes, it was a shock of course. I'd like to visit with Liam today. What I wanted to ask you was whether you think it would be okay if he went to visit his other grandmother – if she's well enough."

He listened for a while, taking a sip of his coffee.

"I'd want to make sure she wasn't in any distress first. When I saw her this morning she was breathing much better and was brighter. Even if she can't understand who he is, I would like him to know who she is. Before she dies."

He nodded as he listened and then smiled. "Thanks, Brenda. I'll make sure not to dwell on anything morbid. I'll tell him that she's sick with a bad cold and had to be in the hospital. I won't mention that she's potentially terminal. And I won't take him to see her if her condition's deteriorated."

Drake listened some more and then glanced over at me. "I think our whole family will take a trip up to see her. Then, we can all go for supper, and maybe ice cream like I promised, if you're okay with that."

I nodded my head, wanting him to know I was happy to go with him and Liam.

"Okay, we'll be by around three. If my mother is too ill, we won't go to the hospital but there's lots we can do down at the beach. Thanks. See you later."

Drake ended the call and turned to me, smiling. "Well, that's all settled."

"I'm glad. I just hope she's not too agitated so Liam can see her."

"They're giving her medicine that is calming her so I hope she'll be fine. She may still be unaware of who we are, and unable to understand who Liam is but he should see her at least in case she passes."

I leaned over to Drake and slipped my arms around his shoulders. "I love you," I said, my emotions getting the better of me.

"When I met you, I told you I was pretty much an orphan" Drake said, brushing hair off my cheek, "but now look at how much family I have. I have us, I have your father and Elaine, I have Brenda and Liam, and now I have my mother and her family."

My eyes teared up at that. "I'm glad for you."

We kissed, the kiss warm and full of affection and emotion.

FOR THE REST of the morning and early afternoon, we did family things together, eating our lunch on the patio and then we put Sophia down for a nap that never happened. She was used to going down around three, but we wanted to spend time with Liam when he got home from school. It would mean she'd probably sleep in the car on the way home and it might mess up her sleep schedule at my father's, but I felt assured he and Elaine could deal with it.

We got ready to go and pick up Liam, the two of us standing at the mirror in the bathroom, brushing our teeth and getting dressed.

"I hope things go okay and that my mom is good enough for Liam to see her."

"You can only check and see. We've got lots to do even if he can't meet her today. There will be other days perhaps."

"We'll see."

I kissed him, brushing his hair out of his eyes. "That's all we can do."

. . .

We finished dressing Sophie in her sunhat and tiny heart-shaped sunglasses and took the car to Maureen's home in the hills outside San Francisco. As we drove, Sophie fell asleep. When we arrived at Maureen's, Drake went to the door to get Liam and I smiled when I saw him. He looked so much like Drake with his fair skin, dark black hair and blue eyes. He was truly a mini-Drake and it made my heart squeeze to see them side by side. Drake spoke with Brenda for a moment and she turned and waved at me.

I waved back, smiling, glad that Brenda was so understanding and so positive about Drake and Liam establishing a close bond. Even if Drake didn't get shared custody of Liam, I knew that Brenda would always be open to him seeing Liam as much as possible. It hurt me to think Drake might not get shared custody because of his past, but we had to face that possibility.

Father and son came to the vehicle, and Drake opened the door for Liam, who climbed in beside his sleeping sister. Drake helped him on the booster seat and fastened his seatbelt. Liam had on a baseball cap with the Giants logo on the front, a pair of jeans and a t-shirt with a Batman logo. He smiled at me.

"Hello, Kate," he whispered, holding his finger up to his lips. "Sophia's sleeping."

I nodded, realizing that Drake had told him to whisper so that Sophie could get her nap in. "She is," I said and held my finger up to my lips in reply.

He turned to Sophie and stared at her like she was something special – and she was something special to him. His half-sister. Beside him in her car seat, she slept, her pacifier in her mouth, her head tilted to the side.

I knew he wanted to talk to her and to us but he was a big enough boy to understand that we didn't want her to wake up just yet and so he was patient, waiting until she did wake up to talk.

Drake got back in the vehicle once Liam was secured, and off we drove, on our way to the hospital.

"I told Liam that we wanted Sophie to sleep so we'll try to be quiet until we get to the hospital," Drake said in a quiet voice.

I nodded and turned to glance back at Liam. He was sitting in his seat, happy to be out with us even if he did have to be quiet. I winked at him and he smiled back at me. He had a backpack with him and fished inside it, pulling out a comic book and a Batman toy. He held them both up for me to see.

"It's Batman," he whispered, his eyes wide when he examined the doll.

"Cool," I whispered back, realizing he had graduated from being a fan of Despicable Me to Batman. Behind us, Liam settled in to read his new comic while we drove, the comic in one hand and Batman held tightly in the other.

I turned back and reached over to take Drake's hand. We really were a little family. I squeezed his hand and he squeezed back, turning to me and smiling.

I knew that for Drake, this was heaven.

WE ARRIVED at the hospital and Drake parked in his spot near the ER. Sophie woke up when the car stopped and we got out, the slamming of the doors waking her. Drake lifted her out of the car, still in her car seat, and placed her on the pavement while Liam put his things away in his backpack and got out of the car. Sophie smiled widely at Liam when he bent down to her in the parking lot, while I gathered up the diaper bag and Drake locked up.

"Hi Sophia," Liam said, his face a few inches from hers. Then he reached into his backpack and pulled out a stuffed toy. It was another minion, this time with two eyes. He handed it to her. "This is for you. His name is Jerry. I was going to give you a transformer but my grandma said it would be better to give you something soft."

Sophie took the minion from Liam's hand and bashed it against the side of her car seat. Liam laughed.

"She likes it!"

"She does," I replied and stroked his hair affectionately.

While Drake went up to check on his mother, Liam, Sophie and I went to the cafeteria to get Liam a cookie while we waited. I didn't want the trip to be disappointing to him if it turned out that we couldn't see Louise. We sat at a table and waited, Liam entertaining Sophia by talking about Jerry and telling her all about the minions and who they worked for. She was happy just to watch him, smiling periodically.

Then, he changed to his latest obsession – Batman. He talked away to Sophie, his brow furrowed as he informed her about the new Batman comic he had. He reached into his backpack again and pulled out the Batman figurine to show her.

Sophie seemed excited to see the doll so Liam handed it to her. It went immediately into her mouth like everything else she picked up. Beside her, Liam looked horrified at the prospect of baby drool on his prized possession so I took it away from her. I wiped it off with a baby wipe from Sophia's diaper bag. Liam looked relieved when I handed it back, no worse for the wear.

Drake returned about ten minutes later and by the expression on his face, I assumed that Louise was in pretty good shape.

"Let's go," Drake said, his hand on one of Liam's shoulders. "Your other grandma is feeling better today. The medicine they're giving her is working."

"She has Alls—high—mers," Liam said carefully. "My grandma said it makes people forget things."

"That's right," Drake said and led Liam down the hall, hand in hand. "She may not even know who we are, but I wanted you to meet her and know your other grandma."

"I have three," Liam said, looking up at Drake. "My grandma, your mom and my other dad's mom."

"You're lucky," I said and smiled. "Most people only have two."

Liam smiled, and I could see his mind working. "I am lucky, I guess."

We took the elevator up to the medical ward where Louise was staying and went to the room. My stomach was full of butterflies as I wondered what she would be like when she saw Drake and the rest of us.

Could she understand who we all were or would it be too much for her?

Inside was Louise's husband, who was sitting by her side, her hand in his. She was no longer restrained, her hands free but her arms were wrapped in bandages. Drake had told me that she tried to rip out her IVs...

"Hello," Herb said when he saw us. He came right over and extended his hand to me and we shook. "You must be Kate. Nice to meet you."

"Nice to meet you," I said and smiled at him. He had a pleasant face, with a balding hairline and warm brown eyes. "Sorry it had to be under these circumstances."

He nodded. "Yes, but we're all so glad to have found Drake." Then he turned to Sophie in the car seat and Liam who was standing beside Drake, their hands clasped. "And this must be Liam. Hello, Liam. My name is Herb. Nice to meet you."

Liam smiled up at Herb and they shook hands, and it was so cute to see Liam being so formal.

"You have the same name as Herb Overkill."

"I do but I'm not nearly as skinny."

Liam laughed and glanced at Herb's belly, which was substantial. "No. But you're as tall as him."

Herb smiled down at Liam. "You look like your dad. And your grand-mother. She had that black hair when she was younger and those blue eyes."

Liam nodded and glanced at the bed where Drake was standing, Louise's hand in his.

I watched Drake, who bent down and kissed Louise's cheek. She looked somewhat more aware than Drake's description after he saw her the first day we found out she was in the hospital. Her hair had been brushed and her eyes were bright. She had a nasal cannula supplying her oxygen, but otherwise, she looked like a normal patient recovering from a disease.

"How are you, Mother? It's Drake, your son from your marriage with Liam."

When he spoke, she looked at him like he was speaking in gibberish, her brow furrowed. She muttered something, her eyes confused. Then Drake ushered Liam over and Liam stood on the stool beside the bed, moving close enough so that Louise could see him clearly.

"This is Liam," Drake said, his voice emotional. "This is my son from a previous marriage. Liam, this is your grandmother."

Liam extended his hand, expecting to shake Louise's hand. She changed demeanor as soon as she saw Liam, her face lighting up.

"Drake, Drake, Drake..." She reached out and touched Liam's head, running her fingers over his hair. Then she took his hand, and squeezed it, all the while she kept chanting *Drake* over and over, and then it hit me that she was remembering Drake as a boy.

She thought she was holding Drake's hand.

"No, I'm Liam," Liam said, enunciating the word. "Li-am. Drake is my other father. He's your son."

"Drake, Drake, Drake..."

"It's okay," Drake said and bent down, taking Liam's hand out of hers. He clasped her hand instead, letting Liam move out of the way. "Grandma is a bit confused. She hasn't seen me since I ten. She thinks you're me."

"I know," Liam said. "That's okay. She's old. She forgot."

"She did."

Drake leaned down and kissed Louise once more on the forehead and she looked up in his face and continued whispering. This time, she kept repeating Liam, and I figured that she must have thought that he was Drake's father.

He did look very much like Drake's father Liam had when he was Drake's age.

I felt so bad for all of them – for Louise, for not being able to understand that she was seeing her son, Drake. For Drake, for being unable to get through to her and her to understand who he was. And for Liam, having to deal with the whole situation. He didn't seem too upset and was quite willing to just accept things. I supposed that after all he'd been through in his short life, this mix-up was nothing.

Drake stood beside the bed and spoke to Louise, telling her all about his first marriage and how Liam was his son with his first wife. He had already told her all this, but he probably felt a need to tell her again, hoping that she'd comprehend.

I didn't see even a hint of understanding on her face – only confusion.

"So, tell me about Liam," Herb said and sat in a chair beside the bed. Liam stood in front of him and talked about himself. He pulled out Batman from his backpack and showed it to Herb, who took it and examined it closely.

"I sure wish we had such great toys when I was your age. This is fantastic."

"You liked Batman when you were a kid?"

"He was my favorite. We could only watch on television or read comics."

Liam smiled, pleased to find another Batman fan. He reached inside his backpack and pulled out the Batman comic, showing it to Herb, who made a big fuss about it.

"We should go," Drake said to Herb, once he handed the comic back to Liam and took his place at Louise's side. "I'll come back and see her again tomorrow."

"Come whenever you like. The doctors are hopeful for the first time that she may recover so we'd be pleased if you come as often as you're able. In fact, we wanted to invite you and your family over to our place as soon as things settled down. We have a big pit barbecue right beside the beach and could cook up a mess of ribs, as my family back home in Louisiana would say."

Drake smiled and shook hands with Herb once more. "That sounds wonderful. I'd love to come and meet everyone, and introduce my family to them." He turned to Liam. "Would you like to go for a barbecue, Liam?"

Liam nodded, taking Drake's hand once more. "Yes. Could I bring my boogie board and surf?"

"Of course, you could," Herb said and smiled.

"We look forward to it," I said, pleased that Drake would get to meet the rest of his siblings.

We said goodbye and made our way out of the hospital and to the car. When we got there, Drake put Sophie's car seat in the back and Liam got in beside her, on his booster seat.

We both got inside and he closed his door, then inserted the key and started the engine. Then, he sat there for a moment, his head bowed. I reached out to touch him, knowing he was overwhelmed.

He turned to me, his eyes wet. "That went better than I hoped."

"It did."

He leaned over and we kissed.

"Other than her mistaking Liam for me as a boy. Probably that's all she can do — draw on deep memories at this point in her disease progression. She thought I was my father."

"I know," I said, my own emotions overflowing. "She didn't seem upset."

"No," he said and shook his head. "She didn't."

He sighed and we drove off, on our way to the beach so we could enjoy the afternoon with Liam. He was a sweet boy who showed such composure during the visit to the people he did not know.

I glanced to the back seat and sure enough, Sophie fell asleep, the motion of the car working every time. Beside her, Liam was reading his Batman comic book, turning pages, his eyes wide.

While we were driving, Drake's cell let out a loud ding, indicating an incoming text message.

"Can you check that for me?"

I grabbed Drake's cell and opened it up, using his passcode. I flipped screens and found his text messages. There was one from his lawyer in Manhattan.

JUDE: Court date coming up. You'll be called by the prosecutor. Need you here so we can go over your testimony. Let me know when you can get here. The sooner the better. Court is in three weeks.

I read it to Drake, a sinking feeling in my gut.

"So soon?" he said, frowning. "I thought it wouldn't be until next month."

"I guess not. We can all go together," I said, not wanting Drake to have to do it himself. "It's a good thing you only have five shifts left. You could go once they're done."

Drake nodded, but his demeanor changed from that point on.

Our special day with Liam, and with Drake's new-found family had gone so well. I didn't want it to be ruined by a text so I took Drake's hand and squeezed.

"It'll be straightforward. You'll meet with Jude, go over your testimony, attend court and then we'll come back. Nothing to it. You did nothing wrong. Nothing illegal. We'll come back to San Francisco and we'll spend the rest of the year getting to know your new family and spending time with each other."

He smiled finally and kissed my knuckles when we pulled up to a stoplight.

"There's a reason I love you so much," he said softly.

"There is," I replied. "It's because I love you so much."

"We're a hopeless case. Hopelessly in love."

I smiled back. "Hopeless as charged."

We drove off to the beach and the spent the rest of a great day with family, thoughts about the upcoming trial put behind us both for now.

CHAPTER 14

DRAKE

MY DAY with Liam and the rest of our family was wonderful. It was exactly what I needed.

After our visit to the hospital to see my mother, we went to Ethan and Elaine's and spent time on the beach in front of their house. The weather was warm, the sky blue with only a few clouds and was perfect. Liam had his boogie board and put on a wetsuit Brenda had packed for him, spending time in the surf, riding the small waves in. Sophie and Kate stayed a little farther up the beach from the surf and built sandcastles, Sophie wearing her floppy brim hat and heart-shaped sunglasses. Above us, on the deck watching over everything was Ethan and Elaine, sitting on the patio chairs under an umbrella.

After an hour of surfing, we all went up to the house for supper, gorging ourselves on barbecue ribs, potato salad, and an assortments of grilled vegetables. We sat around the table on the deck and talked, laughed and had a great time together as one big family. When it was time to take Liam home, I wished we could have arranged to have him sleep over. We had a guest bedroom at our house and could have accommodated him, but I hadn't talked to Brenda about it so instead, I planned on doing so another night. It would be a good thing to get Liam used to staying with us now, so when I got shared custody – and I was determined to get shared custody – he would be ready for it psychologically. We could move in some toys and decorate it in whatever kind of superhero motif he wanted – Batman or whoever it was by the time I got shared custody.

I was eager to get that process started, but until the trial was over in Manhattan and that was put behind me, and the publicity from that died down, I wouldn't push anything. The last thing I needed was to go before a judge and plead for shared custody of my son with that trial in the media.

So, my plan was to go to Manhattan, see the trial to the end and then return to start work on getting shared custody. Until then, I'd make sure we spent as much time as we could with Liam so that he got totally comfortable with everyone – with me, with Kate and Sophia, and with Ethan and Elaine. If I could establish an ongoing relationship with my other family – with Herb and Amanda, Kent and my other two half-brothers I'd yet to meet, I'd want Liam to know them as well.

I envisioned big family dinners in the fall and could imagine us all sitting around a huge dining table on Thanksgiving and Christmas Day. It was a dream for me and I was going to make it happen. It might take a lot of work, but I had been used to working hard at my career. I could turn that focus to getting shared custody of Liam and creating the big family I always dreamed of having.

As we finished our dessert and sat around the table on the deck, the patio lanterns turning on and lighting the area, I felt satisfied that although I had to give up my position at the hospital, things would work out eventually. It was for the best that I quit. I had so much going on in my life that I needed the breathing space. There was nothing stopping me from going back into practice once I could get hospital privileges. That could wait.

I had other priorities – like Kate and Sophia – and Liam. Plus my new family.

At the end of our evening together, we drove Liam back to Maureen's place. The trip was a long one and Sophie fell asleep. When we arrived, I slipped the car in park and walked hand in hand with Liam to the door. Brenda opened it wide and invited me in.

"Come in, come in," she said and peered out around the door to the car. "Tell Kate to bring in Sophie as well."

"Sophie's asleep and we don't want to wake her," I said. "Thanks for the offer but we really should get back home." I handed her Liam's backpack and turned to Liam. "I think we had a great time today."

Liam nodded.

"Oh, that's great," Brenda said and bent down to Liam. "Thank your father for the day."

Liam turned to me. "Thank you, father. I had a fun time at the beach. And the supper was pretty good, too."

"I'm so glad you enjoyed yourself," I replied and ruffled up his hair. "We'll get together again soon and maybe you can do a sleepover if your grandmother says yes."

I leaned down and gave him a quick squeeze then I released his shoulder, said goodbye to Brenda and went to my car. Maybe one day, he'd feel like giving me a hug on his own, but I wasn't going to push it and expect him to.

I waved at them both and got back in the car, driving off into the night, a lump in my throat. Beside me, Kate smiled and took my hand.

"That was fun."

"It was," I said but for the moment, I was too emotional to talk and so we held hands and drove in silence through the darkened streets.

"We should just bring her home," I said after a few moments. "I'd like to wake up with both my girls in the morning. She can go to stay with Dad and Elaine tomorrow night, if they're okay with that."

"I'll call," Kate said and took out her cell. She dialed and the call went over the car's Bluetooth speaker.

"Hi, Elaine. Sophie's asleep in her car seat so we think we'll just take her home with us tonight. Maybe tomorrow night or the next night?"

"Whatever works best for you. Your father and I don't have any plans. Let us know tomorrow if you want to bring her over for the night."

"Thanks. I'll call you."

They said goodbye and Kate ended the call, slipping her cell back into her bag.

I took her hand and squeezed. "I feel like I need to sleep for twenty-four hours."

"It's all the stress of the last few days, plus your workload. You need to sleep in tomorrow morning."

"I will," I said and kissed her knuckles. "I had plans for a real romantic night but honestly, I'm so exhausted, I feel like I could fall asleep the moment my head hits the pillow."

"You should sleep as long as you need."

I squeezed her hand once more and drove back to our place by the ocean.

. . .

I CARRIED Sophie into the house in her car seat and once we were in her room, in the dark, I removed her from her seat and laid her in her crib, pulling the cover up over her. Her pacifier was gripped tightly in her mouth and she didn't even blink an eye open, remaining asleep the entire time.

Kate and I stood beside the crib and watched her for a moment and I marveled at how much she'd grown since she was born. I pulled Kate against me and kissed her forehead, filled with happiness that I had her and Sophie – and everyone else in my life.

"Let's have a nice warm bubble bath and go to bed," I said.

"Sounds perfect."

I kissed Kate on the mouth this time and despite all the emotion of the day and despite my exhaustion, I wanted to make love with her before going to sleep.

So I did.

After our bath, which was soothing and relaxing after a long day at the beach, we made love in the moonlight coming in from the picture window in our bedroom, the shafts of grey-white light flowing over our naked bodies on the bed. It wasn't a BD scene like I had planned, using my lambswool cuffs to restrain Kate on the bed. It was instead plain old vanilla and more a quick but intense release that I needed to completely exhaust me and let me sleep after so many emotions of the day.

Afterward, as Kate lay beneath me, her legs wrapped around my waist, her hands stroking up my back, I kissed her tenderly.

"I needed that, Mrs. Morgan."

"You did, Dr. Morgan. Will you be able to fall asleep now? No ruminating on everything?"

"None," I replied and kissed her neck. "Totally brain dead, I'm afraid. Don't ask me anything more challenging than do you want a glass of water because I'll probably be incoherent."

Kate smiled beneath me and ran her fingers through my hair.

"You could never be incoherent."

We kissed once more before reluctantly pulling apart, our bodies no longer joined.

After we cleaned up and got back into bed, I pulled her against me, my arm around her from behind. I kissed her shoulder and closed my eyes.

"Good night, my love," I said and sighed, the last vestiges of stress evaporating.

"Good night."

And so it was with Kate in my arms and Sophia asleep in her bedroom, that I finally fell asleep after a long memorable day that I wouldn't soon forget.

THE NEXT MORNING dawned and our bed was empty. Both Sophia and Kate were already up and I was surprised that I'd slept through Kate leaving the bed. I must have been extremely tired not to wake up because I was usually a light sleeper. I rolled around in the warm sheets and contemplated getting up or sleeping longer. My watch on the beside table read seven thirty a.m. I would normally get up at that point, but this felt like the true first day of my five days off and I didn't want to waste the opportunity to sleep in, so I turned over, put the pillow over my head and tried to go back to sleep.

Of course, I couldn't. I had to get up. Once my mind started going, it was impossible to go back to sleep. Instead, I got up and went for a quick shower before joining Kate and Sophie in the kitchen. When I arrived, Kate was texting on her phone and Sophie was seated in her highchair, feeding herself Cheerios. She smiled when she saw me so I went right over and kissed her cheeks.

"Good morning, sweetheart," I said and rubbed my hand over her soft fluffy baby hair, which was starting to curl around the nape of her neck. If Liam looked like me, Sophia looked like Kate, with chestnut brown hair.

"Good morning, Dr. Morgan," Kate said teasingly. "I thought you'd be so weak after last night that you'd sleep in."

I laughed. "You think a bit of vanilla sex tired me out? You are sadly mistaken. That was only a warm-up. Tonight, you're in for it."

"Promises, promises," Kate said, smiling down at her phone.

I went over to her and pulled her against me from behind. "I am a man of my word."

"You are," Kate replied and leaned back, her head resting against my shoulder. "I look forward to you keeping your promises. Many times."

Kate finished typing and then put her phone down. "So, what's on the agenda for today?"

I poured a cup of juice and grabbed a croissant then sat beside Sophie at the kitchen island.

"We should go for a nice walk along the beach like you guys do every morning, have a nice lunch on the patio, and then," I said and pulled Kate closer, "I want you to go to the studio and spend a few hours there. Sophie and I will spend our time together, she can have a nap, and when you get back, we can have dinner, and then drop Sophie off at Grandad's and Grandma's place for a sleepover. How does that sound?"

"It sounds totally indulgent."

"Good. We should be indulgent. Both of us have been through a lot in the past year. We deserve it."

Kate kissed me. "If you insist."

"I insist. I want you to feel like all the sacrifices have been worth it."

Kate frowned. "What sacrifices? I have you. I have Sophia. I have my parents. I have my studio. What sacrifice have I made?"

I stroked her cheek. "You know what I mean. You had to take a leave from your Master's degree. You lost a lot."

"I did, but I have so much. How can I feel ungrateful?"

I kissed her again, because she was so accepting of everything. "I won't argue with you. I just want you to be happy and fulfilled."

"I am," she said and leaned her forehead against mine. "You don't have to worry about me anymore. Whatever baby blues I had are all gone now. I couldn't be happier. Honestly, Drake. I'm over the post-partum depression."

I didn't argue anymore. I'd still watch Kate to make sure she wasn't hiding her emotions in order to spare me. She did that before we left Manhattan, and I would make sure things didn't spiral down again. It was completely understandable that Kate had PTSD after the attack and almost losing her life and that of Sophia. Luckily, we had recognized it in time and Kate recovered, but I would always be on the lookout for signs that she was becoming depressed.

WE TOOK our usual walk along the beach to a spot that was sheltered from the wind, and sat on the sand so Sophie could crawl around and make sandcastles. The weather was unusually warm for that time of year and so we had to watch out for Sophie's fair skin, and made sure she had on her floppy brimmed hat and sunglasses. The beach

174

umbrella provided a lot of shade for us and we spent an enjoyable couple of hours out either walking or sitting on the beach.

By the time we got back, I needed another cup of coffee and so we sat in the living room and watched the news while the coffee brewed.

After lunch, we went to the living room to catch up on news headlines. We sat side by side on the sofa while Sophie played on the floor with her toys.

Kate turned to me once we were settled in. "Do you want to go up to the hospital and see your mom? You should go after lunch and see her in the afternoon before I go to the studio. When you get back, I'll go. Sophie will be napping and you can take it easy and do whatever you'd like."

"I would like to go," I said and kissed her. "Thanks."

"Elaine's excited about having Sophie spend the night, so we can do whatever we want. Do you feel like going out for dinner? Maybe go and see a gallery exhibition? There are a number down by my studio."

"That sounds perfect," I said. "Ask your studio mates where is a good place to eat."

She nodded and took out her cell. "There's a gallery a few blocks away from my studio with a new exhibit this week. There's a wine and cheese at six. We could take it in and then go for dinner."

"Sounds good. I'll go to see my mom for an hour or so. You can go to the studio until five. We can drop Sophie off with Dad and Elaine and then go to the opening."

With that settled, I finished my coffee and left for the hospital, hoping to see my mother improve over the previous day. If she kept improving, she'd be able to go back into her nursing home and then I'd have a better idea of how far her disease had progressed.

I wouldn't give up trying to get her to understand who I was. It would be nice to see recognition in her eyes at least once before she passed but I didn't want to put too much hope into it. Alzheimer's disease was impossible to predict and patients varied. They didn't all respond to the latest treatments in the same way. In the end, I'd have to be thankful that I found her again and equally as important, I found my other family members as well.

As I drove to the hospital, I thought about Herb and Amanda, Kent and Craig and Andrew, the two half-brothers I hadn't yet met and who would be arriving in the city today.

In the space of a week, I'd gone from having no siblings to having four.

It was a good week.

CHAPTER 15

KATE

DRAKE SPENT an hour with his mother and when he returned, I left for the studio, taking along some more supplies I picked up during one of my shopping sprees in the art supply store. I was excited to be back at work on my canvas, and spent at least an hour before I even looked up from my paints. I was happy with the way the painting was progressing but needed a break for something to drink. I went to the small bar fridge in the tiny kitchen area and took out a bottle of water and sat at the workbench to check my email.

There was one from a surprising source: Dawn.

I hadn't heard from her for months.

DAWN: Hey, old friend! How are you? I hope all is well. I'm keeping busy finishing my nursing courses and expect to be working this summer full-time at Harlem General. I hope to move to a surgical ward after I put in my time and get some seniority. I understand that the trial is coming up. Are you and Drake and Sophie coming to Manhattan for it? I'll be attending on my days off. Hope to connect with you when you get back if you're willing. I would love to see Sophie – she must be getting big! Love you, Dawn.

I wasn't sure how to respond. There was still a part of me – a big part – that resented Dawn for her meddling in my life when Drake and I were first together. I knew she was doing so out of what she thought was love, but what I needed wasn't a hall monitor but a friend to help me figure things out. Instead, she had been like a nun at a Catholic girl's school, scolding me for liking boys. Of course, that had been her strict upbringing but still...

At least she was no longer so prejudiced against kink. What a shock it must have been for her to realize that she might enjoy a bit of B&D now and then. I hope it humbled her and made her less judgmental. She seemed to want to still maintain our friendship and the truth was that I missed her. I missed having a best girlfriend I could gossip with. I loved Drake and he was my best friend as well as husband, but still. A woman needs a woman friend and I had no one at the moment who fit the bill.

I decided to text her back.

KATE: Hey! Long time no hear. Yes, Drake and I are planning on coming to Manhattan for the trial as soon as Drake finishes up his latest shift cycle. Drake is going to testify in two weeks, so we have to get there early so he can meet with the prosecutor and go over his testimony. I am not looking forward to the trial as you can imagine. It will probably just upset me, given the focus on Drake's past. But I want to be there with Drake and support him. Yes, Sophie is getting big! We should reconnect. I'll contact you when we're in town. Take care.

I just couldn't bring myself to return the *Love you* part and I felt bad. Before all this happened, I would have relied on Dawn to get me through any trying period in my life, but I guess we had grown apart and her attempts to break Drake and me up didn't help. I still felt resentment that would probably never go away.

I had no idea where I might meet a new female friend, but at the moment, I was really too busy with Sophia and Drake and my art to worry about it. Life was full. I wanted to give each part of my life my whole attention and so worrying too much about girlfriends was not going to occupy too much of my mental energy.

When I was finished with my work for the day, I cleaned my brushes and locked up, taking the trash to the trash room before I left. On my way out of the small room, I ran into none other than my fellow artist, Sean.

"Fancy meeting you here," he said and smiled, standing in the doorway blocking my exit.

"Oh, hello," I said and stopped up suddenly so I wouldn't run into him. "It's you."

"Yes, it's me. Let the bells ring out and the banners fly."

I frowned despite remembering my childhood watching Looney Tunes.

"Sorry, can't talk, gotta run!"

Then, I rushed past him and out the building entrance. Unfortunately, he followed me.

"How's the elephant painting coming? I haven't seen you around for a few days."

"It's fine. I've been busy with life. Bye!"

I slipped quickly into my car and slammed the door, making sure the window was rolled up completely and the door was locked. He stopped at the car nonetheless and leaned against it, smiling down at me through the window.

"Running away so soon? I hope you're not trying to avoid me..."

I frowned. "Why would I be trying to avoid you?" I said through the window.

"Because I hit on you the other day. Don't be offended. I hit on all beautiful women. It's my nature."

"No offense taken," I said and pressed the ignition. "Now, I have to leave. Big night planned."

"You going to the gallery opening? My work will be featured."

"I don't know," I said and put the car into drive, my foot itching to let off the brake. "I'll have to see."

Damn... I didn't realize that Sean's work was being featured at the gallery exhibit and that he would be there. I'd have to rethink going. But then again, if Drake showed up with me, surely Sean would get a big hint and leave me alone.

"If you do come, pop by and say hello. We each have a table and are happy to take commissions and sell our work."

"See you later," I said and forced a smile.

"I hope so. Bring along your husband, if you want, but it's always optional."

I laughed at that. "Not with me."

"A man can dream, right?"

I drove off. "Dream on," I said under my breath, watching him in the rear-view mirror.

WHEN I GOT HOME, Drake was asleep on the sofa and Sophie was in her room taking a nap. I quietly tip-toed around the house, trying not to wake either of them. I went to the kitchen and took out some frozen chicken breasts for supper and then started to wash and prepare vegetables for a salad. In the background, CNN was muted, but I could still read the ticker tape along the bottom. Then, a headline caught my attention.

BREAKING NEWS: Suspect in slaying found dead in cell...

The news story showed a picture of Jones, Lisa's lover and co-conspirator in the attack on me and the murder of Derek Richardson.

"Oh, my *God*," I said, louder than I intended. On the sofa, Drake stirred and sat up, glancing at me where I stood in the kitchen, the chef's knife in my hand and a head of romaine in the other.

"What?" He rubbed his eyes.

"Look at the television."

Drake took the TV remote and turned up the volume.

"...sources say that the suspect was put on suicide watch the previous week, but that he had been taken off heightened surveillance when doctors okayed his mental condition. The day after the more restrictive conditions were lifted, he managed to hang himself with his own shirt, dying before guards could get inside his cell and rescue him. The warden at the facility said that he had been in recent contact with his co-accused, Lisa Monroe, despite being ordered not to have any contact with each other. Preliminary evidence suggests they met on a forum and private messaged each other using pseudonyms so that their activity wouldn't be detected."

I had a very bad feeling about the suicide. Had Lisa encouraged him to kill himself? I'd read of cases before where a lover had convinced a suicidal partner to commit suicide and I could actually believe Lisa might do something like that.

"Do you suppose Lisa talked him into killing himself?"

Drake shook his head. "From what I know about her, and what I've read, I wouldn't put it past her. She's a sociopath and would think nothing of it. If Jones is dead, he can't really testify against her in court, can he?"

I finished chopping the romaine and dried off my hands so I could go and sit beside Drake and watch with him. When I was done, I plopped onto the sofa and he slipped his arm around my shoulders, pulling me against his body. He kissed me and then we turned back to the television. The station went to a commercial break so we switched channels to see if the news was being covered on any other channels. There was nothing, so we turned back and waited for CNN to continue its coverage.

"I wouldn't have thought he would kill himself," I said and snuggled closer to Drake. "He was quick to blame Lisa for planning the murder."

"She must have had something on him," Drake said, turning up the volume. "Something he either couldn't face coming out or was just too incriminating."

"What a witch."

"You're right about that," Drake said, sighing. "I had no idea she was this deranged. When I met her, she was this meek submissive, and never spoke a word. We performed for Derek and that was it."

"Derek never said anything about her?"

"Just that she liked to be used. He liked to watch her with other men. It was their kink. I'm glad I never did become involved with her beyond those few times at Derek's parties, but even so, what little did happen between us never warranted her becoming fixated on me."

"Erotomania isn't rational," I said, having read up on the issue after the attack when I was trying to understand everything. "It's an obsession and isn't based on reality but on the fantasy life of the individual with the obsession. The object of the obsession may not have even spoken with the individual."

Drake nodded. "In our case, I actually had sex with her in front of Derek. Unfortunately, he's no longer around to testify in my defense."

"You don't need a defense," I said and stroked his hair back. "You did nothing to encourage her. This is all on her, not you. The police know that. They may not approve of the lifestyle, but they understand that you're the victim in this as much as I am."

"I'm so glad that we're no longer there to be seeing this every day. I'm sorry we have to go back and face it. I'd rather stay here and just enjoy our lives."

"Me, too, but we have to get this out of the way and then we'll be free."

We listened as they moved on to another story and both of us sighed.

"If Jones is dead, do you suppose they'll postpone the trial?"

"They'll cancel his trial, but they'll go ahead with hers for Derek's murder. Who knows? They might even charge her with a crime for encouraging him to commit suicide."

I sighed, wishing we could avoid returning to Manhattan as well. I didn't relish the paparazzi hounding us when we went to the court-house to testify. I had put those memories, such as they were, behind me out in sunny California. Dredging up everything, enduring the lurid gossip about Drake and BDSM, was not something I looked forward to. Still, we had to get it over with, and so I steeled myself and decided to try to get as much enjoyment out of our trip as possible.

"You'll never guess who contacted me," I said and raised my eyebrows when Drake turned to me.

"Who?"

"Miss Priss herself – Dawn."

Drake's eyes widened. "And?"

"She heard about the trial and wanted to connect with me when I'm in town."

"You should meet with her," Drake said softly.

"Do you really think so? After what she tried to do to break us up?"

Drake leaned back and exhaled. "Honestly, if I'd been her and had her background, I'd probably have warned you off as well."

"She did a bit more than warn me off you. She threatened to expose you to my father and to the hospital administration."

"Oh, yes, that's right," Drake said and rubbed his chin, which was a bit scruffy in a very sexy way. "Maybe I'm being too nice." He turned to me, mischief in his eyes. "You should kick her ass."

I laughed out loud at that. "Nah," I said and leaned in to kiss him. "I don't feel like resorting to violence anymore. It does no one any good."

"You know I was just kidding," Drake said and kissed me back.

"I know," I said and scratched his chin and jaw. "I would have liked to at one point, but now? I just want it all to be behind us. All of it."

"It'll be behind us, soon," Drake said and while I hoped he was right, I had a feeling that we would be fighting old battles for quite a while longer.

WE DROPPED Sophie off at my dad's and Elaine's and went right to the gallery. On the way there, I told Drake about my encounter with Sean.

"He's one of those guys," I said. "You know the type – won't take no for an answer."

Drake chuckled. "I seem to recall I wouldn't take no for an answer with you. Was I one of those guys?"

I shook my head. "No, because I wanted you to not take no for an answer. I was just afraid to admit it. I was afraid that if I admitted that I was attracted to you, and wanted to be one of those women in your letters to your new subs, that it would mean I was a fraud. That I wasn't really a feminist."

Drake shook his head. "Feminists are for freedom and equality for both men and women. Freedom means being able to choose what you prefer – as long as it's legal. Too often, those who call themselves feminists think it means that women have to act and feel a certain way, but that's exactly what patriarchy did to women – and men – for ten thousand years."

I turned and looked at him, amazed at what I heard coming out of his mouth.

"Drake Morgan, MD. I could have sworn I was in a Women's Studies class and not a Mercedes SUV on the way to a gallery exhibition."

"I studied social science in college, you know. I have this stuff memorized and filed away waiting for the right time to pull it out and impress during dinner conversation."

He gave me this brilliant smile, pleased with himself.

I smiled to myself and watched out the window at the passing scenery. I always knew Drake studied the social sciences. He once considered becoming a psychiatrist when he went into medical school. I had no idea he was up on feminist theory. My gaze moved over him, dressed in a crisp white button down shirt, black chinos and casual shoes. His hair was longish, his jaw covered in a few days-worth of scruff. He was gorgeous. I smoothed my sundress as I sat beside him, adjusting the light sweater I wore over top against the evening's cool breezes. The sundress was his favorite – thin straps, a

185

built-in bra, and a back zip that he liked to slowly undo when he helped me undress. I hoped it would bring back fond memories of other times I wore it and he undressed me after.

We arrived at the venue and found a parking spot about a block away. Drake rushed around to my side of the car and opened the door for me, taking my hand and helping me out. Then, we walked arm in arm down the street to the gallery, which was lit up with floodlights and bright decorative lights at the entrance. The front door was open and we could hear music coming from inside – something soothing and classical. It sounded like a Mozart string quartet.

We went inside and picked up a glass of wine and brochure from a table just inside the front entrance, which gave the names of the exhibitors and a brief biography as well as one of the works of art. Then, we went from exhibit to exhibit, examining the works and discussing what we thought of each piece. There were watercolors and acrylics and sculptures and collages. The subjects were diverse and ranged from complete abstract to complete photo-realism and everything in between.

Drake held my hand the entire time and I felt relieved when, after half an hour had passed, we hadn't run into Sean. It was when Drake slipped into the men's washroom that I did run into someone familiar.

I was admiring one of the watercolors of a local redwood trunk when I felt someone behind me. I turned abruptly, fully expecting to see Sean there with that grin on his face, but it wasn't him.

It was Sefton.

Sefton deVilliers.

Just as I remembered him from Africa – smiling like he was the king of the world. Dressed in a dark blue suit with crisp white shirt, opened to display a thick gold chain. His hair was a bit longer, still blond, his eyes still a piercing dark brown.

Just the sight of him gave me shivers – but not the good kind. The creeped-out, bad news kind.

"Oh, God," I said and covered my heart with a hand. "I thought you were someone else."

"Sorry, but it's just me." He smiled, standing just a bit too close to me. "Fancy meeting you here. I guess it really is a small world."

"It is. Checking out the competition?" I said, glancing around at the other paintings, hoping that Drake would arrive quickly and rescue me.

He looked around as well, his hands in his pockets. "Some of them are good, but I'm not too worried." He turned back to me, a quizzical expression on his face. "You don't seem all that surprised to see me."

I shook my head. "I saw a flyer announcing your North American tour and that you were going to be in town this week. Quite impressive."

He smiled and seemed to puff up a bit.

"I looked you up when I was in Manhattan, but sadly, I was told you and Drake and your baby left for San Francisco. I thought I might find you here but I didn't expect to find you so easily."

"You were actually looking for me? After what happened in Africa?"

"*Nothing* happened in Africa, much to my chagrin," Sefton said, a quirk of a grin. "But I did want to see if I could find you."

I shrugged, not wanting to display any emotion towards him but disdain.

"I have a studio across the street." I gestured to the building where my studio was located.

"A studio?" he said and raised his eyebrows. "You're getting serious. I'll have to stop by and see your work."

Just then, Drake walked up and put his arm around my waist.

"I don't think so," he said, giving Sefton a curt nod.

"Are you speaking for your wife or do you let her make her own decisions?"

I squeezed Drake to indicate he shouldn't let himself get baited by Sefton's cracks.

Drake glanced at me quickly so I raised my eyebrows suggestively. He turned back to Sefton and I heard him exhale softly.

"I'm only letting you know so she doesn't have to. You're one of those guys who can't take a hint. Last time I saw you, I believe I bloodied your nose because of it. I should have done more, considering how you practically assaulted my wife in Africa."

"You did, and she wasn't your wife yet, if I recall," Sefton said and ran his hand over his chin. "You threw a lucky sucker punch or I would have taken you down. I am taller and heavier than you."

"That you are," Drake said and stood a bit taller. I could feel his body tensing under my hand. "I figured you could take me, so I had to use whatever advantage I had at my disposal."

I glanced between the two of them, amazed that even now, they were acting like two cocks of the walk. They were both smiling, but their smiles were cold and didn't reach their eyes.

"Hey, you two," I said and slipped my arm through Drake's, pulling him away gently. "I'd like to see the rest of the exhibits. Sefton," I said and gave him a nod. "Good to see you again. Maybe Drake and I will drop by your exhibit and see your latest works."

Sefton had locked eyes with Drake and held his gaze, not looking at me.

"I look forward to it."

Then he turned and walked off. I felt the tension drain out of Drake's body, his muscles relaxing under my hand.

"Let's go," I said softly. We walked in the other direction, and were barely ten feet away when Drake muttered something under his breath.

"What did you say?" I asked, leaning closer.

"I said he's a fucking jerk."

"Drake!" I pushed him as he walked beside me, his hands stuffed into his own pockets. "You were ready to get into a fight with him. I could tell by the way your body tensed."

"Damn right I was. He did practically assault you in the tent in Africa. You texted me right after and were really upset, Kate. By all rights, I should plough him one now."

"Drake!" I stopped him and rested my hands on his shoulders, looking deep into his eyes. "I'm a big girl and was able to look after myself."

"He could have raped you," he said, his voice deep and emotional. "Out there on the savannah. What could you have done to stop him?"

"Scream? Hit him? Luckily, Claire came in and that shocked him back into reality."

"That's my point. If Claire hadn't come in, what then?"

I sighed. "I'm fine. Nothing more happened and it was all just a bad memory I tucked away in the back of my mind. Seeing him again brought it back and I'm glad nothing more came of it, but let's not allow Sefton and his pompous snark ruin our evening."

Drake leaned closer to me, his eyes half lidded. "When I get you home tonight, I'm going to tie you to my bed and make you come three times without a break."

That sent a jolt of lust to my core. Drake hadn't spoken to me like that for a long time nor had I seen the possessiveness in his eyes like that for a while either.

It totally turned me on.

"When we get home, I promise you can do whatever you want to me, especially if you look at me like that when you do it."

"Oh, yeah?" Drake said, his tone lightening a little. "How am I looking at you?"

"Like a lion regards the lamb he's just about to eat."

He smiled slowly, but not a full smile. It was a lusty smile that promised so much pleasure.

"You like it when I look at you like I'm just about to eat you, do you Ms. Bennet?"

"Oh, yes, I do, Dr. Morgan. I do, very much."

"Hmm," he said and quirked an eyebrow, totally ruining the effect. Then he chuckled. "I'm sorry I was such an idiot, but the thought of any man touching you makes me feel like a raging bull."

I ran my fingers along the lapel of his sports jacket. "Raging bull, hmm?" I said in a soft voice, aware of the people milling around. I leaned closer so that only he could hear me. "I think I like that image almost as much as the hungry lion image. You with your nostrils flared, examining my naked body with salacious intent, standing over me like you own me."

"Salacious intent?" Drake leaned down and kissed me, a smile on his lips. When he pulled back, I could see the humor in his eyes. "I do own you, Mrs. Morgan," Drake said. "In a totally feminist, full equality, sort of playacting ownership way."

"You do, Dr. Morgan," I said and stood on my tiptoes, my mouth beside his ear, "and you could put a collar on me and lead me around a dungeon and I'd do anything you asked of me."

"Oh, God," Drake said when I moved back. He leaned down, his mouth beside my ear this time. "Are you *trying* to make me hard right here in the middle of the art exhibition? Because if you are, you're succeeding. I'm going to have to walk bent over and with a limp the rest of the evening because of all the hard inches I'm going to give you later..."

I smiled up at him, my own eyes half-closed. "You know what I'd love to do with all your hard inches, Dr. Morgan?"

"No, I don't, Mrs. Morgan. Please, do tell..."

"I could describe it to you," I said and licked my bottom lip suggestively. "Or, we could find a broom closet somewhere in the building and I could show you."

His eyes widened at that and he grabbed me, pulling me close, his mouth against my ear. "Now, that would be sweet justice. You with your beautiful mouth and tongue wrapped around my cock while Sefton deFuckingVilliers walks around imagining being with you."

He pulled back and grinned, his eyes narrow.

I smiled back at him and we stood like that for a moment, and I imagined that both our hearts were beating a little faster and our bodies were both aching for each other. I know mine was aching for him.

It felt like old times – like when we first met and I couldn't wait to be with him, for him to take control over my body and take me to places I'd never been before.

"I'd love to find a broom closet somewhere in this building and have you show me exactly what you'd do with your lips and tongue, Mrs. Morgan," Drake said, his voice almost a whisper, "but alas, I think we'll have to wait until we get home. The last thing I need is for someone to walk in on us and for the gossip to get around that I was caught having public sex with my wife at an art exhibition."

I nodded in understanding. That would be the very last thing Drake needed – being found in a compromising position at a public event. If he wanted custody of Liam, he'd have to live an exemplary life from now on – not that he hadn't already.

I couldn't understand how Drake's willingness to save Liam's life wasn't enough to reassure a judge that he would be a great father, but many judges were social conservatives and any hint of kink could be a threat. If it hadn't been for the publicity surrounding the trial, Drake might have been able to coast through a custody hearing, but that was a game-changer.

Drake took my hand, kissed my knuckles, and then led me through the gallery to the door.

"We're leaving all of a sudden?" I said. "What about dinner?"

"We're going to that new restaurant downtown – Soirée. The one I told you about. Everyone raved about it at the hospital. But first, I'm going to take you home and fuck you."

I smiled to myself. I was a bit breathless from our little tete-a-tete about sex. Both of us were seriously deprived. We'd forgo food if it meant mutual orgasms.

The drive back to our house was silent, but Drake held my hand the entire time. When we finally pulled up into the driveway, I was very uncomfortable, nearly squirming in my seat in anticipation of what was to come.

Drake hopped out of the vehicle and came around, opening my door and taking my hand, leading me out and over to the front door. He disarmed the lock and the alarm system, and before I could even take off my heels, he pushed me up against the wall beside the entry. His kiss promised everything and more.

"I need you, now."

"I'm yours," I replied because I was his. Every inch of me.

AFTERWARDS, while we lay together on our bed, Drake turned to me.

"What do you say I cancel those reservations and we stay home and eat leftovers? I feel like just spending the entire evening lying with you on the sofa and watching Netflix."

I turned to face him and slid one of my arms around his neck, stroking his hair. I moved closer and kissed him softly.

"Whatever you want."

"If you were really looking forward to going out for supper, we can go. It's just that I've been out of the house at night for so many nights, I feel like staying in with you alone. All to myself."

I smiled. "I'm happy to be with you here or anywhere. If that's what you feel like, I'll be happy."

"Don't think you're going to fall asleep on me early. I've got more plans for you later tonight and they involve some lamb's wool cuffs we haven't used nearly enough in the past year."

I smiled and laid my head against the pillow, my eyes locked with his. "I'm at your disposal."

LATER, while we lay together on the sofa watching the news, with Drake's leg draped over me possessively, I thought how nice it was to have Drake all to myself. Just Drake and me, together, as lovers and friends. It was nice to reconnect that way again. The first time Sophie spent the night at Elaine's, I felt guilty for taking time away from her, but I realized that for us to be good parents, we had to keep our relationship alive. Besides, it was good for Sophie to become close to Elaine and my dad. I wanted them to have a great relationship and for Sophie to really know them, to feel totally secure with them and feel their love.

Tomorrow morning when we picked up Sophie and brought her back here with us, both Drake and I would be refreshed and eager to spend the day with her.

For now, it was our time and as Drake stroked my back while we watched the news, I felt such contentment. For a few moments, the upcoming trip to New York and the trial were forgotten and it was just me and Drake.

CHAPTER 16

DRAKE

A FEW DAYS LATER, in the afternoon while Sophie was sleeping, I got an email from Gary Wood, the lawyer who would be taking my case in Manhattan, with a time and date for us to meet to discuss the case. Lara had recommended him from her list of BDSM-friendly and knowledgeable criminal lawyers. He understood the lifestyle and what it entailed. I could feel comfortable talking about my past with him and not fear judgement.

In Lisa's case, I would be a witness for the prosecution and I had to be prepared to face cross examination by Lisa's lawyers, who would try their best to make me look like a bad influence on Lisa – anything to lessen her own culpability in what happened to Kate and Derek Richardson and make her more sympathetic to the jury.

"I know you and Lara have gone over everything that happened between you and Lisa, when you first met her and had those encounters with her and Richardson, back before you met Kate. I have all the dates and times you were alone with her after, when you started working at NYU and she was in the residency program. I want to subject you to the kinds of questions her lawyers will ask you on the stand, so you won't feel flustered and will know what to say."

I frowned. "I'll tell the truth," I said plainly. "That should clear things up. It's her fucked-up psychology that's the cause of this, not anything I did."

"I know that, but you have to remember you're going to be talking in front of a jury and a judge who are scandalized by anything to do with BDSM, the whole Mr. Grey fan club among romance readers aside. You have to explain things in a way that makes clear you barely remembered her, despite the sexual encounters. We have to make sure nothing you say puts your innocence into question."

"I'm innocent, so I don't see how telling the truth could get me into any trouble."

"That's very idealistic, but it's also very naïve, Drake," Gary said, "but I understand your view. She was young when this all happened—."

"She was a consenting adult of legal age who signed a non-disclosure agreement and a contract with Derek Richardson specifying what would happen when they were together."

He sighed audibly. "I know that, and you know that, but her lawyers will try to make her appear as sympathetic as possible. They'll play up her youth and her tragic past as a victim of sexual abuse, and will claim that you two adult men – into dominance and bondage – preyed on her innocence and corrupted her."

"That's not how it was," I said firmly.

"That's how her lawyers will portray it and you," Gary replied. "An older man who viewed her as nothing more than a willing hole for your pleasure."

It was my turn to sigh heavily. Of course, that's how they would present her.

"That's the way many men view women. Some women like that. I don't judge them for wanting it. I understand the psychology of dominance and submission. This is about a sociopath who tried to kill my wife, who did kill Derek Richardson, and who compelled her boyfriend to kill himself. This is not my fault and it has nothing to do with bondage and dominance but mental illness."

"That's all true, but since you aren't on trial, I don't want to get into any long-winded discussion of the finer points of BDSM if we can avoid it. It can only make things more complicated. The defense will probably already be calling experts in on the psychology of BDSM and they'll be critical, bringing up other cases where young women have been exploited and have gone on to do things against their own best interest. I don't want you to start arguing the case. That will be for the DA's own experts to worry about. All we want is for you to lay out how you met her, and the extent to which you had any private encounters with her after she started at NYU as a resident."

"Of course. I'll stick to whatever script you think is best, as long as I'm truthful."

"Don't worry," Gary said. "You'll be truthful, but as you and I both know, there are different ways to tell the truth. Some ways will portray you more favorably than others. This is going to do a hell of a job on your career prospects, Drake. I hope you're prepared for the publicity from this to follow you for years."

"I know," I said, a knot in my gut over it. "Luckily, I don't have to worry about money. I can always go into private practice and be extremely selective about clients if I want to keep practicing medicine."

"And if you can't practice medicine any longer? What will you do?"

I shrugged. "I'll volunteer in Africa. I'll volunteer in clinics where people don't have health insurance. I'll volunteer at a homeless mission. Don't worry about me."

"Okay, Drake. I just want you to be prepared for what's coming. It won't be fun. It will be very upsetting and potentially – most certainly damaging to your reputation and career prospects."

"I understand. It already has, so I don't see how this will make things worse."

"I wish I could tell you that things will go back to normal after the trial, but they won't. Not for a few years, anyway."

I frowned at that, because I thought that once the trial died down, I would be able to go back to my life the way it was before everything happened.

"You really think it will take several years?"

"I do," he said. "You could probably get by if you moved away, maybe to Canada or Europe where they aren't as... how shall I say... puritanical about sex. But here? Every hospital will do their due diligence before they hire you and will be reluctant to piss off their donors or board of directors by hiring you."

I thanked him for his advice and we went over the itinerary for my return to Manhattan and what dates we would meet to go over my testimony and a mock cross examination. I said goodbye and sat alone in my office, ruminating on what lay ahead for me – and for Kate. This would affect her as well, for she'd have to leave her studio for a couple of weeks and we'd be without Ethan and Elaine for support and to sit with Sophie when we needed a break.

Instinctively, I knew that what he said about the publicity affecting my career was right, but I hadn't wanted to believe it. I thought my credentials would be more important, but I was coming to realize, with great reluctance, that I was screwed – at least for a few years. Everywhere I went, the trial and scandal would follow me. My only hope to practice was to find a place somewhere that needed me more than it cared about my personal life. Somewhere that neurosurgeons with skills like mine were in short supply and high demand. That somewhere was either in poor rural areas of the country or in under developed countries with few resources where I would be considered a life-saver rather than bad news for potential donors.

It upset me that, through no fault of my own, I was going to be untouchable for a while, but that was the risk I took when I first became involved in the lifestyle. Lara warned me, back in those first weeks that I wanted to learn more about D/s and bondage, that I had to keep my personal and professional lives scrupulously uncon-nected. I should never ever have a submissive in the medical profes-sion. I should be very careful with whatever submissives I did use. That was the biggest reason that I let Lara find my submissives. She vetted them for me, basing her suggestions on how trustworthy and stable the women were.

She didn't find Lisa Monroe and Derek Richardson for me. I met Derek at one of his private dungeon parties and it was because of mutual business interests that we connected. I did scenes with Lisa because of him and it was not through Lara.

Of course, Lara also warned me off Sunita. She felt concerned about her, but thought she was more stable than she turned out to be. That was a huge regret of mine and hers. It was Sunita who released the video of me caning her. That could be the end of my career. That video had probably already affected my career but I wasn't yet ready to face the truth.

I refused to face that prospect. I'd find something to do that used my skills as a neurosurgeon. I wouldn't let Lisa defeat me.

That afternoon, Kate was at her studio and so while I was waiting for Sophie to wake up, I spent my time catching up on work for the foundation. While I had taken a serious back seat there, I still had to read over monthly reports from Dave about what projects were being finished, what projects were underway and what projects were in development. There was a mountain of material to cover and I was behind because of my work at the hospital. I rolled up my sleeves and settled in, reading over each report and sending Dave my comments so he'd know what my thoughts were when he went before the board to defend the new projects he was developing.

It was while I was writing an email to Dave Mills that I got one from Ken O'Riley, whom I hadn't talked to since Kate and I left Manhattan. I'd sent him an email earlier in the week to let him know we'd be back in town for a few weeks and that I'd love to get together with him and see the family. Maybe we'd be able to stop by for one of their Sunday dinners.

DRAKE!

So good to get your email. Of course, we'd be thrilled to have you for Sunday dinner. Anytime – you know you have an open invitation. Mom is dying to see Sophia and Kate – and you of course. If you feel up to it, why not get in some practice with Mersey? We still haven't found a replacement bass player who knows our repertoire as well as you so we'd love to do a few gigs while you're here. I spoke with the other guys and we're in if you are. We can practice for a week and then get in a couple of gigs, if you're game. Sounds like you have a lot on your plate, but it might be good for the soul to play some Brit Invasion. Paint It Black, Under My Thumb. The Stones seem like a good way to let off steam. Let me know if that sounds like a plan and I'll set things up. You haven't been gone too long so you shouldn't be very rusty. Give Kate and Sophie our love,

Ken

I smiled to myself as I re-read the email, glad I'd contacted Ken. We'd be in Manhattan for a month during the trial. Getting in a few gigs during that time would be manageable. Hell, I used to play a few gigs with Mersey when I worked full-time at the hospital and did everything else. It would be no problem if I was there only for the trial.

Of course, I'd stop by the foundation and corporate HQ and do some catch-up with everyone, but I had time to play if I wanted.

Ken,

Thanks for the reply. Of course, I'd love to jam with Mersey again while I'm in Manhattan. I'll have to check what my schedule will be like re: the prosecutor and any testimony I have to give but we can work around that. We miss everyone and look forward to Sunday dinner with you and your family. On that note, I've discovered my other family – my mother remarried and had four children so I've now got more family than I could have dreamed of when I was growing up. Three half-brothers, a half-sister, and a step-father. My mother is ill and suffering from Alzheimer's Disease so she doesn't understand who I am, or remember much but it was good to see her and meet everyone.

I'll let you know about my schedule once I speak with the prosecutor.

Cheers,

Drake

I'd speak with Kate and make sure she was fine with it, although I knew she'd encourage me. She often suggested I try to pull together another band like Mersey while we were in San Francisco. I'd been too busy with my shifts in the ER to do any serious planning for it, but maybe I would work on that once we returned from Manhattan. If I wasn't going to be working in the ER, I'd have time on my hands. What better way to fill that time than to play music?

I heard snuffling on the baby monitor and checked my watch. She'd been asleep for about forty-five minutes. Usually, she went down for an hour or hour and a half, so I left her alone in case she was going to go back to sleep. While I waited, I surfed the news sites for the latest and was dismayed to see coverage of the suicide of Lisa's partner in crime. I tried to avoid anything to do with the trial and case, but it was making national news and so I faced an uphill battle. When Sophie continued to babble to herself in her crib, I decided to go and get her up.

When I went into her room, she was lying on her back, a stuffed toy in her hand, her pacifier between her teeth. She was making sounds around it and the image of her lying there with the Stuart minion from her half-brother warmed my heart.

"Hey, baby," I said and went to her side. "Time to get up?"

She smiled and reached up when I came to the side of the crib. I picked her up and brought her over to the change table to check her diaper. It was wet so I put on a new one and changed her outfit. Then I carried her out to the living room, slipping her into her ExerSaucer so she could play with her toys while I got things ready for our trip to the beach.

WHEN WE GOT HOME from our trip down the beach to make and destroy sandcastles, Kate was already home and was sitting in front of the television, watching the news. She took Sophie from me and kissed her, then sat with her, watching the television intently.

On the screen was a reporter standing in front of the courthouse in Manhattan. Apparently, Lisa had been indicted on a charge of Reckless Endangerment in the First Degree for encouraging Jones' suicide.

"She was indicted," Kate said, handing a toy to Sophie while I got myself a drink of water. "Apparently, there are emails between them that encouraged him to kill himself."

"She's evil," I said, shaking my head. "They need to put her away for a very long time. I bet she'll be hell in jail and will probably be one of those women who runs the place. Pure sociopath."

I stood beside the sofa and watched the news for a moment, amazed that she had gone from a successful surgical resident to being incarcerated and waiting trial for attempted murder, murder and now reckless endangerment.

I realized once again that Kate and Sophie were lucky to have escaped with their lives.

"Turn away," I said and sat on the sofa beside Kate, my hand on her shoulder. "I don't want to waste a moment thinking about her. I want to spend my time with you and Sophie."

Kate tore her eyes away from the screen finally and turned to me after changing channels to one of the music stations.

"I'm sorry," she said, her voice soft. "I can't stop thinking about her and what happened. I feel a bit obsessed about it. I'll try not to think about it too much."

"I understand," I said and slid down the arm of the sofa to sit beside Kate, pulling her into my arms and kissing her forehead. "It's morbid curiosity. Perfectly natural but not healthy. As your doctor, I'd advise a healthy dose of making love to your husband to distract yourself from the coverage."

She smiled up at me, her eyes narrowing. "That sounds like a very self-serving prescription, Dr. Morgan."

"It is. It's extremely self-serving. It's a prescription I plan on delivering once Sophie's asleep tonight."

Kate smiled up at me, the hungry expression in her eyes telling me everything I needed to know.

WE HAD a dinner of grilled fish, salad and fresh baguette and spent an hour or so with Sophie, taking an evening walk along the beach while the sun set. When it was time for Sophie's bath, I took over, running the bath and getting everything ready. I loved bath time and if I could, I would always be the one who took over. Kate had been responsible when I had been working and so I wanted to give her a break. Besides, it was fun. Sophie loved her bath and it made me feel like a real father to be so involved in Sophie's day-to-day care.

I held her after she was dried off and in her jammies, giving her a bottle. Her eyes were heavy and when I saw that she was going to fall asleep, I carried her to her crib and put her to bed. Kate joined me and we stood beside the crib and watched her for a moment.

We left the room, turning off the hall light so that the back of the house was in darkness.

"We're lucky she's such an easy baby," Kate said, her voice soft. "I don't know if I would have survived if she'd had colic."

"We would have managed. It would have been a lot harder, but we would have found a way. I do admire parents who have colicky babies, though. Adjusting to parenthood is hard enough, let alone with a baby who can't settle and has digestive issues."

I took Kate's hand and led her not back to the living room, but to our bedroom and the master bath.

"And now, Mrs. Morgan, I gave you a prescription to divert your attention away from other matters. It involves pampering you, giving you a nice warm bubble bath and then a full body massage followed by multiple orgasms. I aim to deliver on my promise."

"You're the doctor," Kate said, her voice all throaty with desire.

"I am," I said and pushed her gently into the bathroom, intent on delivering my prescription exactly as described.

CHAPTER 17

KATE

THE NEXT FEW days passed quickly as we prepared to travel to Manhattan for the trial. I spent as much time as possible with my dad and Elaine. I'd grown used to seeing them at least once a week and now we'd be away for a whole month. I worried about my father. He was frail and weaker than I liked to see, although he was in good spirits. I had to remind myself that Elaine was a nurse and took good care of him. She was aware of any sign that he might be sick. But still, I felt anxious that something would happen to him while I was away and there would be nothing I could do about it.

I got quite weepy when I finished packing my bag and it was time to go to their place and say goodbye before we left for the airport. Drake was there of course, to comfort me.

"Hey, hey," he said, his voice soft. "Come here." He pulled me into his arms and let me snivel against his shoulder. "Your father's fine. He's got Elaine there all the time. She knows what to do if anything happens. He's in good hands."

"I know," I said and wiped my eyes. "It's just I'm afraid that he'll die and I won't get the chance to say goodbye."

"I know," Drake said. "I know how that feels. Not good. I don't see that there's anything immediate to worry about. He's not ill and at his age with his condition and on his meds, I'm more worried about him getting the seasonal flu than anything else happening to him. Okay? I'm the doctor in this family, remember..."

"Okay."

I squeezed Drake because, of course, that's what happened to him with his father. Liam died in a remote part of Ethiopia when his small plane went down during a volunteer mission. I wish I'd met Drake before his father died, because I would have loved Liam. My father loved him. I know I would have, too.

Finally, I wiped my eyes and let go of Drake, taking in a deep breath and putting on a brave face.

Drake took my hand. "If anything happens, you'll be on the first flight to San Francisco. How does that sound?"

I nodded. "That sounds good."

We drove to my father's place for a quick visit.

I practically ran inside because we were running late, to find Elaine and my dad on the patio, sitting in the shade under the umbrella.

I went right over to him and gave him a kiss and then kissed Elaine as well. Drake handed Sophie to Elaine, who gave her a big hug and kiss and then held her for my dad to kiss as well.

"Goodbye, chipmunk," my dad said to Sophie, who had her two front bottom teeth and seemed to like to show them off to us like they were a prize. Her top ones were due out next and she was teething, drooling over everything like crazy so we had to keep a bib on her at all times. She gave her grandpa sloppy kisses as a result but he didn't seem to mind.

"See you when you get back, sweetheart. Drake, take care of my girls."

"I will, Dad," Drake said and leaned down to kiss my dad on his forehead, clasping my dad's good hand in his briefly.

We hugged Elaine and said goodbye then we were off. It was a considerable detour, but I couldn't imagine not seeing them before we left.

OUR FLIGHT DEPARTED mid-morning and we wouldn't arrive until late in the afternoon. My hope was that Sophie would fall asleep on the flight and would be easier to manage than if we left earlier in the morning when she was always wide awake. Luckily, Sophie seemed to be a good flying baby for she didn't make a fuss and seemed to enjoy sitting in our laps, reading books and playing with toys on the long flight from San Francisco to JFK. She fell asleep briefly after lunch and slept until about an hour from our arrival time.

We touched down and I watched through the window, pointing it out to Sophie, who was beside me next to the window. I was happy that we could travel first class and could afford to buy a seat for her. I always hated the thought of not having her in a car seat in case of turbulence so she was in her familiar car seat for a lot of the trip.

I sighed and turned to Drake, who sat across from me on the other side of the aisle.

"Well, we're back. I feel like saying home, but I don't know if it is home anymore."

Drake took my hand across the aisle. "It feels strange. Like home is wherever Ethan is."

"I know," I said and nodded. "It does feel like San Francisco is our home now. But still, I was here all my life."

"I was here most of my adult life."

We were silent the rest of the way, while the plane was taxiing to the terminal.

AFTER WE GOT OUR BAGS, we found our Uber waiting outside and piled in, suitcases in the back. After getting Sophie seated, we drove off toward the city. I was glad to see the Manhattan skyline again after months in San Francisco, and realized that I did miss it. Living in San Francisco felt more like an extended vacation but I didn't think I'd want to live there if my dad and Elaine weren't there. Heath was here with his family and there were the O'Riley's...

Still, home was where family was and my dad and Elaine were the closest thing Drake had as family. Of course, now we had Drake's new family. I hoped we could all become closer and spend time together, especially on the holidays.

That would make Drake very happy.

By the time we were a few blocks away from our place on 8th Avenue, I noticed we were nearing the spot where Lisa attacked me.

"Can we stop?" I asked, my hand on Drake's arm. I pointed to the block where it happened.

Drake leaned forward and asked the driver to stop ahead for a moment. Once we were parked, I got out and walked over to the place where I had been hit. From what I had heard, I just stepped off the curb and Lisa accelerated, striking me before I got more than a few feet in the crosswalk. I was thrown several feet and landed on the pavement a few feet away from where I stood.

I had no memory of the events surrounding that day. The last memory I had was calling Drake in the morning before I went out for a walk. The next memory I had was waking up in the ICU, and Drake telling me what happened. The rest was a big blank.

"This is where it happened," I said to Drake when he joined me, Sophie in his arms. "I don't remember anything."

"That's good," Drake said, turning around in a circle with Sophie held up high. She laughed and waved her arms around. He stood still and kissed her cheek. "You don't want to remember that. It happened and changed many things but we're here now, alive. With our beautiful daughter. I'd like to forget that day. It was the worst day of my life," he said and met my eyes. He rubbed my cheek with the backs of his fingers, his gaze moving over my face. "I almost lost you. I almost lost both of you." He leaned down and kissed me and then he kissed Sophie.

"We're glad you didn't." I smiled at him. "Don't worry. This is just a bad story told to me since I remember nothing."

Drake exhaled heavily and I knew that the accident and everything that happened afterward had been very hard on him, even if the horror of it seemed lost to me, other than my injuries and the fact I couldn't have any more babies. That was upsetting to me but truthfully, I felt blessed that I did have Sophie and she survived the attack. If we got shared custody of Liam, we would have the kind of family that would make Drake very happy and me as well.

How could I be anything less than thankful?

I *was* thankful. I knew how lucky I was, and any lingering PTSD was of the unconscious variety. I no longer walked around feeling like something bad was going to happen, so I was glad that was dealt with soon after we realized I was suffering from PTSD.

"We should get going," Drake said and gestured with his head back to the car where the driver was patiently waiting.

"We should. I just felt a need to stop and remember how lucky I am."

Drake kissed me again and then we went back to the car. After I closed the door and fastened my seatbelt, I sighed as we drove off. It felt so strange that such a momentous event in my life was a total blank to me, but as Drake said, it was for the best.

I turned away, seeing a small jeweler on the street and that was more my memory of this part of the city rather than the accident.

We stopped at the same small grocer where I always used to shop, to pick up some supplies we'd need for the night and the next morning – tea and coffee, cream, bread, cereal, and food for breakfast and lunch. I'd do a more thorough shopping trip once we were settled.

We arrived at the building on 8th Avenue, and after the driver helped us with our bags, we climbed the stairs to our apartment. I felt butterflies in my stomach at the prospect of staying there for a month. I loved that apartment. There were so many good memories there when Drake and I were first together and he introduced me to real pleasure, D/s and a bit of kink.

I felt like my life really began in that apartment – my life as a woman who was coming into her own. Discovering what she needed and wanted. Drake was the one who helped me become that woman.

"Here we are," he said and smiled while he turned the key in the lock. "Our old home."

"Home sweet home," I said to Sophie in her car seat. "You won't remember this place because you were too young, but I'm filled with memories – so many memories."

We went inside and I stood in the entry, taking in the apartment. It was exactly as we left it, of course. It smelled a little dusty, but it was otherwise welcoming. Every renovation we had made was to our tastes and it felt like us.

I got a bit teary because I hated that we no longer felt at home in Manhattan because of the trial and scandal associated with Drake's past.

"What's this?" Drake said and put Sophie's car seat down. He pulled me into his arms and wiped the tear off my cheek. "What are the tears for? This is a place of happiness for us."

"I know," I said and laid my head against his shoulder, squeezing him more tightly. "I was the happiest I'd ever been here. I'm just so sad that we can't live in Manhattan because of Lisa. I *hate* her." I looked up into Drake's eyes. "I hate her guts."

"I hate her too, but there's no reason we can't come back in time. I'll be able to have a private practice again. I'm sure once this all blows over, we'll come back for part of every year.

"But my dad is going to stay in San Francisco."

"We can come for a few months every year if we want. We're free, Kate. We can do whatever we want. And maybe if we had a better situation for Ethan, he'd feel okay about coming here for spring, summer and fall. Maybe something that is more wheelchair accessible. I'll talk to him about it. They could sell their apartment on Park Avenue and find one that is more accessible with a nice big patio so he could sit outside in the good weather. Maybe even Brooklyn..."

"Brooklyn?" I said with a laugh. "Sacrilege! My father would never live in Brooklyn." I grinned up at Drake, seeing the gleam in his eye, knowing full well that my father would never leave Manhattan except for a place like San Francisco.

"He might not live in Brooklyn, but maybe a nice townhome some-where in the upper east side in a building with a huge patio and easier access than a penthouse in an apartment block. Somewhere close to a park where he could go and sit when the weather was good. I'm sure he just wants to be able to get outside more than he was when he was up in the penthouse."

I nodded, and let go of Drake, wanting to get unpacked as soon as possible so we could settle in for the evening.

Afterwards, I went to the drawer in the kitchen where I kept all our takeout menus and found my favorite – an organic restaurant that only sourced organic and humane produce and meat.

"Should I order our favorite? Ribs and salad and rice?"

"Please," Drake said, glancing up from the floor where he was playing with Sophie. "I'm salivating at the thought of those ribs."

"Me, too," I said and called up. The owner still recognized my phone number and was happy to fill our usual order. Not much had changed since we'd been away and before long, I felt right at home.

After dinner, we played with Sophie for a while, Drake gave her a bath and then she had a bottle and went to bed for the night. I wondered if she'd be fussy and not go to sleep well, but she was fine, falling asleep quickly. I returned from her room and stood in the center of the great room and just took it in.

I loved our apartment. Sure, I enjoyed our place in San Francisco, but this was us – this was Drake's and my home. I wanted us to return someday and have a life here.

"Do you want a glass of wine? There's a bottle chilling in the refrigerator."

"I don't think so. I think I'd rather have a cup of hot tea."

"Coming right up," Drake said and went to the kitchen to turn on the kettle. I stood at the window and just watched the pedestrians on the sidewalk across the street. I knew every store and corner by heart and was caught up in the sounds of the traffic filtering in through the open window.

We had our tea and crashed for the evening on the sectional, putting some favorite old music on the stereo system. I was too tired to go out anywhere and all I really wanted was to have a nice warm bubble bath in our tub and then go to bed in the bedroom in the apartment where Drake and I first fell in love.

"Our first night back," Drake said and stroked my arm. "Are you tired? Do you want to watch something or do you want to go to sleep early?"

"I didn't sleep well last night. Maybe we should go to bed early. You have a busy day tomorrow. You've got to go see your lawyer and then visit the foundation and corporation."

"Do you mind?" Drake asked. "I wanted to get it over with so we could focus on spending time together."

"Not at all. I'll take Sophie for a walk and visit all my old haunts. It'll be fun."

After our bubble bath, we crept into our bed and I sighed when Drake wrapped his arm around me from behind, feeling strange to be back again despite the fact I'd spent much of the past two years there. And then, even though I thought I was too tired to make love to my husband, the way he touched me, kissing my shoulder, his hands sliding down my hip and around my buttock, aroused me.

So I did.

CHAPTER 18

DRAKE

When I woke in the morning, for a moment I was disoriented and wasn't sure where I was. I slept on the same side as usual, but the window wasn't in the place I'd grown used to. The room wasn't nearly as bright as it usually was back in San Francisco. The open window brought in sounds of car horns and traffic. Somewhere, a jackhammer banged away on cement.

I was used to the sound of waves breaking on the beach and the cry of seagulls. I was used to waking up at six in the morning and finding Kate and Sophie beside me, but Kate was already up and I was alone in the king-sized cherry wood four poster bed. I rolled over onto my back and checked the clock on the bedside table. It was eight. I'd slept in despite falling asleep hours earlier than usual.

I got up and after a quick trip to the bathroom, I went downstairs to find Kate and Sophie already up and sitting at the island in the kitchen, eating breakfast.

"Good morning, Dr. Morgan," Kate said when she saw me come down the stairs. "Rise and shine, sleepyhead."

"Good morning, Mrs. Morgan," I said and went to her for a kiss. "How did you sleep? Why didn't you wake me up?"

"You were sleeping like a baby. I wanted to let you sleep in as long as you needed. Obviously, you needed it."

"I did," I said and stretched my hands up over my head. "I feel good, if a little disoriented."

I went over to Sophie, who was playing with her Cheerios, and gave her a kiss.

"How's my baby? Did you sleep all night again?"

"She did," Kate said with a smile. "I was surprised when I woke up at seven that she was asleep. I even went in to check to make sure she was still alive."

I laughed and went to Kate, who was pouring water for coffee.

"You're joking, right? You know she's very healthy and there's nothing to worry about."

"I know," Kate said and poured me a cup of coffee. "I can't help it. I guess it's just lingering anxiety after her spending time in the NICU. I keep worrying that she'll stop breathing."

"She doesn't have sleep apnea. That was just due to her prematurity. She's totally healthy. You can sleep as well as any other new parent."

"I'll try," Kate said and she looked at Sophie with doubtful eyes. "I'm not looking forward to all the childhood illnesses she'll get."

"She won't get many at all because well make sure she gets all her vaccinations. Really, Kate. I'm trained in pediatrics. Sophie is healthy. She was only premature because of the accident not any underlying disorder."

I took her in my arms and kissed her, wanting to quell her fears. She had no reason to be concerned. I realized that it was her lingering PTSD that made her worry so much about Sophie. I hoped that as time passed, she'd grow less and less worried about Sophie and could enjoy her more without the constant fear of something bad happening.

We had breakfast together and I had to rush to get ready for my meeting with my lawyer to talk about the case. I had a quick shower and selected a grey suit and white shirt and then gathered my laptop and briefcase before giving Kate and Sophie a kiss goodbye.

"I'll meet you for lunch," I said when I got to the door. Kate followed me with Sophie in her arms. "We can go to that deli down the street if you want some smoked meat."

"That sounds good," Kate said and leaned in for a kiss. "I thought pasta for supper?"

I nodded. "Sounds good. Whatever you feel like."

I left them and took an Uber to rent a car for our month in Manhattan. After I was finished with the paperwork, I drove to the offices of Gary Wood, my lawyer, who was a partner in a prestigious criminal law firm in the upper east side. Although I had nothing to worry about regarding the trial, he was right that I had to be careful to phrase things so that people didn't get the wrong impression of me or what happened between Lisa and Derek and me. My demeanor had to be impeccable so that I wasn't seen as a crass exploiter of psychologically vulnerable, barely legal women.

She wasn't barely legal. She was a med student and had to be close to twenty-four at the minimum. I didn't see myself that way and had always demanded that my submissives were at least twenty-one or older. I didn't want someone who was virginal. I wanted a submissive who knew what she wanted but hadn't found someone with whom to explore it yet. So that had been one of my rules.

It would require a delicate hand dealing with questions about BDSM. Most people probably viewed it as perverted and oppressive to women. While it could be that way, it wasn't always that way and many men were the submissives in the relationship and the power dynamic flowed in the opposite direction to patriarchy. But I found over the years that people saw what they wanted to see. There was only so much you could do barring an epiphany to change their minds, especially on such a contentious issue as sexuality.

As I drove through the streets of Manhattan, I looked back over my years as a Dominant in the community. The first year I did some SM as part of my training, but it was always with who I assumed were consenting and willing adult women who signed NDA forms and waivers. They knew what they were signing up for because they were usually vetted by members with experience, to exclude those who might be underage or mentally ill. While the NDAs and waivers didn't have any real weight in court, they demonstrated state of mind of the participants.

Unfortunately, not everyone who signed those NDAs and waivers were of sound mind, despite being vetted. Sunita was one such case. She was conflicted about her sexuality and desires. She felt torn between her religious upbringing and her need to be dominated to be able to enjoy sex fully. Many women felt that way.

I wished I could go back in time and not try Sunita out as a partner. I wished I could go back in time and not do several scenes with Lisa but there was no way to undo the past. I had to focus on the future.

My future was with Kate and Sophia, and hopefully, with Liam. That was what held my attention and towards which I would focus all my energies.

I parked on the street and made my way into the law offices after signing in at the front desk and getting a visitor pass. There was high security in the building and people couldn't just pop into the offices.

These lawyers dealt with high profile clients and needed to maintain security and complete discretion.

I checked in with the receptionist at the front desk of the law office and sat in the small lobby to wait for my lawyer to come and get me.

After about five minutes, he popped out of an office and came over to where I sat.

"Drake," he said and extended his hand. "Glad to finally meet you. Sorry to keep you waiting. I had a Skype meeting and I couldn't get the client to stop talking. Come on in."

We shook hands and he led me down the hall to his office in the corner of the floor. We were on the 23rd floor and had a great view of the East River and Roosevelt Island.

"Take a seat."

I sat on the chair across from his desk and waited while he flipped a file open and scanned the top paper inside briefly.

"So, I've been going over the police reports on the attack on your wife and the witness statements and those of the accused. Seems like she's maintaining that you encouraged her to kill your wife, so that the two of you could be together."

"Of course, that's false," I said, my hands folded. I took in a deep breath to calm myself. Whenever I heard that claim, I grew incensed and didn't want to appear too upset. "I never saw her once between the time we had our last encounter and when she started as a resident at NYU."

"You two were never at a function together? Any parties that you might have both been at?"

"No," I said. "At least, at none that I was aware of her presence. I'd gone to a few costumed parties where people wore masks, but if she was in attendance, she never made herself known to me."

"You did say that Derek Richardson attempted to involve you in an ongoing relationship but that you refused?"

"Yes, that's the case. He said that Lisa enjoyed our experiences and wanted them to continue. At that point, I decided I wasn't really interested in being involved in a voyeur scenario where the focus was on pleasing an external viewer who directed our actions. I met a new partner and was happy with her and so I turned him down. Derek and I remained friends because we were both at the head of businesses in the medical industry. We'd occasionally play racquetball or meet for a drink to discuss business. Nothing more happened with Lisa and me after that time. In fact, it was a total shock when she showed up at the NYU residence program for neurosurgery. I knew she was a medical student but had no idea she had chosen neurosurgery as a specialty."

We went over the steps I had taken to try to avoid her and all the claims Lisa had made about me and the lies she told, insisting that we had been together. I refuted them all.

"You'll be asked about your time with Lisa. I want to run through some sample questions with you so we can think of how best to phrase your answers."

For the next hour, we went over questions that he thought I would be asked by the defense, to try to cast doubt on my testimony and to try to paint Lisa in the best possible light so that she could use the defense that she'd been coached to kill Kate. While the police didn't believe that, and I had never been charged, the defense could still try to push that narrative to make Lisa appear more sympathetic to the jury for when the sentencing came around.

They would play up her vulnerability, her traumatic past as a victim of child abuse, her age, and the fact she was a submissive to an older man, Derek Richardson, who they would likely claim dominated her and abused her. His death was not part of the current trial, and would not be brought up of course, but he would be painted as a controlling man who abused her. I would be painted that way as well and my background in BDSM would ensure that label would stick.

People would be sympathetic towards Lisa even if they thought she was guilty. They would see her as a victim as well as an accused because of her age and gender and past. Above all, I had to be brief with my responses, and not spend any time arguing the case for BDSM. I would speak about it as a small part of a busy life that I explored for a few years and left behind after my marriage to Kate.

The defense would try to unsettle me and make me stumble or admit something to make Lisa look less culpable. I'd have to keep my cool and not let them do that.

I didn't relish the thought of having to defend myself but I had to do it.

When we were finished going over the facts of the case and my involvement with Lisa, Gary stood and extended his hand once more.

"I'm sorry we have to go over this, but it's necessary if you want her to be convicted and sentenced to a maximum. It's clear to me that she's mentally unstable and calculating. She needs to be put away for a long time. You want to do whatever you can to make sure the prosecution is able to do that."

"I'm meeting with the prosecutor tomorrow to go over my testimony. Will you be there?"

"I will. We should meet again the day before your appearance so we can go over this again."

"I'll be here."

I left his office and made my way out to my car, steeling myself for my meeting the following day with the prosecutor who would go over my testimony and ensure we had all the facts straight.

. . .

My next stop was at the foundation to meet with Dave Mills and catch up on the projects completed, ongoing and in the pipeline. It felt strange to walk into the building after several months away. Everything was familiar but at the same time, I felt like everything was new. Janine, one of the receptionists, was seated behind the counter as I got off the elevator and walked past the walls of posters depicting our different projects around Africa and now, in the USA.

"Hello, Dr. Morgan," she said with a smile. "Welcome back."

"Thank you. It's great to be back. How are you?"

"I'm fine. Dave's in the boardroom, waiting for you to arrive. Would you like a coffee or water?"

"Water would be great," I said. "Thanks."

I went down the hall to the boardroom, which looked out over the Hudson. Inside, Dave sat at the head of the long oval table, his laptop open and a projector on the tabletop beside him.

"Drake," he said and stood up, coming to meet me at the door. "Welcome back. It's good to see you. We've missed you around here. Staff have mentioned that they noticed your absence. You used to come by at least once a week."

"Good to be back," I said and we shook hands. I clapped him on the back and we went to take our seats at the table. "How have you been?"

Dave spent the next few moments catching me up with his private life. He was seeing a new woman and was selling his apartment and going to buy a house in Brooklyn.

"That's a change," I said, surprised at this development. "Why Brooklyn?"

"Time to settle down. I want a garden. I want a home, not a bachelor pad."

"You're getting old."

"I am!" he said with a laugh. "I want a life, not just a living."

"Understood. And this woman you're seeing—."

"Lila," Dave said, smiling when he said her name. "A beauty. She's a policy wonk for one of the non-profits we fund. We met last year and I've been circling around her for months but she resisted my manly charms until she didn't."

I raised my eyebrows. She sounded like just Dave's type. Probably smart and pretty. Someone like Kate.

"She's the reason you want to settle down and have a life and a garden?" I asked, grinning at him.

"Something like that."

We exchanged a knowing smile.

"How are Kate and Sophie? And you're near Liam. How are things going on that front?"

We covered all the personal stuff and once we got that out of the way, we went over the projects that had been completed since I left, the ones that were ongoing and those that were just ideas being developed.

When we were finished, it was lunch time. I wanted to get home so I could spend some time with Kate and Sophie before I had to pop over at the corporate headquarters to get a briefing on the last quarter's performance.

We shook hands once more.

"We should go out for a drink some night while you're in Manhattan and play a game or two of racquetball."

"Sounds good. I'm busy preparing for the trial in the next few days but after that, I'll have time. Send me a calendar appointment and I'll let you know."

"Will do."

He walked me out to the elevator and waited with me for the elevator to arrive.

"Maybe we can all go out for dinner some night," he said. "I'd like you to meet Lila. My aunt could probably sit with Sophia for you, if you'd ask her."

"Absolutely." The elevator door opened and I went inside. "I'll talk to Kate and get back to you with a Friday or Saturday night coming up."

"Later," Dave said as the elevator door closed.

As I left the building and walked to my rental car, I realized how much I enjoyed learning about the projects and all the business of the foundation. If I wanted, I could probably keep myself busy just working on the Board – if they would let me, that is. I'd have to keep a low profile until the trial was finished and the news blew over, but once it did, I could find real, rewarding work at the foundation.

I kept that in mind, in case Kate and I talked more about moving back for part of the year if we could find better situation for Ethan.

While I loved our place in San Francisco, being back at the 8th Avenue apartment and visiting my old haunts felt surprisingly good. I'd spent most of my adult life in Manhattan and leaving it for good just didn't seem right.

CHAPTER 19

KATE

D RAKE SPENT the first few days back in Manhattan meeting with his lawyer and catching up on work at the foundation and corporate headquarters. On my part, I spent my time with Sophie, enjoying my beautiful apartment once more, and when I could, I took Sophie out for a walk around the neighborhood. Sophie was fine and adjusted well to being in a totally different location. She fell right back into her usual sleep/wake patterns and other than the constant drooling due to her teething, she was her usual happy self.

On day three of our return, I got a call from Dawn and while I hesitated to answer it, I finally gave in on the fourth ring.

"Hello, Dawn," I said, trying to sound happy to hear from her.

"Hey, girl," she said, sounding just as forced as I sounded. "I thought I'd give you a call and see if we can meet for coffee or if I could come by and see you and Sophie."

"Of course," I said and glanced around, trying to decide whether I wanted to meet her at our favorite coffee shop or have her over. "When are you free?"

"I work the evening shift at Harlem General so I'm free until three."

I glanced at the clock. Drake was out meeting Dave for a game of racquetball and wouldn't be home until supper.

"Why don't you come over here before you go to work? You can see Sophie and we can have a cup of tea like old times."

"Sounds good. I'll be there is twenty. Thanks, Kate. I know we haven't been close since you and Drake got together and everything but I would really love to see you and Sophie while you're in town."

"Me, too," I said, my heart warming just a bit for her. "See you when you get here."

I ended the call and turned to watch Sophie, who was lying on her back on the blanket, playing with her stuffed toy. Frozen was playing on the flatscreen and she was watching it on and off. I was amazed at how addictive the movie was. Sophie couldn't get enough of it and when it was playing in the background, she seemed happy, turning to watch at certain parts – especially the singing.

I got out my mother's tea set and got everything ready for making tea for Dawn. When the buzzer sounded indicating that Dawn was outside the building, I went to the security panel and checked. Sure enough, it was her, standing at the front door waiting for me to buzz her up. I did and watched as she entered the building and started up the stairs.

I opened the door and there she was, coming up the last flight of stairs.

"There you are," she said and came to me, a bouquet of wildflowers in her hand, dressed in her colorful nursing jersey and pants, her hair pulled back into a bun. "Come give me a hug."

I went to meet her with Sophie in my arms and we hugged, patting each other on the back. I took the bouquet from her and she took Sophie, who seemed quite calm being held by a complete stranger.

"Come on in and I'll make the tea," I said and took the flowers into the kitchen. I turned on the electric kettle and then put the flowers on the island counter so I could cut the stems and put them in a vase of water.

"These are pretty," I said and smiled at Dawn. "Did you get them at the grocer down the street?"

"The very one," she said and sat at the island with Sophie in her arms. "She's getting so big. I half expected to see her being smaller than she is but I guess she was only premature because of the accident. Not because of anything organic."

"That's what Drake said. She's perfectly healthy and is in the top 75% of her age for weight and height."

"Good. She's doing really well." She talked to Sophie, asking her about Frozen on the television and telling her about the crucifix on a chain around her neck when Sophie pulled at it.

"No, that's my mother's," she said softly. "You have to be careful with that."

Dawn's mother had died when Dawn was young, and like me, had been motherless until her father remarried a few years later. It was something that bonded the two of us together, because she completely understood how I felt when my own mother died of breast cancer.

Dawn finally tore her gaze off Sophie and turned to me, her eyes soft.

"How are you doing, Kate? How are you really doing? I know you had some problems after Sophie was born. Dave told me."

"You and Dave?"

She shook her head. "No, we just met up in Starbucks one day and I made him sit down and talk to me about you. He told me you'd been diagnosed with PTSD, which is totally understandable, considering what happened."

"Yes, I was," I said and nodded. I poured the hot water over the tea infuser and watched as the hot water turned a deep orange-brown. The aroma of black tea filled the room. "I was obsessed for a while with Sophie's health, worried that something terrible was going to happen to her. I had a hard time sleeping and was having panic attacks. Drake finally figured it out and I got some counseling. I'm much better now. I still occasionally worry about Sophie when she sleeps late, but I know she's healthy and probably nothing bad is going to happen."

"That's good," Dawn said and played with Sophie's minion. "How is Drake doing, anyway? This must be hard on him, with all the publicity about his past."

"It is," I said and poured her a cup. "It's really affected him – even at the hospital in San Francisco. He had to quit because of the harassment from one of the nursing supervisors who claimed to be watching Drake, warning the nursing staff to beware of him."

"Really? That's terrible. That nursing supervisor should be fired."

I shrugged. "You didn't like Drake when I first started to see him. In fact, I seem to recall that you threatened to report him to my father and the administration at NYP..."

Dawn sighed audibly. "I know," she said softly. "I can't ever expect you to forgive me for that. All I can say is that I was a bit unreasonable about it, because of my sister."

"A bit unreasonable?"

She looked at me sheepishly. "Okay, a lot unreasonable. He's been good for you, other than the whole murderous ex-sex partner trying to kill you out of jealousy."

"That's not Drake's fault. She's nuts. She's a sociopath."

She sighed. "I don't want to argue with you about this," she said. "I understand more about BDSM now than I did before. I don't blame Drake for what happened. You can meet a nut job in any situation who can hurt you. It's not Drake's fault."

"It isn't. Drake's been a rock, but he's decided to take some time off and wait until the publicity from the trial blows over and then he may try to go into private practice. He doesn't need to work. He does it out of love for neurosurgery."

"He's lucky he has the flexibility."

We drank our tea and ate some of the fresh scones I made, along with some strawberry jam.

"How are you liking San Francisco? It's beautiful there. I bet you love it."

I smiled, thinking of our place overlooking the bay. I told her about our place and my studio, and what I'd been doing while Drake worked.

"It's so good that you're painting again. That makes me happy. Have you thought about finishing your MA?"

"I have," I said. "The thing is that I've been so busy with Sophie that I barely have time for anything. But Elaine was really good and took Sophie in the afternoons occasionally so I could go to my studio and get some work done. I might finish my MA if we come back to Manhattan for part of the year."

"You're thinking of that?"

I nodded. "I miss Manhattan. San Francisco is great but this is my home."

"That's great. I'd be so happy if you moved back and we could try to be friends again. I miss you."

I smiled. "I miss you, too."

I did miss Dawn. I missed having a best girlfriend who understood me and was there for me. Dawn had crossed a line when it came to Drake, and at one time, I wasn't sure I could forgive her completely, but now, I felt that I might be able to forgive her, even if I couldn't forget. We could have coffee or tea now and then if she showed an ability to accept my life for what it was.

"Let's not let too much time pass between visits," she said. "I know I was wrong in the past, but I hope you can forgive me and we can be friends again – real friends."

I nodded, my heart squeezing just a bit at the thought we might be friends again.

"How about you?" I asked, wondering whether she had someone special. "Are you seeing anyone? I know you and Kurt were seeing each other for a while."

"That ended pretty quickly, but we're still friendly at least. But no, I'm still an old maid." She shrugged. "Always the bridesmaid, never the bride."

"You'll find someone," I said and took her hand, giving it a squeeze. "When you least expect it, you'll look up and see someone and he'll see you and that will be it."

"That's what happened with you and Drake, right? Although, you were a bit more reluctant at first. You fought it."

"I did," I said, smiling to myself as I remembered meeting Drake and finding out he was the Dom I was going to meet for an interview. "I overcame my reluctance pretty fast. I never looked back. Not once. He's a perfect match for me."

"You're lucky." She sighed. "I hope I can find my own perfect match."

We talked some more about my father and how his health was and what Heath was up to in Haiti and then she glanced at her watch.

"Well, I guess I better get going," she said and stood up, carrying Sophie to the door. She gave her a big kiss on the cheek and then handed her to me. After she put on her shoes, she stood up and gave me a hug.

"I hope we can do lunch one day, before you leave."

"I'll talk to Drake. He can take Sophie for a few hours and we could go to Katz's Deli if you'd like. I feel like some good corned beef."

She smiled. "I'd love that. I haven't been to Katz's Deli for years."

We hugged again and then she left, taking the stairs back down to the entrance.

I watched her on the security monitor and saw that she waved before she exited the building.

I went to the window and followed her as she walked down the street to the subway stop. From there, she'd take the train to Harlem General for her shift as a pediatric nurse.

I took Sophie over to the living room and put her back down on the floor with her toys. Then I went to get a bottle ready for her afternoon nap. While it was heating up in the bottle warmer, I watched out the window at the street traffic, the sounds of the city coming in through the open window. I loved the city.

I wanted to move back. But I wanted my father and Elaine to come back as well. I hoped Drake was right – that if we could find a better place for my father to live, he might be quite happy to come back to Manhattan for part of the year. As much as I loved and missed Manhattan, I wouldn't leave my father for very long. I knew he was ill and probably didn't have a lot of time to live. I wanted to spend as much time with him as I possibly could. I wanted him to watch Sophie grow and to remain close to Drake.

Drake had lost his father too soon, and so I wanted us to be as close a family as we could possibly be.

So, we'd try to spend as much time with him and Elaine as we could.

That was one thing Lisa had taught me – life was too short and humans too fragile to waste.

CHAPTER 20

DRAKE

For the next few days I divided my time between Kate and Sophie and preparing for the trial. That meant meeting with my lawyer and with the prosecutor to go over my testimony.

The day of my testimony at the trial arrived. Late that morning, I spent an hour sitting in on the trial, tucked away at the back of the room, in a seat close to the door so I could leave quickly in case anyone recognized me. I didn't want to be the subject of gawking. At one point, someone recognized me and turned, taking out their cell to videotape me. A murmur went through the courtroom and so I got up and left, determined not to give anyone any gossip material.

Earlier that morning, I spent some time with the ADA going over my testimony to nail down the main points we would make. I did my best to keep a calm level head while I sat in the hallway outside the court-room, waiting to be called.

When I was called and went inside, I felt the eyes of all those in the courtroom on me as I walked to the witness box and was sworn in. On my way to the stand, I passed Lisa, who sat next to her attorney. She glared at me, her eyes narrow. She was dressed in a very prim women's pin-striped suit and white blouse, no makeup on her face and her hair pulled back into a bun.

She looked nothing like a crazed delusional murderer, out to kill anyone who got in her way, and certainly not like anyone in love with me. I felt like she would have killed me then and there if she could have reached me.

After being sworn in, I sat in the witness box and the prosecutor went through the questions we had prepared. As I answered, I glanced out and saw Lara sitting in the rear of the courtroom dressed impeccably in her blue suit, her platinum blonde hair pulled back into a bun, her dark glasses making her look very brainy.

She smiled at me and gave me a slow nod.

Strangely, she left abruptly. I imagined that she got a message and had to leave to attend to business.

I felt I answered calmly, clearly and without any defensiveness. I admitted that while I had a few sexual encounters with Lisa Monroe before meeting Kate, I had never seen her again privately or in public until I learned she was a student in the surgical residency program at NYU. I denied any romantic or sexual relationship with Lisa while she was a student in the program or any time after we first met and had several encounters at parties at Derek Richardson's mansion in Yonkers. I described how once she became a student at NYU, she made suggestions about us being 'friends' or more, had tried to encourage me to be alone with her, and had made a physical pass, but that I told her I was currently happily married with a pregnant wife and wasn't interested.

I recounted how I had gone to my supervisor in the pediatric neuro-surgery program to withdraw because of Lisa's ongoing inappropriate behavior but had been encouraged to stay. Ultimately, because Lisa had continued to show interest and wouldn't accept no for an answer, I had gone to withdraw but had been told that Lisa would be asked to withdraw instead, because she was deemed to be not working out as a candidate in the residency program.

I also went over how I had no idea it had been Lisa who attacked Kate until I was called by my supervisor, who apologized and expressed fear that it had been Lisa who struck Kate.

My voice broke when I described being informed about Kate being hit by a car in a crosswalk while she was out walking and how I watched the surgery to save her life and that of Sophia, our unborn and seven-week premature baby. After a moment, I recovered and finished my testimony.

All that was left was the cross examination.

I was glad I spent time with my lawyer going over my testimony so that I was prepared for the kinds of questions the defense would ask. However, it was worse than I expected.

Lisa's lawyer was a stern-looking woman with dark hair and dark-rimmed glasses. She kept asking leading questions, suggesting that I had maintained a relationship with Lisa from the time we met at Derek Richardson's until Lisa had attended NYU as a surgical resi-dent. She suggested that I had been encouraging Lisa, wanting her to "take care of Kate for me" according to Lisa's claims. She repeatedly had her questions objected to and finally, the judge cautioned her when she asked a question that had no evidence to support the accusation.

"Isn't it true that you were at the same public events as Ms. Monroe and that you secretly met with her and engaged in sexual activity while your then-fiancée was present?"

"Objection!" the prosecutor called out, losing his patience. "Your Honor, there is absolutely no evidence presented that Ms. Monroe was at the concert in question. There was no record of any ticket being purchased by Ms. Monroe or receipt presented as evidence of Ms. Monroe's attendance. This is hearsay."

The Judge, looking tired, agreed. "Sustained."

Lisa's lawyer persisted. "Your honor, it is the Defense's contention that Ms. Monroe was encouraged to believe that if Mrs. Morgan was no longer in the picture that she would have a relationship with Dr. Morgan and would be married to him."

The prosecutor stood up to protest. "Your Honor, the defense has produced no evidence that Dr. Morgan and Ms. Monroe were ever at the same event. There is no evidence in writing or on tape that Dr. Morgan ever made any promises to Ms. Monroe."

The Judge responded wearily. "Dr. Morgan is not on trial and has not been charged with any offense. Move on from this line of questioning, Ms. Mackenzie."

The defense tried their one tactic of suggesting that I had coached Lisa and promised that if she killed Kate, we would be together. It wasn't meant to get her off. It was meant to make her look like a victim, and that I was the evil mastermind for when she was convicted and it was time for sentencing. That was its sole purpose.

One claim they didn't bring up, that the prosecutor demolished during his presentation of the case, was the emails that were purportedly from me, which detailed our relationship and spoke in derogatory terms about Kate and glowingly about Lisa.

Of course, police had already determined that those emails were written and sent from the IP associated with Derek Richardson's cabin where Lisa and her boyfriend were staying. From what I understood, those emails were subject to no cross examination by the defense. They gave up on those emails because they could not put me in the cabin at any time the emails were written, the way Lisa suggested. In fact, the only person who could have written them was either Lisa or her boyfriend.

I was amazed at her mind and how she had concocted an entire fantasy of me conspiring with her to kill Kate and for us to be together. I still couldn't believe she thought that might happen, but apparently, she did. She thought that once Kate was out of the way, I would be free to be her lover. She'd throw over her boyfriend and together, she and I would work in a private practice as two neuro-surgeons.

How someone as bright and with such promise could be so mentally delusional, I would never understand. Perhaps it was her past that made her vulnerable to erotomania. According to evidence presented by the defense, she had been neglected by her parents as a child, and had been in foster care for some period of her childhood before being taken back after her mother remarried.

The roots of her delusion about me and about men were laid down due to her history of sexual abuse in foster care – a sad story too often told. I had no doubt they were connected. Of course, that meant that she should have received psychological counseling to help her over-come her issues.

That she didn't get counseling pointed to the inadequacy of our mental health programs in the US health care system.

I suspected that she might plead not guilty due to insanity but she didn't, which suggests that she had a bad lawyer despite her family connections. She also thought she was too smart and could direct her defense herself. She wasn't insane. She was definitely mentally ill. But she was sane enough to plan a murder and cover-up, even if she didn't do it well enough to escape detection and imprisonment.

Instead of being just delusional, I suspected she was also a sociopath and just didn't think anyone was as smart as her. Sociopaths often thought everyone else was stupid in comparison. They over-estimated their own intelligence and underestimated everyone else's. It was a very dangerous combination because they didn't know how much they didn't know.

That was Lisa's failing. She was arrogant and thought she knew better than everyone -- including the police, the prosecutor, her own lawyer and the judge.

When the cross examination was finished, I was dismissed and asked to remain available in case there was a need to have me testify again. I left the courtroom, glad to be out of that environment.

I heaved a sigh of relief as I walked down the long hallway to the front entrance, but wasn't ready for what awaited me. At the bottom of the steps leading from the courthouse stood a gaggle of reporters with their associated camera operators, waiting for me. They approached me when they saw who I was and I wished I had someone with me, but I'd assured my lawyer that I was fine and could handle myself.

"Do you have anything to say about the trial, Dr. Morgan?"

"Why did you continue to work at NYU if you didn't want a relation-ship with Ms. Monroe?"

"Did your wife know about your affair with Ms. Monroe when she married you?"

I stopped for a moment, and they crowded around me. When they were silent, their microphones shoved as close to my face as they could get without blocking their camera's views of my face, I spoke.

"I feel very bad for Ms. Monroe's family. She and her lover killed Derek Richardson and almost killed my wife and unborn baby. She most likely encouraged her boyfriend to commit suicide. She's hurt many people and will have to pay for her crimes. That's all I have to say."

Then I pushed past the reporters and made it to my car without feeling the need to respond to any of the questions they shouted after me.

"Dr. Morgan, there are reports you were forced to quit your position at San Francisco General Hospital because of allegations of harassment on the part of the nursing staff supervisor. Do you have anything to say?"

I frowned and turned to face the reporter.

"That's completely wrong. I left voluntarily to spend more time with my family."

Then, I got inside my rental car and slammed the door, glad of the car's tinted windows.

As I drove away, I had to acknowledge to myself that I had given the typical excuse used when someone was forced to retire or quit their job due to a scandal. At that moment, I had to admit that I quit because of a scandal. In my anger, I drove a bit too fast and had to slam on my brakes when a pedestrian stepped out into the crosswalk and I didn't see her until the last second.

Luckily, I stopped in time but I got a real glare from her. A well-deserved glare.

I pulled over when I got far enough away and tried to calm myself. I texted Kate to let her know my testimony was done and that helped. After my pulse calmed down, I continued driving.

Back when I first considered getting involved in BDSM, I never truly thought it would mean I had to give up my career. Lara warned me of the need for the utmost discretion in my dealings with people in the lifestyle, but I always trusted myself to make the right decisions and use good judgment in my participation in BDSM. You could control yourself, but ultimately, you couldn't control other people.

I had the bad luck of running into a very damaged sociopath who fixated on me and could never take no for an answer. Little did I know when I had sex with her at Derek's dungeon party that I was laying the foundation for my future – a future where I almost lost the love of my life and my daughter. As it was, Kate was damaged and had PTSD. Although she was better than she had been, she would be affected by the attack for years. I had a future which was increasingly looking like I would not be able to work as a neurosurgeon again – at least for a few years.

That hurt more than I realized. I'd often thought I could do whatever I wanted, when I wanted – that I had so much freedom due to my specialty in neurosurgery and my wealth, but I was realizing that the publicity from the trial and my past in BDSM might take away that freedom.

I arrived back at the apartment on 8th Avenue and sat in the car for a moment, trying to let go of my stress about the trial. I didn't want to bring that negativity into our home, so I sat in the car for a few moments and just breathed in deeply. It was at that moment that my cell dinged and I checked to find a message from Lara.

LARA: How are you doing?

I remembered seeing Lara leave abruptly and was surprised that she left in the middle of my testimony. I thought she would have stayed for the entire time and waited for me afterwards, but she didn't.

I texted her back right away.

DRAKE: I'm fine. I saw you in the back of the courtroom. Why did you leave?

LARA: *Someone I didn't want to see came in and so I left at the first chance I had. Sorry about that. I wanted to stay but believe me, I didn't want to stay and have this person do anything to disrupt the trial. Let's just say he's a bit of a nutcase about BDSM. I'm surprised he didn't disrupt the trial anyway. He usually raises a stink and is taken out by security guards. If he saw me there, he would have gone crazy.*

DRAKE: *He did nothing while I was there.*

LARA: *That's good. I'm glad. If he saw me, he might have interrupted your testimony. I suspect he's really more interested in Lisa. He's on some kind of crusade... Listen, I'm busy the rest of the day today but I want to meet up with you two. Can you and Kate meet with me for dinner? I'll be in meetings all day tomorrow but afterward, I would love to relax with the two of you and have a drink, some good food and catch up.*

DRAKE: *I'm sure Kate would love to see you. I'll talk to her and if we can get Dave's aunt Karen to sit for us, I'd love to. I'll let you know as soon as I hear back from Kate and Karen, okay?*

LARA: *Sounds good. Take it easy.*

DRAKE: *You, too.*

I got on my cell and called Karen Mills. Luckily, she answered on the third ring.

We said our hellos and I asked if she would be able to sit for us on short notice.

"You know I'd love to sit for you. How is that little sweet pea doing?"

"She's wonderful. Really, we're really lucky to have such an easy baby. It's still been exhausting, which is to be expected, but she's sleeping through the night and that makes a big difference."

"It does. I'll be there at six thirty and can stay as late as you want."

"I really appreciate this, Karen. You're a godsend."

"Don't mention it. How are you doing, Drake? I've been watching the news. The coverage can't be very easy on you guys."

"It's hard but we're trying to just lay low and hope that once the trial is over and some time passes, things will get more back to normal for us."

"How is San Francisco? Do you love it there?"

"We do," I said. "But we miss Manhattan of course. We may come back for the good weather in the fall if we can find a better setup for Ethan. But we'll probably spend winters in San Francisco. So much better for Ethan to be able to go outside in the fresh air and sun."

"No doubt. Okay, I'll see you tomorrow night."

I said goodbye and ended the call. I wanted to have the details arranged before I asked Kate if she wanted to go. I knew she'd feel comfortable leaving Sophie with Karen.

I parked my rental in the parking garage and then walked the rest of the way to the apartment, whistling to myself, feeling better than I had for a while. I had my testimony out of the way, and it was all downhill from here. The trial would be finished soon, Lisa would be convicted and sentenced and put away. The headlines would die down and then, maybe in a year, I could return to my life and continue where we left off. I still had the confidence of my supervisor at NYU if I wanted to continue the Fellowship. I could qualify as a pediatric neurosurgeon and start a practice doing what I loved. I could schedule as many or as few patients a week as I saw fit, since money was no object.

I climbed the stairs to the apartment, relieved that my role in the trial was over, eager to see Kate and Sophie.

CHAPTER 21

KATE

I DIDN'T WANT to go to the courtroom and watch the trial or Drake's testimony.

Some may have seen that as me not supporting Drake, or me not being interested. The truth was that I didn't want to have to face the paparazzi. I didn't want to have a microphone shoved in my face and to be asked stupid and insulting questions about my sex life and my marriage to Drake. I just knew what the tabloid reporters would ask:

How did you feel when you found out Drake was carrying on an affair with Lisa while you were pregnant?

Did you know that your husband was a notorious Dom in the BDSM community before you married him?

Did you ever suspect that he was secretly seeing Lisa Monroe while you were pregnant with your baby?

How does it feel to be married to a notorious womanizer?

Did you know about the restraining order his ex-wife filed before they divorced?

Of course, I knew Drake wasn't the man the tabloids tried to make him out to be but some of the press picked up on those allegations from Lisa and ran with them because all Drake could do was deny them. When people looked at Lisa, they saw a beautiful young woman. Probably most of them couldn't believe that Drake wasn't having an affair with her. After all, I was pregnant. They wouldn't and couldn't know that Drake found me exceedingly sexy while I was pregnant and that it was even easier for me to orgasm while I was pregnant than before.

If they knew that, they might understand that there was no way Drake was interested in Lisa. But I wasn't going to tell them so they continued pushing false gossip about our relationship to sell copies and get clicks on their news stories or websites.

I didn't watch coverage of the trial on television, deliberately avoiding the news so I didn't have to see the headlines. Instead, I listened to calming music and spent my time with Sophie.

I was glad when I got a text from him.

DRAKE: Well, it's over. Now, we can move on.

I texted him right back, smiling, a sense of relief filling me. He was right. Now, our lives could re-start and we both could move on.

KATE: I'm so glad. I hope you were okay with me not coming to court. I just couldn't face seeing Lisa or the press afterwards.

DRAKE: No, don't worry. We already talked about this and I meant what I said. I didn't want you there. You're my wife and Sophie is my baby and none of it is anyone's business.

KATE: Okay. I'll see you when you get home.

He understood. I had to keep telling myself that but I just couldn't face the prospect of having everyone watching us, watching me, and what they'd say and ask me. Drake didn't want to have to face those questions or cameras either but he had to do it. He had no choice. But at least now, it was all over.

We could both move on, whatever that meant.

I hoped it meant that Drake could finish his Fellowship and that he could eventually practice as a pediatric neurosurgeon. It might mean that I could finish my MA and write and paint. We could go back to living our lives, whether that was in San Francisco part of the year or in Manhattan part of the year.

Liam could come and stay with us in Manhattan if Drake got joint custody and the rest of the time, he could stay with us in California. Because he was in school, we'd have to choose where to live that would be best for him.

We'd work it out. I knew that Drake wanted it and so we would do whatever it took to make it our reality.

WHEN DRAKE ARRIVED HOME, he came right over to me and hugged me, pulling me into his arms and kissing me. The kiss was warm but needy, like he needed reassurance that everything else in his life was okay.

"I'm so glad that's over," he said and stroked my cheek, his eyes on mine.

I squeezed him. "Me, too. How did it go?"

He shrugged, sighing a bit. "As well as could be expected. Lisa's lawyer tried to make me sound like a rogue and rake, suggesting I coached her into killing you, but luckily, the judge shut her down."

"How long will the trial go on?"

Drake shook his head and brushed a strand of hair from my cheek. "I'm not sure. The rest of the week and then the jury will convene and deliberate. We should know next week what the verdict is and then there'll be sentencing. If you wanted, you could do a victim impact statement as part of what the judge hears when it comes to sentencing."

"No." I leaned against Drake, enjoying the way his body felt warm and solid against mine. "I don't ever want to see Lisa again. I'd have to see her if I gave a witness impact statement. I don't want to go to the courthouse, I don't want to be followed by reporters or cameras." I looked up into his eyes. "I just want our old life back."

"Can't get that back, I'm afraid," Drake said, his voice soft. "But we can have our new life. It can be a better life. Us together with Sophie and maybe Liam part of the time. In Manhattan part time and in San Francisco the rest of the time."

"That sounds like a dream."

"We'll make it a reality." He kissed me again. "And now, Mrs. Morgan, I hope you don't mind that I made plans for us. Lara texted me after my testimony and invited us out for dinner with her. I called Karen Mills to see if she could sit for us for a few hours and she was happy to."

I raised my eyebrows. "I'd love to see Lara. That sounds great. When? Tonight?"

Drake rubbed my shoulder. "Tomorrow night. Tonight, I want to put Sophie to bed and then ravage you. I *need* you, Ms. Bennet."

"I'm yours," I said, my body responding to the sound of need in his voice and words. "To ravage as you see fit."

"Good, because I need you. You don't get pampered enough so expect to be pampered tonight."

I narrowed my eyes playfully. "I thought you said 'ravage' not 'pamper'..."

He smiled. "Ravage. Pamper. For me, they mean the same thing. You will have multiple orgasms. That's all you need to know."

"Did anyone ever tell you that you're awfully confident in your ravaging skills?"

He grinned. "They have. For example, you." He kissed me again. "All this talk of ravaging and I'll be unable to wait." He pulled me more tightly against his body so that I could feel his hardness.

"Patience is a virtue," I quipped. Then Sophie let out a yelp and we turned to see that she'd crawled under the side table and banged her head when she sat up and now, couldn't get herself out.

Drake let go of me and went right over, picking her up and kissing her cheeks.

"That'll teach mommy and daddy to kiss and hug when Sophie's on the floor crawling around," he said and rubbed her head. "What were you doing? Getting trapped in the corner? You have to learn how to turn around. It's a great skill."

"She's trying to pull herself up on things," I said, smiling as I watched them together. "The days of putting her down and being able to leave her are gone. We're going to have to watch her every move."

"They are and we will. She's getting so mobile so fast. I'm glad I can be here to watch her instead of being away all the time she's awake. Maybe all this is for the best. If I was still at NYU, I'd be working twelve-hour days at the hospital and would be away from you both all the time. Now, I'll have more freedom."

"You should still be at NYU. It's not fair that you've had to give up your career because of all this."

"I haven't given it up. I've just put it on hold for a while. I'll be able to go back to finish my Fellowship next year. I'll be able to work again. Right now, I have other things – family things – to figure out. I feel blessed despite the trial and everything."

We smiled at each other and I knew what Drake was thinking. He was thinking how lucky we were to have each other and to have Sophie.

"We are blessed. We have Sophie. You now have a relationship with Liam, and one day, maybe even Liam can live with us. I can imagine him playing with Sophie, showing her his toys and enjoying being a big brother to her."

"You can't believe how much it warms my heart to imagine that day," Drake said, his voice breaking. "I have to do everything right for the next six months so I can go before a judge and convince him that I'm fit to be a custodial parent. I hope all this dies down by then."

Then his cell dinged to indicate a new text. He removed it from his jacket pocket and read for a moment.

"Our cup runneth over. An invite for a special dinner at the O'Riley's place this Sunday." He glanced up at me. "Sounds like a good diversion. I know Mrs. O would love to see Sophie and both of us."

"We should go," I said. "Weren't you going to practice with the band this weekend?"

"We are planning to practice on Sunday afternoon. I could go and then we could have dinner afterwards. We're playing on the following Tuesday night at O'Rileys to get me back into the swing of things."

I went to him while he texted a response. "I want us to move back."

"I know," he said and kissed me. "We have to talk to Ethan. See what we can arrange for the fall. If Maureen is going to stay with Chris, we could move Liam to Manhattan to start school in August. Ethan could spend spring, summer and fall in Manhattan and winters in San Francisco."

"That sounds perfect. I can wait until August to return. Maybe by then things will be figured out with Liam."

"Maybe," Drake said and sent his email message. He glanced up. "There. We've got our weekend planned. Maybe we can go to Coney Island on Saturday."

I nodded, happy to be doing a few touristy things since we were only in town for such a short time. I wanted to move back right away, but I didn't want to leave my father and Elaine... It would be a few months and we could move back. That wasn't too long.

I'd find more than enough to do in San Francisco to keep me occupied until then. Now all we had to do was convince my dad. It would be easy enough. After all, his entire life was in Manhattan, just as mine was. His friends, his son and grandkids. His associations. Elaine's family was there, too.

We'd have to find the right place for him and Elaine to live. Wheelchair accessible with access to a big patio or yard.

Until then, I'd have to be patient.

THE NEXT DAY, Karen arrived at six fifteen to sit with Sophie and walked right in, taking her from my arms like a pro. She had Sophie on the sofa playing and reading a book in no time.

"You two go out," she said, glancing in our direction. "I know my way around your apartment. I'll give her a bottle before she goes down. What time do you want me to put her to bed?"

"She usually goes down at about eight."

"Sounds fine. Now, off you go. I have my cell in case you need to stay later or anything. Let me know."

"Thanks," Drake said and put his arm around my shoulder. "We really appreciate you helping out. We'll be home after nine."

"Like I said, call me if you need more time. I'm happy to stay."

We left the apartment and I felt only the slightest twinge of guilt at going out. Sophie seemed quite happy to be with Karen and so I took in a deep breath and tried to stop worrying about Sophie. Karen was a retired nurse. If anyone could look after her, Karen could. She was trained in CPR and knew babies inside and out.

Drake took my hand and led me to the car outside on the street. We drove to the restaurant Lara had chosen and found a spot in a parking garage a few blocks away. The sun was still high and the air warm. I breathed in, enjoying the early evening.

The restaurant specialized in modern French food and the décor was upscale and trendy. We entered and Drake gave Lara's name to the hostess who took us back to a booth in the rear of the dining room, next to a bank of windows. Lara greeted us, standing up, dressed in her usual navy pinstripe suit and white blouse, her platinum hair in a tight bun. She looked every inch a defense lawyer you wouldn't want to mess with. I was glad we had her on our side.

"Drake, Kate," she said and gave us both a hug and kiss. "Good to see you. Please, sit down. I've been here for fifteen minutes catching up on personal email and drinking vodka martinis. After the day I had, I needed them."

We sat in the booth, with me between Drake and Lara.

"Bad day in court?" Drake asked, opening his menu.

"The worst. Some people just cannot understand what's in their own best interest."

She proceeded to tell us about a case where she was defending a man charged with involuntary manslaughter.

"I always tell people to keep it succinct. Less is more. Don't get into any long, convoluted explanations of your behavior. Keep it simple. My client started explaining too much and screwed up his case. I needed a drink or three. Maybe four." She held up her martini glass and winked at me.

"Speaking of cases, I have it on good authority that you were very good on the stand, Drake. One of my assistants sat in while you were giving your testimony. He said you were cool as a cucumber and that your voice broke at just the right place."

"And that was?" I asked, curious about Drake breaking down.

"When he described the phone call he got about you being struck by a car. My assistant said Drake was calm and clear up until that part and his emotion showed through when he described seeing you when you were wheeled into the ER trauma room and they had to force him out. It was classic and it sounded totally genuine so I was very happy to hear Drake did so well."

I turned to Drake and he bent down and kissed me.

"It's still hard for me to remember that day or talk about it."

"I have no memory of it so it's like a story that's been told about me," I said softly. "Nothing more."

"It's like a bad dream – a nightmare that you want to wake up from but can't," Drake said. "It was the worst day of my life, thinking I might lose you and Sophie."

We kissed again and then both of us turned back to Lara, who was smiling.

"I knew she was perfect for you, Drake, when she walked into our meeting that first time. Perfect."

We ordered and had a lovely dinner. The food was great, the wine flowed freely and the talk ranged from the trial to my studio back in San Francisco and the problems Drake had with the nursing supervisor at UCSF.

"You did the right thing," Lara said, taking a sip of wine and eyeing Drake over the rim. "It would have been uncomfortable for you knowing that people were warned about you. Honestly, I wish I could have been there to put that woman in her place."

"I appreciate your support," Drake said, studying his own glass of wine, swirling the liquid in his glass. "I made a few mistakes and they've followed me ever since. I should never have tried to stop Maureen from leaving that day. I should never have allowed Sunita to videotape our session or take photos."

"I should have never matched you with her," Lara said morosely. "It's my fault. You trusted me to vet your partners. Sorry, Kate," she said and turned to me. "I'm sure you don't like to listen to us talk about all this."

"No, that's all right. I'm familiar with his past and his partners, especially after the investigation. But I already knew it all. Maybe not all the specifics, but I knew how many partners and what he'd done. It was a selling point," I said and turned to Drake. "It made me feel safe."

"Unfortunately, it was my trusting Derek Richardson's taste in submissives that made you unsafe. You can't realize how bad I feel about that."

"It wasn't your fault that she's a sociopath."

"Yes, Drake," Lara said and leaned forward. "We all run the risk of running into the path of a sociopath and being harmed by them. We're just lucky that you hired a security detail for Kate and he probably saved her life."

I nodded and reached out to take Drake's hand, squeezing it. "That's right. So you saved my life, probably, because you were worried enough about Lisa to hire security for me."

Drake exhaled and squeezed my hand back. "I'm glad my paranoia was higher than normal or you and Sophie might not be with me today."

He leaned over and kissed me tenderly. When the kiss ended, I glanced over at Lara and saw that she was smiling like a proud matchmaker.

"You two will have to invite me over to your place before you go so I can see that beautiful little girl of yours. Drake showed me some pictures he has of her. She's really grown and she looks like you, Kate. Same soft brown hair. But she has Drake's eyes and fair skin."

Lara glanced between Drake and me, smiling like she was our parent.

"I know you don't really care much for Brit Invasion music but Mersey is getting back together for old time's sake for a few gigs," Drake said. "We're playing at O'Riley's on Tuesday night in case you want to come and have a drink."

"Will you be there, Kate?" Lara asked, turning to me.

"I will," I said and smiled. "We have our sitter all lined up already."

"Maybe I'll pop in and listen to a song or two. What's your lineup?"

Drake shrugged. "We'll wait and see what we're least rusty at, I expect. Can't say yet. Might be The Beatles. Might be The Rolling Stones. I haven't even picked up a guitar since I left Manhattan so I know I'll be rusty as hell."

"You'll be fine," Lara said and waved her hand. "It's like riding a bike or sex. Once you do it, you never forget how."

"I hope so," Drake said with a laugh. "Wouldn't want to forget how to do any of those." He winked at me and I smiled back.

When we'd finished our coffees, we said goodbye and promised to get together again for dinner at our place.

"I'll see you on Tuesday," Lara said to me when she gave me a hug goodbye. Then she turned to Drake. "If you have any questions about the trial, you can always call me." She gave Drake a hug and kiss on the cheek and then we split up, Lara walking north and us south to our car.

"That was a good night," Drake said, his arm around my shoulder as we walked down the block. "I'm glad we got together with Lara."

"Me, too," I said and slipped my arm around him. "She feels like a big sister to me."

"I'd say she felt like one as well, except we had sex, so that would be wrong."

Drake gave me an evil grin and we arrived at the parking garage and waited while the attendant brought our car out.

I laughed lightly. "She's been a great friend and mentor."

"She has."

As we drove through the streets of the city, I felt grateful that despite the terrible thing that happened to me – the attack, the emergency C-section, and the long recovery – I was now surrounded by friends and family who loved me.

CHAPTER 22

DRAKE

Practice at the O'Riley's bar on Sunday afternoon went well despite the fact I'd been away for months and hadn't picked up an instrument the entire time.

We started out playing some really old stuff – The Dave Clark Five, early Beatles, and then some Zombies.

It went well enough considering.

"I'm a bit rusty," I said, apologizing when I flubbed a few songs, my fingers not quite as nimble on the strings due to lack of practice.

"You're slipping, Doctor Morgan," Ken joked while I played the riff a few more times to get it down.

"Hey, old man," I countered. "This is a battle you don't want to fight. You'd lose."

"Oh, yeah?" Ken said, laughing. "Wanna have a go at it?"

Of course, the two of us couldn't resist a play off and so we did a battle of the guitars, him on lead and me on bass. It was all in fun, and of course, a lead guitar will beat a bass guitar any day.

When we were finished, we both laughed and slapped each other on the back. I was considerably more warmed up as a result and the rest of the practice went smoothly.

Kate would join us for dinner and so when we felt we'd gone over our repertoire enough, and had crossed songs off our playlist, we put our instruments back in the basement below the restaurant and went upstairs to the dining room to wait for family to arrive.

"I've got to finish inventory," Ken said and waved me off. "I'll join you in fifteen. Go say hi to Mom. I know she's eager to see you."

"I will."

I passed through the kitchen on my way to the office to talk to Mrs. O, enjoying the scent of the meal preparation. As usual, the cooks were busy, finishing meal service for the restaurant and preparing the family meal on top of it. Once everyone arrived, we'd go to the special private room off to the rear of the main dining room for our meal.

I found my way through the back of the restaurant to the office and Mrs. O's desk. She turned when she saw me and stood, giving me a huge hug and kiss.

"Drake," she said and smiled. "When are you two moving back? We miss you terribly and Ken has been morose ever since the band broke up. They can't replace you, you know."

"I'm irreplaceable," I said with a laugh and sat beside her at the desk. "We actually may be moving back sooner than we thought."

"Really?" Her eyes brightened. "How come?"

I shrugged. "There's some drama on the family front with Liam and Maureen."

She frowned and peered at me over the top of her reading glasses. "That's too bad. Is she giving you a hard time about seeing him? He's your son!"

I shook my head. "She wants to go to Indonesia with her husband, but can't take Liam until he's clear for five years after the transplant. It's why they split the first time. I guess he was unhappy back in California and wants to go back to his job in Indonesia. More money and seniority or something. That means that Liam has to move back to Manhattan to stay with his grandmother. Unless I can get joint custody and he stays with me. But, I've had some issues at the hospital in San Francisco and quit. So..."

"Oh, Drake, that's terrible. I feel selfish wanting you back but under happier circumstances."

"Kate wants to move back but doesn't want to be too far away from her father, given his health. I don't want to be too far away from Liam. We're going to work on Ethan and see if we can get him to come back for the fall but maybe finding a better place to live where he can get out more than his penthouse on Park Avenue allows. He's wheelchair bound now."

She nodded. "He needs a house with a garden. Maybe a townhouse somewhere nice."

"Kate's really torn. She wants to move back but can't imagine leaving her father. I don't want to miss being in Liam's life and Maureen will fight me if I try for custody."

Mrs. O sighed heavily. "You have to try, right?" She took my hand and squeezed. "If you need anything, let us know. You're like a son to me, Drake and a brother to the kids."

"I know," I said and leaned over and gave her a kiss. Then, I told her all about my new family in California.

"That's amazing," she said, her eyes wide. "I'm sorry your mom is so sick, but to find your brothers and a sister? That's priceless."

"It is. So, you can understand how torn I am between staying in California and coming back to Manhattan."

"What a decision. I don't envy you but at the same time, how exciting to discover your new family and your mother..."

I thought about how confused my mother was and how there was no recognition in her eyes when she saw me. "She doesn't recognize me but I like my brother and sister. But Liam and Ethan are the priorities."

"Family is always the priority. Everything should be viewed through that lens. In the end, your business and your accomplishments will mean little if you're alone."

"I know. I learned that lesson when my father died. We didn't spend enough time together and then he was dead. I think Kate feels that really acutely and is afraid to be away from her father for too long."

"You guys will find a way to balance things. Kate, Sophia and Liam – they're your priorities. Then us old fogies."

"Old fogies," I said and kissed her cheek.

For the next half hour, while we waited for the last diners to finish their meal and the wait staff and bus staff to finish their shifts, I helped out in the private dining room getting it set up for our family dinner. Every Sunday it was the same – serve the guests supper from five until seven, and then have a late supper prepared by the cooks. We would sit down after and eat.

I was finishing setting the table when Kate arrived with Sophie. Of course, there was a huge fuss made over them, with everyone crowding around them, helping them with the diaper bag filled with toys and the car seat. I went over to them and kissed Kate and Sophie, proud that they were my family. Once everyone said hello, we all went into the dining room and sat at our places. Mrs. O had the table set up so that Kate and I were the center of attention, and we sat and had a drink and waited for the first course to arrive.

The meal was fantastic – high end but still family food. Two different roasts – beef and chicken plus all the trimmings. The wine flowed, the plates were passed and passed again, and everyone was smiling and laughing. I sat beside Mrs. O and watched her family talking and enjoying themselves. This – this is what I wanted for myself and for my family. Big family meals around a table like this one, with great food and conversation. Everyone felt comfortable with each other and truly liked one another. I had been denied a family like this one growing up but I was determined to make a family like this for myself – and become a part of every other family I could, whether that was with Ethan and his family, the O'Rileys, or my new family in California.

One day, if we were lucky, Kate and I could host a big family dinner like this one in our house. I imagined the day and all the preparations, choosing the menu and wine, buying the food and preparing it and then welcoming everyone into my home. Our home.

One day...

When we finished dessert and had our coffees, we talked about the future and what was on the agenda.

"Drake, we hope you move back and take back up with the band but I realize that things are up in the air right now," Mrs. O said.

"They are. We'll figure it out. We'll probably come back for the temperate weather and maybe visit Ethan and Elaine in San Francisco during the holidays. If Liam does live with me, he'll be going to school and we can't be going back and forth between the two locations. His school would come first.

One thing I did appreciate was that no one asked me about the trial. They all knew it was a sore spot with me and a personal embarrassment. Luckily, I didn't have to think of any answers.

They asked Kate how she was doing with her art, and she was pleased to talk about her studio and the pieces she was working on.

"We saw that you had an exhibition at the Ballantine Gallery before you went to San Francisco. Will you do more?"

"I hope so," Kate said. "I'm going to finish this series of paintings from Africa and then I might finish my MA. I'll play it by ear. It depends on so much – what my father decides, what happens with Liam."

"Whatever you decide will be great, my dear," Mrs. O said, always the supporter.

It was getting late so we said our goodbyes and left the O'Rileys after ten, driving through the streets of Manhattan to our place on 8th Avenue.

"That was fun," Kate said and took my hand, squeezing it. "There's so much love for you in that family, Drake. You're lucky to have had them."

"I know," I said and kissed her knuckles. "I survived and thrived because of them and my friendship with Ken and the boys. Mersey really helped me make it through the years after my father died."

"Speaking of which, I can't wait to come and listen to you play on Tuesday night."

"I'll love to have you there, watching us play."

She smiled. "I always get a little giddy when I see you up on the stage."

"You do, do you, Mrs. Morgan? Giddy?"

She narrowed her eyes. "Like I'm a groupie and you're my rockstar crush. I'd do anything you wanted when I see you standing on the stage with the guitar strapped around your shoulder."

"Anything?"

"Anything," she replied with a knowing grin.

"This sounds like a role-playing scenario I'd love to play out. How about if I wear that white shirt you like so much and my leather pants. You show up dressed in that little black dress I really like – the one that's really sexy and shows a lot of cleavage? I'll pick you up and we can get it on in a limo then I can bring you home and tie you up and torture you with pleasure."

I wagged my eyebrows at her suggestively and she laughed.

"You don't know how much that appeals to me."

"Oh, but I do. And that's exactly what's going to happen on Tuesday night."

We drove up to the parking garage where I kept the rental car, both of us smiling and imagining it.

After we parked, I took her hand and we walked to the 8th Avenue apartment, enjoying the sounds of the city at night time, the traffic still busy even at that time of night, people out walking along the streets. When we arrived back in the apartment, Karen was sitting in front of the television, a magazine in her hand.

"How was everything?" Kate asked after taking off her shoes.

Karen stood up and stretched. "She went down for the night at nine. I know you said eight but she was wide awake and so we read a lot of books until she started to pull at her ear. She went down without a fuss once she got her bottle."

"That's the sign," I said and hung up my jacket. "She always tugs at her ear when she's tired."

"Thanks so much for agreeing to sit for us on Tuesday when Drake plays with his band," Kate said. "We'll need you for about three hours from nine until midnight, if that's okay."

"Absolutely," Karen said. "Like I said, I have nothing scheduled this week so I'm totally free."

"I'll make sure she's already down for the night so you can come and watch a movie or whatever you want," Kate replied.

"Sounds good," Karen said and we said our goodbyes.

When the door was closed, I wasted no time. All the talk about Tuesday night had me aroused and so I pushed Kate against the wall beside the door, my hands splayed against the wall on either side of her.

"And now, *Katherine*, I think I need you on your knees."

She smiled slowly, and the look in her eyes told me everything I needed to know.

"Yes, *Sir*."

She slid down to her knees and began to unfasten my belt, her moves slow and deliberate, her gaze moving from the considerable bulge in my pants to my face and back again. Before she unzipped my pants, she pressed her face against my groin, her mouth open around the outline of my cock, which strained against the fabric of my pants, running her lips along the length from the tip to my balls.

She knew how to tease me.

I closed my eyes and just enjoyed the sensations. When I heard the sound of the zipper, my cock jumped, and I had to watch once more as she pulled my slacks and boxer briefs down over my buttocks, exposing my erection. It sprung out of its confines and hung heavy in front of her face, the tip wet with pre-cum.

"May I suck you, Sir?" she asked, her lip running over her bottom lip suggestively.

"You may."

I couldn't suppress a groan of pleasure when her tongue reached out to lap the head, a throb of lust making me exhale. She took the head in her mouth and sucked, running her tongue around the rim. With her other hand, she cupped my balls.

"Oh, Katherine, you do know how to please me."

I guided her head as she moved on my length, taking in more and more with each attempt until she gagged. She pulled back and recovered and then began once more, her lips tight around my cock, one hand stroking the shaft while she sucked and licked.

"That's so good," I murmured, the pleasure building inside of me.

She pulled off, stroking my length. "May this one finish you with my mouth, Sir?"

Usually, I'd say no, preferring to make her orgasm before I did, but tonight, I thought we'd reverse the order so I could focus entirely on my own orgasm and then on hers.

"Yes," I said, my hand tangled in her hair.

She sucked my cock back into her mouth and began her motions once more, stroking and sucking, faster, harder, and before I knew it, I was ready, the pleasure building inside of my balls, my body tensing.

"I'm coming," I managed to grunt as the pleasure spread white hot from my balls to the tip of my cock, the feel of her mouth on me making it all the sweeter. I spasmed with her lips around me, ejaculating, groaning in pleasure.

"Oh, God..."

She took me, all of me while I came, swallowing me eagerly.

I leaned against the wall, my cock still in her mouth, and recovered.

I pulled her up finally and kissed her, my arms around her.

"Was that to your liking, Sir?" she said coyly when our kiss broke. She gave me this playful expression that suggested she knew damn well that it was very much to my liking.

"Yes, it was, Katherine. It was very much to my liking. And now, I think you deserve something special as well. I think I'd like to strip you naked and eat you until you scream out my name."

"That would be very much to my liking, Sir."

And so I did.

CHAPTER 23

KATE

I CALLED my father the next day.

"How are you, sweetie? We've missed you this past week or so."

I smiled and rubbed Sophie's head as she played in her chair. "We missed you, too. We're going to be here another two weeks so I hope you two are all right there."

"We're lonely," he said and his voice sounded sad. "We realized how much we rely on you two and Sophie for entertainment. What's going to happen when you move back?"

"You know we're planning to move back?"

"Yes, Drake called me to talk about options."

"He never said anything."

"He knew that this would be one of those hard conversations and even harder decisions. But I think Elaine and I have come to a decision. We think we'd like to move back and maybe spend a couple of months farther south in January and February. Maybe we'll do what Drake suggested and get a better home with wheelchair accessibility, so I can be more mobile and get outside more than I could in the penthouse."

"Oh, Daddy, that makes me so happy." I got actual tears in my eyes at the news. "I've been so torn about all this. You know I really love our place in San Francisco, and I liked the studio but when I got back here, I felt like this was my real home. Plus, if Liam is going to be here living with Brenda, Drake would want to be closer to him. Drake doesn't think he should try for custody until the publicity around the trial dies down and it goes out of people's minds, so that means we'd want to be back in New York for the start of the school year."

"My thoughts exactly. The autumn is the best time of year in Manhattan. I like California, but nothing can compare with Central Park in the autumn. We'd likely stay until the new year and then come out here for a couple of months. You two could visit when you had the time."

"That's exactly what I was thinking. It would be different if Drake got full custody but that's not likely, so..."

"So, moving back to Manhattan makes sense. I thought Elaine and I would be fine out here alone but even ten days feels like a long time without you two and without Sophia. I haven't seen Heath and his family for a while. My friends are all in Manhattan... I guess I'm not ready yet to give up the ghost."

"We'll stay in San Francisco until Liam is finished with the school year. Drake could go back to finish his Fellowship after Christmas and I could even finish my MA. We'll get a nanny to look after Sophie when I'm on campus. It'll work out."

"It will. You two have to follow your dreams and we old fogies will follow you wherever you go."

"That makes me so happy," I said. "The thought of us moving back and you staying in California was making me feel really sad."

"That's why Drake called. He knew you were upset. We'll find a great place and have big family dinners and celebrate all the holidays together, like we always do. One of Drake's new brothers lives not too far away in Massachusetts, so there's opportunity to invite them down for holidays. I guess I was upset when I lost my ability to walk and felt I wanted to be somewhere I could spend most of my time outside, but home is where the heart is and my heart is with you and with our family."

"Mine, too." I wiped my eyes, my emotions almost overwhelming me at the thought we'd be back in Manhattan and all together instead of spread apart.

We spoke for a few more minutes about the trial and then said goodbye until the weekend when I'd call again.

I ended the call and sat for a moment, wiping my eyes. It was then that Drake arrived back from the store with a bag of bagels and cream cheese from the local deli as well as some fresh oranges for our juice.

He put the groceries onto the island in the kitchen and came over to where I sat with Sophie.

"What're the tears for?" he asked and sat beside me, turning my head to face him.

"I was just talking to my dad," I said and smiled. "He told me that you called him and talked about him moving back and finding a better place to live. Thank you," I said and slipped my arms around his neck. "I love you, Drake."

"I love you," Drake said and kissed me warmly. "I'd do anything for you. Anything."

"I would for you, too."

We kissed again and when our kiss ended, we pressed our foreheads together for a moment and I tried to enjoy the moment.

Of course, at that moment, Sophie decided to bang her toy against her tray as if to get our attention. We both turned to her to watch her for a moment. Drake leaned over and lifted her out of her chair and for the next half an hour, we sat and played with her while we waited for lunchtime, discussing the logistics of our move back and all the preparations we'd need to make to get back into our lives – Drake restarting his Fellowship and me my MA.

I had butterflies in my stomach just thinking about it.

Sophie would be turning a year old, at least in terms of gestational age, rather than birth age. She was sleeping through the night which meant I was getting enough sleep for a change.

I couldn't wait to get back for good, although I'd miss the beautiful California beaches and weather.

On Tuesday afternoon, Drake grabbed his change of clothes for the set, packed up his gear and went to O'Riley's for his gig.

Karen was coming over at 8:45 P.M. and I'd take an Uber to the O'Rileys to watch his last set. We were going to rent a limo and do the whole role playing of me meeting a hot musician at a concert and going home with him. It would be fun. I'd wear his favorite dress, with no underwear on, and sit alone. He'd drop by between sets and chat me up, and then after the set, I'd wait for him behind the restaurant at the 'stage door' and go home with him.

We'd have sex in the back of the stretch limo.

It would be fun.

I spent the afternoon with Sophia, walking around the streets with her in the stroller, visiting all my favorite neighborhood haunts. I felt good that we'd be moving back for September. It was my favorite time of the year. Our second anniversary would be coming up and it would feel strange not to be celebrating it in Manhattan in Central Park, so I was happy to imagine spending time in the park with all the colors of autumn around us.

We had supper alone, the two of us sitting at the kitchen island, eating leftover pasta from the previous night. When I was finished cleaning up, I gave her a bath and put her in her jammies and then read to her for half an hour. By the time eight came around, she was sleepy and her eyes closed when I laid her in her crib with her bottle. She was asleep soon, her pacifier firmly in her mouth.

On my part, I had a shower and dressed in my little black number that Drake liked so much. I did my best to look as sexy as I could, even wearing more makeup than usual. I wanted to play the part of a groupie, wearing big earrings and high heels and lots of lipstick. I wore my hair in a half-up half-down updo. When I looked in the mirror, I almost decided to take it all off again and go as my usual self, but this was going to be a special night for Drake – his first performance with the band again. He'd be excited and would be looking forward to our 'date'.

Karen arrived precisely at 8:45 p.m. and got set up in front of the sofa with Netflix on to watch the latest episodes of her favorite series.

I said goodbye and went to the street to catch my Uber, which thankfully was right on time. We drove through the streets of the city, and the closer we got to the restaurant, the more the butterflies in my stomach grew.

I arrived at the O'Riley's in time for Drake's final set at 9:30. Because it was a Tuesday, the last set ended at 11:00 P.M. and so we'd have time to say goodbye to everyone and then we'd play out our little musician/groupie fantasy. After I paid my driver, I went inside and said hello to Colin, Ken's brother who tended bar, and then Sarah, his pretty dark-haired sister came by and said hello when I took a seat at a lone table at the back of the bar. Lara had been at the early set and left, so I was alone. Drake told me to sit at the back alone so he could come by and talk to me like I was a stranger.

"Why don't you go sit at the front of the tables beside the stage? That way Drake could see you better."

"No, that's all right," I said and waved her off. "We'll let the customers sit up close. I'm fine here."

"If you're sure, because I can move you if you want..."

"No, that's not necessary," I said and squeezed her hand. "Thanks, but I'm fine here."

"What would you like to drink?"

I bit my bottom lip, trying to think of what I wanted.

"A vodka martini with a twist of lime."

"Coming up," she said and threaded her way through the tables, taking new orders and picking up empty glasses on her way. I sat in the dim room and watched while couples and small groups arrived and left, taking seats and being served. Just before 9:30 P.M., Cliff Walters, one of Drake's band mates, came out on stage and a thrill went through me. Drake would come out soon to tune his guitar and I would get to see him the way other women saw him. As a musician, a hot looking musician, coming out on stage to get ready for the final set.

I glanced around and saw the patrons were busy talking and drinking, but there was a table of young women off to the left of the stage, all dressed up and talking a little more loudly than the other guests. When Drake finally came out from the back of the restaurant to take the stage, the women seemed to perk up and whispered to each other. One wolf-whistled him and my gut clenched, jealousy rising in me in a way that surprised me.

Yeah, he was that good looking...

His dark hair was a bit longish and falling in his eyes in that really sexy way. He wore his black leather pants and a white linen shirt untucked and open a few buttons. If you added a tux jacket, he would have been dressed as his Master D persona and it made me a little breathless to realize he was all mine. Underneath his shirt, when he reached up to adjust the mic, his thick leather belt with the heavy buckle was visible and beneath that, his rather ample package captured behind his leather pants.

Just watching him aroused me.

Drake was gorgeous. He was good looking enough to be a model.

The table of women giggled and laughed to themselves, clearly giving Drake the eye.

One of them called out and at first, I didn't understand what she said but she repeated it more loudly.

"Hey, Doctor D!"

There was a pause and the three women laughed together, their heads bent closer to each other. Then another spoke up, clearly trying to get Drake's attention.

"Hey, Master D!"

If Drake heard them, he didn't show it. Instead he picked up his bass guitar, slid the strap over his shoulder, plugged it into the amp and then began to tune it, playing scales and chords and adjusting the tuning. He had his head bowed and was listening to the notes, seemingly unaware of the table of women off to the side of the stage clearly ogling him.

Or, maybe he was just outright ignoring them.

I wanted to go over to the table and wipe the ridiculous grins off their faces but of course, I wasn't that kind of person so instead I sat and fumed, sad that they were going to try to ruin Drake's debut back with Mersey.

Whatever those women wanted to achieve with their catcalls, they didn't succeed. Drake and the band were great. Their set was tight and Drake sounded wonderful. God, he was so hot...

During the break, after the applause died down, one of the women at the table yelled out to Drake.

"Hey, Dr. Dangerous, come over and talk to us!"

Drake put his guitar down, bent closer to Ken, with whom he exchanged a few words. Then, to my utter surprise, Drake actually did go over to the table of women. He went over and knelt beside the woman in red who called out to him, a huge smile on his face. The women were totally shocked and their mouths dropped. He spoke with them and I would have killed to listen in to what he said. Finally, he pointed my way and everyone at the table glanced over to where I sat.

Then Drake stood up, said something else to them all, and left.

The women watched him walk directly over to my table. He had a determined expression on his face. He arrived at my table and took my hand, pulling me up and into his arms. He kissed me, deeply, and when my arms went around his neck, he lifted me up so that my feet weren't touching the ground.

When he put me back down and sat on the chair beside me, he leaned closer and took my hand.

"Drake," I said, trying to catch my breath. "What was all that about?"

"Other than the fact that I love you madly and can't wait to get you home alone tonight so I can drive you mad with pleasure?"

I smiled and fanned myself dramatically. "Other than that, yes."

"I went to the women and said I appreciated their attention, but that I was taken and wasn't interested in any of them. I said that the love of my life, my goddess and the woman who rules my heart, was sitting in the back of the restaurant waiting for me to get off the stage so we could go home together. That seemed to shut them up."

"It sure did shut them up, but they're whispering to each other like crazy," I said and glanced over to the table. One of had taken out a cell and was recording us. "They're recording us."

Drake didn't even look at the table. Instead, he took my hand and kissed my knuckles, smiling at me, his eyes locked on mine.

"I don't give a fuck about them. I only care about you." Then he leaned over and kissed me. "I can't wait for the set to finish so I can take you home in the limo and make you dizzy with lust."

"Me either," I said, grinning, my heart rate increasing. "But you should enjoy the rest of the set. Don't let them stop you from doing what you love. They don't matter."

"No one matters except us."

We kissed again and then Drake smiled. "Now, I have to use the men's room and then have a glass of water before we start back again. Wait for me?"

He stood, but kept my hand in his.

"I'd wait for you forever."

He walked to the back and went through the door to the staff area and I couldn't resist watching the women watch him.

They glanced at me and I couldn't help but smile to myself.

He was mine.

WHEN IT CAME time for the last song of the set, Drake took the microphone and stood at the front of the stage.

"This final song is for Kate, the love of my life, my soul mate and the mother of my beautiful daughter, Sophia. Kate, my life was changed the day you fell and scraped your knees and I looked after your wounds. I didn't realize it at the time but you, and now Sophie, healed me and made me whole. I love you. This song is for you."

I covered my mouth as the song began – the first bars of *And I Love Her* – and tears filled my eyes. It was my favorite song and Drake sang it so well and with so much emotion. I felt the eyes of those women on me.

I knew what they were thinking. They were thinking what I was thinking: Drake Morgan, MD, neurosurgeon, bass player and philanthropist, was one of the hottest and most desirable men on the planet.

He was mine.

AFTER THE SET WAS OVER, and the applause died down, I did what I was supposed to do – I left the restaurant and went out the back to wait at the rear exit into the back alley. When I arrived, I saw a stretch limo idling, the driver standing beside the passenger door, waiting, smoking a cigarette. When he saw me, he dropped it and crushed it under his boot.

I stood at the back door and waited, my heart beating just a little bit faster at the prospect of seeing Drake come out the door. When the door opened and I saw him, his dark black hair shining in the light from the overhead lamp, I got a surge of desire that went from my chest right to my core.

We were going to play this out. I tried hard not to smile too widely when our eyes met. Instead, I put on a sultry expression, my eyes half-lidded. I leaned against the brick wall and put one hand on my hip, trying my best to look slutty. As he walked down the stairs to the alley, I flipped my hair and licked my lips.

"Dr. Morgan," I said, trying to make my voice sound all breathy. "I've been waiting."

"You have?" he said and stood in front of me, his eyes moving over my body from head to foot and back. "What were you waiting for?"

"For you."

"And who are you?"

"My name is Katherine."

"And what did you have in mind, *Katherine*?" he asked, his hand resting on the wall beside my head.

I knew that the use of my name like that meant I was supposed to fall into submissive mode.

"Whatever you want," I replied. "Sir. Anything."

"Oh, yeah? Anything?"

I licked my lips again. "Yes, sir. Anything."

"Hmm," he said and took a lock of my hair in his fingers, sliding down the length until he reached my breast. He let his fingers fall onto the exposed skin, stroking lightly. "That gives me a lot of ideas. Kinky ideas."

"Those are the best ideas, Sir," I said, fighting not to smile.

"I see that smile," he said and I could see him fight his own smile. He frowned. "I might have to punish you for impertinence if you keep smiling like that."

"Really?" I replied, biting my bottom lip. "What did you have in mind, Sir?"

"That's for me to know and you to be quiet, *Katherine*, and let me lead. Now, be quiet because I'm going to take you home in that limo and I'm going to shut up that saucy mouth of yours with my cock."

A surge of desire filled me at the tone of his voice and the leer in his eyes. Then, he leaned closer and kissed me, one hand slipping behind my head, his fingers tangling in my hair.

When he pulled back, he grabbed my hand and pulled me over to the limo. The driver had the back door open and was waiting for us. He closed the door once we were inside and Drake didn't waste any time. As we drove off, Drake pressed me back, lying on top of me, his weight a comfort, one of his hands sliding up my body from my hip to one breast, which he squeezed.

He kissed me deeply and ground himself against me so that I could feel his erection. He was aroused by our little role playing game. I was as well, my body swelling in response to his touch and to his tongue on mine as he kissed me deeply. When he pulled back, he tugged at my sweater.

"Take that off. I want to see your breasts."

I did as he commanded, slipping the sweater off my shoulders and pulling down my top to expose my breasts, my nipples hardening in the cool night air. He nuzzled me, sucking my nipples, squeezing my breasts like he couldn't get enough.

The car drove through the streets of Manhattan while Drake and I played our little groupie-rock star game and it was only because there was a dark glass partition between us and the driver that I felt able to let myself go and enjoy what he was doing to me.

"Get on your knees," he said in a hoarse voice. I complied, sliding over him so that I was on my knees between his thighs. I unfastened his belt and unzipped his leather pants, pulling him out of confinement, his cock thick and so hard. I paused for a moment, his shaft in my hand and glanced up to meet his eyes. I slowly licked my lips, wanting to tease him a bit before I took him in my mouth.

"You're a saucy one," he said, gruffly. "If you don't take me into your mouth soon, I might have to punish you."

So I did, licking the head of his cock slowly, running my tongue around the rim before sucking the head into my mouth.

"Oh, that's good, Katherine," he said, his voice a little strained. "That's very good. Keep it up."

I did, stroking his shaft while I sucked the head. He slipped one hand behind my head, urging me to take more of him into my mouth and I complied, swallowing as much of him as I could manage before gagging.

"Now, I want you to sit on me," he said, pulling me off his cock. I licked my lips and nodded. I crawled up onto his lap, already so aroused from the build up to that moment that I knew I wouldn't need much to orgasm the first time. "I want you to fuck me until you come."

"Yes, Sir," I said, breathless, my heart pounding.

I got into position, my hands on his shoulders, and lowered myself down onto him while he held himself in place. I was already so wet that I slid onto his cock, the pressure from his girth making me shiver.

His fingers found my clit and when I started to move up and down on his cock, he stroked me deftly, knowing exactly what I needed.

"Fuck me, Katherine. Come on my cock."

"Yes, Sir," I managed, my eyes closed as I moved on him. He kissed my throat, stroking me with one hand while squeezing my breast with the other.

Soon, I felt the pleasure build in my core and I knew it wouldn't take long for me to orgasm.

"I'm going to..." I said with a gasp as my pleasure crested.

Drake said nothing but he sucked one nipple, squeezing my breast and that sent a jolt of pleasure right through my body to my clit and sent me over.

"Oh, God," I cried, exhaling as my body tensed and my orgasm started.

I stopped my motions while my body convulsed, unable to keep moving. When I was finished, I stopped moving completely, my face beside Drake's.

Then Drake lifted me up and turned me over so that I laid on my back on the bench seat.

"Wrap your legs around me," he said, his voice needful.

I complied, barely able to think, and he began to thrust, hard and fast. I met him with each thrust, and soon, he was breathing hard and I knew he was close.

"Oh, fuck," he groaned and rammed into me, his eyes rolling up in his head. He thrust slowly through his orgasm, and I enjoyed watching his face as he came, his neck strained, his teeth gritted.

He collapsed on top of me, his face beside mine. I smiled to myself as he caught his breath, my arms wrapped around him, his cock still hard and inside of me. I felt such incredible love for him at that moment, my eyes filled with tears. They were tears of happiness.

Everything seemed right in my world again – for the first time in a long time.

We'd be moving back to Manhattan. My father and Elaine would return as well, only leaving for short periods to head south in the coldest part of the winter. We'd be back in my beloved Manhattan, close to where Liam would be going to school.

Most of all, Drake and I were madly in love, with each other and with our lives together.

Drake pulled back and looked in my eyes. When he saw my tears, a dark expression passed over his face.

"What are these for?" he asked, and wiped tears off my cheek.

"Tears of happiness," I replied. "I'm just so happy."

He kissed me, tenderly.

"I love you, Kate," he said, his voice filled with emotion.

"I love you, Drake. So much."

We lay together like that for a few long moments, enjoying each other as our bodies remained joined.

Finally, I felt him slip out of my body and we quickly sat up Drake cleaned me up with a tissue from his pocket.

"You came prepared," I said because of course we didn't have to use a condom.

"Always," he said with a grin. "I'm always prepared for you, Ms. Bennet."

Once we were rearranged, our clothes back in place and we were sitting primly in our seats with our seatbelts on, Drake pressed the button and spoke to the driver.

"Take us home, please," he said, humor in his voice.

Drake took my hand and kissed my knuckles as we drove through the streets of Manhattan back to our home on 8th Avenue.

It had been a memorable night – one I wouldn't forget for a long, long time...

EPILOGUE

DRAKE

Our return to San Francisco was melancholy.

Despite both of us keeping busy adjusting back into the familiar rhythm of life there, I think both Kate and I missed Manhattan more than we realized. I liked the California weather and Kate liked her studio in the downtown area but we both agreed that Liam was a priority. When he returned to Manhattan after the summer ended and he would go to live with Brenda in Manhattan, we would as well.

For our remaining time in California, I spent my most of my days and nights with Sophie and Kate since I no longer worked at UCSF, although I made time to pop in and see how my mother was doing. She never recognized me. I suspected that she thought I was Liam, her former husband, if she thought anything at all. It upset me, but I had to accept that there was nothing to be done about it.

I did see Kent and Amanda frequently at the nursing home and we invited both their families to our place for dinner, getting to meet their spouses and children and establish a relationship with them that I hoped would last for the rest of our lives. I would be sad to say goodbye to them when we left, but at the same time, I had to prioritize Liam. His needs for a stable home and to know his father were primary.

On her part, Kate spent more time at her new studio, and for a while, we kept busy but no matter how nice the weather or our view of the ocean, the house on the coast wasn't home. For the next two months, we spent our time alternating between Ethan and Elaine's for dinner, or dinner with my new siblings at the family house.

Our stay in California had been like an extended vacation – filled with excitement because everything was new and the weather was fantastic – but it wasn't home. Until we returned to Manhattan, I had pretty much free access to Liam and he spent a lot of time with us on the beach on the weekends. Brenda was only too happy to allow a sleepover or two and so Liam became used to being around us and was starting to feel more at home.

Of course, we also spent time with Ethan and Elaine. Kate helped Ethan work with realtors back in Manhattan to find the perfect place for he and Elaine to buy. It took some convincing to get Ethan to agree to sell the penthouse, but neither Kate nor Heath wanted it, and so in the end, Ethan decided to list the apartment and find a smaller, more accessible townhouse in Brooklyn. He didn't want to be apart from Kate or Heath and our two families for more than a month or two at a time. Ethan and Elaine would take the winters off and spend January and February away but they would return for the warmer weather starting in late March so we could all be together as a big happy family.

Finally, the week came when Liam was finished with school. He and Brenda were flying to Malaysia for a week and then he'd fly back with

Brenda to stay in Manhattan. Preparations were underway for our own move back to New York and we were busy boxing up our things so movers could come and take them away.

We had one last big dinner at Ethan's and Elaine's place, the night before our flights back to Manhattan. We arranged things so that we took our flights out of San Francisco at the same time as Brenda and Liam and would meet up with them for a quick visit before their flight.

I could feel that Kate was emotional all that day before we left, and several times, I had to take her in my arms and comfort her. Ethan and Elaine weren't returning for a few weeks due to the timing of their possession date for their new house in Brooklyn. Kate had been hoping that we would all leave at the same time but that hadn't worked out so it would be a temporary goodbye to her father.

Kate hated goodbyes.

We stood in the middle of the living room, boxes of our possessions stacked around us, packing paper crumpled up, a tape dispenser at the ready.

"What are you so afraid of?" I asked, stroking her hair. "Ethan and Elaine will be following us in two weeks. They'll be fine until then. Elaine has everything in hand."

Kate nodded and tucked her face into my shoulder, her arms tightening around me.

"I know. It's just that you never know when it will be the last time you see someone."

"Ethan's fine," I said and rocked her in my arms. "He's healthy enough, all things considered. He's not weak so you don't have to worry."

"I'm trying," she said. "I always expect the worst."

"I understand," I replied and kissed her tenderly. "It's the PTSD. It'll get better with time."

She sighed and we stood like that for a few moments, enjoying the moment. Outside the window, I could see San Francisco bay. I'd miss the view but we could always come out for a visit.

We ended the embrace when sounds of Sophie grousing in her crib came over the baby monitor.

"She's awake," Kate said and slipped out of my arms. "I better get her."

I let go and watched as Kate went to Sophie's bedroom. Then, I returned to packing, slipping a few of our dishes into a box and stuffing paper around them. The movers were coming in the afternoon and the cleaners were coming the next morning to clean the place before our rental agent took back possession. We'd be staying at Ethan and Elaine's for the night and then would go directly to the airport to take our plane to Manhattan once we turned our keys over to our rental agent.

Kate returned with Sophie and we spent the rest of the morning finishing up our packing. Sophie played in the living room, where we'd boxed her off in the center of the room so she couldn't hurt herself. The movers came an hour late, and packed up the truck with our boxes and the few items we'd purchased for the house that we wanted to take with us. By the time five thirty came around, the packing was done and so we did one last check of the house and drove to Ethan and Elaine's for the night, our suitcases in the trunk.

After a last walk on the beach, during which time Kate took pictures of the surf and of Sophie and me walking along in the water, we went up to the house for dinner, which was a somber affair for Kate. I enjoyed Ethan as I usually did, appreciating his dry wit, but Kate was upset at having to say goodbye for even two weeks. At least she knew they'd be following us and arriving not long after. We'd be a big happy family once more when they returned to Manhattan and

Liam arrived back from his visit with Chris and his mother in Malaysia.

When we put Sophie down for the night, we spent an hour going over plans with Ethan and Elaine, and then all of us went to bed, because we had a busy day.

Kate finally crawled in beside me after brushing her teeth, cuddling up against me, her arm across my chest.

"I'm so sad," she said and gave me a pout. "I thought I'd be so happy to be leaving, but now I wish we had more time. I barely got to know your new family. Now, we'll only see them on holidays."

"We can always fly out for a weekend, if you want. Anytime."

"I know. I just wish we could all be together in one place."

I kissed her forehead and thought about my new family and how I enjoyed talking with my brother and sister and visiting my mother, even if she had no idea who I was. I felt like there was this special hole in my life where they were supposed to be all this time, but I'd been filling that hole with other stuff – work and music and the foundation and the corporation. Now, that hole was starting to feel like I'd found what fit perfectly inside. My mother hadn't abandoned me. She saved her own life by moving away and finding a new one. She always loved me but couldn't look after me because of her depression. When she finally got over it, she had a new life that didn't include me out of shame and guilt.

But she did love me. Before she lost her mind, she told her second family of her regret and how she wanted them to meet me one day.

I squeezed Kate and tried to shut off my brain but it was hard. After more than half an hour of lying awake, my eyes open, Kate rolled over and slipped her arm around my neck.

"You still awake?"

I nodded. "Yes. Can't seem to fall asleep."

She moved closer, and draped one leg over mine. "I know what will help."

Then she kissed me, rolling me over onto my back and lying on top of me. The kiss deepened and I ran my hands down her back to her buttocks.

"And what is that exactly, Mrs. Morgan?" I asked in mock innocence.

"I'm going to make love to you. I've heard that when men have an orgasm, it puts them to sleep. I'm going to test it out."

I smiled in the darkness. "An experiment? Haven't we tried this remedy before?"

She kissed me, one hand moving down my body to grasp hold of my rapidly thickening cock.

"You need to test and retest before you can draw any real conclusions."

When I opened my mouth to reply, she covered it with hers and shut me up.

There were no more words spoken between us except for gasps of pleasure.

The morning went fast as we woke and had breakfast on the patio one last time with Ethan and Elaine before we left for our old place to turn in our keys. Elaine and Kate cooked up a big breakfast of eggs, bacon, fried potatoes and toast. The five of us sat at the big table and ate al fresco, shaded from the warm sun by a large umbrella.

After we cleaned up, I packed up the rental car and we said goodbye, hugging and kissing Ethan and Elaine before we left.

"We'll be joining you in two weeks," Ethan said when he saw tears in Kate's eyes. "You'll pick us up at the airport and take us to the hotel for a few nights until we take possession of the house. We'll Skype any time you want. The time will go by so fast, before you know it, we'll be back home."

"I know," Kate said and kissed Ethan once more before giving Elaine a hug and kiss.

We fastened Sophia in the car seat and then the two of us got in the car. Ethan and Elaine waved at us as we backed out of the driveway and turned around.

When we got back onto the main coastal highway, I took Kate's hand and kissed her knuckles because I knew she was still upset.

"Everything will be fine," I said. "Ethan was right. We'll be so busy getting settled back in that we'll barely notice the time passing. You'll see."

"I know," she replied and turned to watch the highway as we drove to the house. The rental agent was there when we arrived. I did one last walk through with him.

"We really enjoyed the house," I said as I handed over the keys.

"Contact me if you want to come back. Any time."

I nodded and we shook before I returned to the car. I took one last look at the house and yard, catching sight of the beach through a gap in the hedge. We'd had a lot of enjoyable times on the beach and at the house. I expected we would return at some point for a month or so when we had time and hoped that we'd find another place like it.

Then, I hopped in the car and we returned to the highway. We drove to the airport where we'd meet Brenda and Liam and say goodbye to them before we each took our respective planes. I let Kate and Sophia off at one entrance, and after getting a cart to carry our luggage, I dropped off the rental car and made my way back to where Kate waited for me.

Together, we walked to the United lounge where we'd arranged to meet Brenda and Liam for a brief visit before our flight.

There they were, sitting at a table for four people beside the window overlooking the tarmac outside, where a plane was being boarded. I reached into one of the carryon bags and removed a small wrapped toy I bought for Liam the previous day. I wanted Sophie to give it to him before they left so he'd have something from her to remember her while on his trip to Malaysia. I placed it in Sophie's hands as we arrived at the table.

"Drake! Kate!" Brenda said and stood up, coming to us to give us both a hug. "There's little Sophie." She bent down and stroked Sophie's cheek. "Come and say hello to your father," she said to Liam.

Liam stood and came over to me like a well-behaved boy. "Hello Father," he said to me.

I knelt and opened my arms for a hug. "Hello, Liam," I replied. He came into my arms and I gave him a quick hug. He laid his head on my shoulder briefly and then pulled back.

I pointed at the present that Sophie was holding, and who looked like she was going to pop it into her mouth at any moment.

"That's a present for you," I said and Liam turned to check it out.

"That's for me?" Liam asked, hesitant but eager at the same time.

"Yes," I said and gently removed it from Sophie's hand. "Sophie doesn't understand the idea of giving a present yet, but it's for you from your sister."

I handed it to Liam, who took it and smiled. 'Thanks, Sophia! I have something for you, too."

He went to his backpack and pulled out an unwrapped toy. It was another minion.

"You can have this. You can put it in your mouth. Grandma washed it so it's clean."

"Why thank you, Liam," I said and rubbed his head affectionately. "I'm sure Sophie will love it."

On her part, Sophie happily took the minion from Liam's hands and it went directly into her mouth as expected.

We sat at the table and watched as Liam unwrapped his present.

"It's another transformer," Liam said brightly, holding up the package with the transformer inside. "It's Drift." He examined the trans-former. "He transforms into a Mercedes."

I helped him open the package and he proceeded to transform it into its different forms while we had a nice time talking with Brenda about their trip to Malaysia.

"We're on United Airlines and make one stop in Hong Kong before our flight to Kuala Lumpur," she said.

"It's a long flight."

She nodded. "Liam has a Gameboy and has become a big fan of Legends of Zelda. He's got three different versions of the game from a used game store plus several comic books. I think we'll be okay."

"Good," I said and watched Liam, hungry to see him for as long as I could before they left to catch their flight. "We're boarding after you so we can spend some more time together before you go."

When the time came to say goodbye, we walked them to security. After a hug, which lasted longer than I intended, I waved as they went out of sight.

"Well, that's it. Now, it's our turn."

I hugged Kate, feeling quite emotional seeing Liam off and knowing it would be the first time he'd seen his mom in over a month. Part of me hated Maureen for leaving Liam with Brenda. My own mother left me when I was older than Liam. I had forgiven her, now that I met her again and realized that she'd felt she couldn't do anything different and that she had been ready to end her own life. At least I could understand what Liam was going through. And I was determined to be a parent to him, no matter what.

We checked in through security and went to the waiting area outside our own gate. I held Sophie on my knee and the two of us watched out the window at the planes landing and taking off. I saw one United plane and while I wasn't sure it was Liam's flight, I imagined it was him and he was smiling as the plane took off, the transformer clutched tightly in his hand.

After we boarded our own flight, we took our first-class seats. Sophie had a seat beside Kate and I sat across the aisle beside her. I would have liked to have sat beside Kate because she was still nervous on airplanes, but with Sophie beside her, Kate put on a brave face and was generally distracted by having her baby with her.

After takeoff, once we were leveled off and the fasten seatbelt signs flickered off, I went to them and leaned over, looking out the window at the passing scenery. I glanced at Kate, who was gripping the arm rests tightly. She gave me a smile, but I could see it was nervous.

"Only a few hours and we have our layover in Denver," I said with a smile. She nodded and turned back to the window. I handed Sophie her minion and then sat back down, watching the two of them and thinking about the upcoming couple of months back in Manhattan.

The Richardson murder trial would be going on and that would be in the news. It would put a damper on any of my plans to try to win shared custody of Liam, but at least I'd be close to him. I could spend time visiting him at Brenda's and he could have sleepovers at our place on weekends.

Once the murder trial was over and the publicity surrounding it had died down?

I'd be going to court to get shared custody. Then, I'd be converting the spare bedroom at our apartment on 8th Avenue into Liam's bedroom. Until Maureen returned to Manhattan or California to live, I was determined that Liam would live with me and Kate and Sophie during the week, and visit his grandmother on weekends. As his biological father, I had every right to that if Maureen was going to spend most of her time in Malaysia. I'm sure a judge would look at my current circumstances rather than my past and decide on that basis rather than on salacious gossip about my sex life before I was married.

I hoped that was the case.

The hours passed quickly, and Sophie was a good traveler for the most part, falling asleep soon after we took off at her usual nap time. I moved her seat and sat beside Kate while Sophie slept, our hands clasped as we watched the clouds outside and talked about our plans for getting settled into our apartment once we were back.

"You'll be able to take up with Mersey again," Kate said and leaned her head back, watching me intently. "You should keep playing with them. Once everything is cleared up with the trial, you could go back and finish your fellowship if you wanted."

I kissed her knuckles. "I do want. I was thinking maybe in the new year."

She smiled. "Whenever you feel ready. We should take the next few months off from any stresses and just focus on enjoying our time back in Manhattan. Liam will be starting school and I'll find a studio and finish my new series."

"Sounds perfect."

OUR LAYOVER in Denver was very short and we had little time except to find our way to our other gate and board our plane. Then, after a meal and time holding Sophie on our laps, we landed in New York, the bright lights of the city at night sparkling like a million diamonds.

As our plane touched down, I held Kate's hand across the aisle. She always closed her eyes until the sound of the reversed engines softened and she knew we had landed safely.

I smiled when she finally opened her eyes and looked at me. As we taxied to the terminal, I pulled her hand up to my lips and kissed her knuckles.

"Well, Mrs. Morgan, we're finally home."

THE END

ABOUT THE AUTHOR

S. E. Lund writes erotic, contemporary, new adult and paranormal romance. She lives in a century-old house on a quiet tree-lined street in a small Western Canadian city with her family of humans and animals. She dreams of living in a warm climate where snow is just a word in a dictionary.

S. E. Lund Newsletter

Sign up for S. E. Lund's newsletter and gain access to updates on upcoming releases, sales and freebies! She hates spam and so will never share your email!

S. E. LUND NEWSLETTER SIGN UP

For More Information:
www.selund.com
selund2012@gmail.com

Everlasting: Book 6

Drake Forever: Book 7

Endless: Book 8

The Unrestrained Series Collection 1 & 2

THE DRAKE SERIES (The Unrestrained Series from Drake's Point of View)

Drake Restrained

Drake Unwound

Drake Unbound

The Drake Series Collection

Military Romance / Romantic Suspense

THE BAD BOY SERIES

Bad Boy Saint: Book 1

Bad Boy Sinner: Book 2

Bad Boy Soldier: Book 3

Bad Boy Savior: Book 4

The Bad Boy Series Collection

Standalone Romances:

Matched: Standalone Romantic Comedy

ALSO BY S. E. LUND

New Adult Romance

THE MR BIG SERIES

Mr. Big Shot: Book 1

Mr. Big Love: Book 2

Mr. Big Daddy: Book 3

THE MACINTYRE BROTHERS SERIES

Tempt Me: Book 1

Tease Me: Book 2

Tame Me: Book 3

Tempting: The Collection

Contemporary Erotic Romance

THE UNRESTRAINED SERIES

The Agreement: Book 1

The Commitment: Book 2

Unrestrained: Book 3

Unbreakable: Book 4

Forever After: Book 5

If You Fall: Military Romance

Paranormal Romance

THE DOMINION SERIES

Dominion: Book 1 in the Dominion Series

Ascension: Book 2 in the Dominion Series

Retribution: Book 3 in the Dominion Series

Resurrection: Book 4 in the Dominion Series

Redemption: Book 5 in the Dominion Series

The Dominion Series Complete Collection: Books 1 - 5

Made in the USA
Monee, IL
01 September 2021